Their lips met. Their mouths fused as they were both firing all-in-a take-no-priso

Hunger roared t... ...eed to give her back ju... ...as giving him.

Angelina tore herself out of his embrace. "Why did you do that?" she asked him finally.

"Because you wanted me to." It sounded arrogant put that way, so he added, "Because I wanted to."

"That is not true."

"Which? That I wanted to kiss you?" One corner of his mouth twitched upward into an engaging grin. "I wanted to. Oh, yeah, I definitely wanted to, since the first moment I saw you."

She shook her head. "Not that. You said I wanted you to kiss me. And that is not true."

Alec's grin faded, and he held her gaze with his steady one. "Oh, yes you did," he told her, accepting the truth even if she refused to acknowledge it. "You wanted to know what it would be like. We both did. And now we know."

And nothing will ever be the same again.

* * *

Be sure to check out the next books
in Amelia Autin's exciting miniseries:

Man on a Mission—
These heroes, working at home and overseas,
will do anything for justice, honor...and love

* * *

If you're on Twitter, tell us what you think of
Harlequin Romantic Suspense!
#harlequinromsuspense

Dear Reader,

When I wrote *McKinnon's Royal Mission*, part of my Man on a Mission miniseries, two characters who intrigued me were Princess Mara's other two bodyguards—Diplomatic Security Service agents and brothers, Alec and Liam Jones. So alike in many ways, and yet so different in others. They are emotionally close, as brothers should be, so I started writing their stories simultaneously, weaving the plots together into a cohesive whole, although each book stands on its own.

But it was the brothers' differences that caught my imagination. While both men are protectors, Alec, the older of the two, is *more*—more assertive, more demanding of himself, more demanding of others, as well. Alec needs a woman who understands what motivates him...because she's motivated by the same things—honor, duty, loyalty and sacrifice. Like Alec, Angelina Mateja has stepped between danger and the person she's guarding. Has been forced to kill in the line of duty. And like Alec, her career is the most important thing in her life...until they meet.

Readers often ask, "Where do your story ideas come from?" We live in a violent world. Tragedies happen every day. In the case of *Alec's Royal Assignment*, it wasn't just one idea, but several, sparked by real-life occurrences and what-if scenarios. And a heroine whose moral stand on right and wrong matches Alec's...and mine.

I love hearing from my readers. Please email me at AmeliaAutin@aol.com and let me know what you think.

Amelia Autin

ALEC'S ROYAL ASSIGNMENT

——

Amelia Autin

H⬧ **HARLEQUIN**® ROMANTIC SUSPENSE

Recycling programs
for this product may
not exist in your area.

ISBN-13: 978-0-373-27932-6

Alec's Royal Assignment

Printed in U.S.A.

www.Harlequin.com

Amelia Autin is a voracious reader who can't bear to put a good book down...or part with it. Her bookshelves are crammed with books her husband periodically threatens to donate to a good cause, but he always relents...eventually.

Amelia returned to her first love, romance writing, after a long hiatus, during which she wrote numerous technical manuals and how-to guides, as well as designed and taught classes on a variety of subjects, including technical writing. She is a longtime member of Romance Writers of America (RWA), and served three years as its treasurer.

Amelia currently resides with her PhD engineer husband in quiet Vail, Arizona, where they can see the stars at night and have a "million-dollar view" of the Rincon Mountains from their backyard.

Books by Amelia Autin

Harlequin Romantic Suspense

Man on a Mission

Cody Walker's Woman
McKinnon's Royal Mission
King's Ransom
Alec's Royal Assignment

Silhouette Intimate Moments

Gideon's Bride
Reilly's Return

Visit the Author Profile page at Harlequin.com for more titles.

For my sister, Diana MTK Autin, Esq.,
whose Edward Everett Hale quotation on
FB sparked an idea, and who helped me get the
legal details correct (any errors are mine
and mine alone). And for Vincent...always.

Though itself part of the US Department of State,
the Bureau of Diplomatic Security
is the parent organization of the
Diplomatic Security Service (DSS). The DSS is
the primary tool by which the DS carries out its
security and law enforcement mandate.
For more information, please visit state.gov/m/ds.

I have the highest regard for the work these
federal agencies perform. Nothing in this story
is intended as a negative representation of the
Bureau of Diplomatic Security or the Diplomatic
Security Service, their duties or their employees.

Prologue

Diplomatic Security Service special agent Alec Jones turned automatically when the front door opened and let a stream of light into the coffeehouse. He and his date were in the vestibule waiting to be seated, along with a couple of her local acquaintances—husband-and-wife schoolteachers. Alec watched with detached, professional interest as two bearded young men dressed as security guards entered. Their garb and their holstered sidearms appeared innocuous enough, but there was something off. And Alex's sixth sense instantly went on the alert.

He glanced over at Darla, but she was caught up in conversation with her friends. Alec had only been posted as regional security officer, or RSO, for a month at the embassy where Darla had been serving for a year as personal assistant for the US ambassador to this tiny Middle Eastern nation, and this was their first date.

Alec's eyes flicked back to the two men. They'd taken seats near the front door as if they were patiently waiting their turn at a table. But one man was peering through the curtained window as if checking out the street. The other was watching the movements of the customers in the coffeehouse with cold, hard eyes. Alec's sixth sense was humming steadily—something was definitely wrong.

His hand slid inside the jacket he always wore, even on the hottest days—and there were a lot of hot days in the Middle East—for his SIG Sauer P229R, one of the standard-issue concealed carry weapons DSS personnel used.

Without warning, the two men abruptly jumped to their feet, drew their sidearms and started shouting commands in Arabic and broken English. Alec's semiautomatic was instantly out.

Nearly everyone in the coffeehouse hit the ground immediately, including Darla's two friends. But Darla was shocked into immobility. She stared openmouthed at the gunmen, frozen with fear. And when the men turned their weapons on Darla and Alec—their faces twisted with hate, a fanatical light in their eyes—Alec fired.

It was all over in seconds. The two young men lay on their backs on the floor, unmoving. Their eyes were open and fixed sightlessly, guns still clutched in their hands. The shots they'd managed to get off had gone wide—only the gunmen had been hit. Blood stained their clothing crimson, pooling around their bodies.

But Alec felt no guilt. No remorse. He knew enough Arabic to know these men were terrorists—their shouted warning to the non-Americans to take cover and leave the infidels to them was easily understood, even with his less-than-perfect knowledge of the language. Their sole intent had been to abduct or kill the only two Americans in the coffeehouse.

Alec moved on autopilot now. He kicked the guns from the hands of both men into a far corner of the room. The training ingrained in him said you *never* take the death of the bad guys for granted. The only way to ensure safety was to neutralize the threat by removing any and all weapons from the vicinity. He didn't think these men had any other partners in the coffeehouse, but you could never be sure. And he wasn't taking any chances.

How had they known Darla and he would be here? The answer to that question would have to wait. Could Darla's so-called friends have set them up? Possibly. This coffeehouse wasn't frequented by Americans from the embassy, but Darla's friends had insisted it had true "local flavor," something Darla was interested in experiencing. It was something to consider…but not right at this moment. Not with the coffeehouse patrons staring at him in horror, as if he'd instigated this confrontation.

Alec bent over and quickly checked both men for a pulse he knew he wouldn't find. Then he rifled through their pockets. He found zip ties, blindfolds, gags and a couple of switchblade knives—confirming their intentions—but no identification. Nothing to tell him who these men were or what terrorist organization they were affiliated with.

He lifted a corner of the curtain and glanced out the window. These two likely had a driver and a getaway car somewhere outside, but he couldn't see anything that looked suspicious. And he couldn't very well leave the scene to check. Not now. He'd have to depend on the local authorities to follow up on the getaway car... if it was still around. The gunfire had to have alerted the driver that things hadn't gone down as planned, and he was probably long gone by now.

Most of the coffeehouse patrons had risen from the floor in the few seconds Alex's back was turned, and many of them had cell phones out. Two of them began sidling for the door when police sirens were heard in the distance. Alec holstered his weapon, turned to them and said coldly in Arabic, "No one is leaving. You are all..." His mind frantically searched for the right word. "Witnesses. You are all witnesses." He culled his knowledge of the language and added, "All of you will give a complete and accurate statement to the police." He stared them down until they returned to their tables.

Alec's eyes met Darla's for the first time since the shooting, and he recognized the familiar look of shock and dismay most civilians displayed when confronted with sudden, deadly violence. Darla wasn't naive— all embassy personnel were briefed on the hazards of working in the Middle East—but she'd never taken a human life. And she seemed appalled Alec had done so. Coldly. Dispassionately.

At least that's how his actions appeared to her, he knew. Alec wasn't cold. Nor was he dispassionate. He regretted the *necessity* of this killing, but the alternative was unacceptable. He wasn't going to second-guess himself or his actions. Not now. Not ever.

As the distant sirens grew louder, Alec sighed softly. No matter what came next, he knew two things for sure.

One, despite the fact that he hadn't instigated this incident, he would now be persona non grata at the US embassy here. The promotion posting as RSO he'd just received a month ago was now shot to hell and gone. Even though there were plenty of witnesses to back up a claim of self-defense, the State Department was hypersensitive about the possibility of reprisals. He would be whisked out of the country as soon as the local officials allowed, in order to hush this incident up.

Two, not as important but still important enough, his budding relationship with Darla had just died a quick death, too.

Which raised another question. Would he ever find a woman who understood?

Chapter 1

Alec deplaned at the surprisingly modern airport in the quaint city of Drago, the capital of Zakhar. His computer bag was slung over his left shoulder as he made his way up the jetway, leaving his right arm free as always—he was one of the few men post-9/11 allowed to carry a firearm on board a plane, and he never went anywhere unarmed. After a quick glance at one of the overhead monitors, he headed down the wide corridor with the rest of the passengers toward Baggage Claim.

His posting as regional security officer to the US embassy here in Zakhar had come as a great surprise, given what had happened at his last posting. As if he was being rewarded instead of punished.

Despite the fact that he already spoke rudimentary Zakharan—courtesy of an earlier assignment guarding Her Serene Highness, Princess Mara Theodora of

Zakhar, before she became an American citizen—he certainly hadn't been expecting this. He'd thought he'd be banished to the diplomatic equivalent of Siberia for a long time.

Instead, it was almost as if someone had pulled strings on his behalf to get him here, but that didn't make sense. Alec didn't have the political connections to make this happen, and it had been bugging him ever since the word came down where he was being assigned next.

He'd heard a rumor the king of Zakhar had specifically requested him, but that rumor was so fantastical he'd discounted it immediately. The king knew *of* him—how could he not, when Alec had been one of his sister's bodyguards in the US?—but the king didn't *know* him.

So the reason why he'd been tapped for this plum assignment was still a mystery to him...for all of ninety seconds. That was how long it took for Alec to exit Security and spot Trace McKinnon behind the barricade, waiting for him. And he began to smell a rat. A large, deadly rat who worked for Alec's brother-in-law, Cody Walker, at the Denver branch of the ultra-secret "agency." Who also happened to be married to Princess Mara. And suddenly the fantastical rumor didn't seem so fantastical, after all.

"I should have known," was all Alec said as he shook McKinnon's hand.

"Hey, don't look at me. I just volunteered to meet your flight, that's all. If you want to thank anyone, thank my wife. She's the one who asked her brother to intercede on your behalf."

Alec's smile morphed into a frown. "Wait a second. I don't want anything I haven't earned."

Trace spared him a cynical glance as they walked toward Baggage Claim. "You know as well as I do that in the real world it's not always *what* you know but *who* you know. But don't think you didn't earn this assignment. Not to mention, you did the right thing taking down those terrorists, no matter what anyone says."

Alec shook his head. "Diplomatically—"

McKinnon uttered a pithy, four-letter word. "You're alive. They're not. Score one for the good guys."

They arrived at the baggage carousel for Alec's flight and stood there waiting for his checked luggage to appear. "So what are you doing in Zakhar? Don't tell me you're on assignment here."

McKinnon shook his head. "No, Mara and I are here on family business. The king's wife just had a baby, hadn't you heard? You'd better believe it's a big deal here in Zakhar—the birth of the crown prince, the continuation of a dynasty going back more than five hundred years. This country has been celebrating almost nonstop for a month. We're here for the christening ceremony, along with a bevy of international dignitary invitees, including our very own secretary of state standing in for the president." He grinned. "You can thank him in person for putting in a good word for you with your boss—Mara made sure you received an invitation to the christening."

Startled, Alec said, "Thanks… I think. Speaking of babies, I hear congratulations are in order for you and the princess, too."

McKinnon's smile deepened into one of intense satisfaction. "Yeah, this summer. I didn't plan on more than one at a time, but as Mara says, children can't help being born—they have no choice in the matter. So we're now the proud parents of twins, a boy and a girl."

"How's that working out for you?"

"It's hectic," was all McKinnon would say. But his grin told Alec he wouldn't have it any other way.

Following the two from a distance, off-duty lieutenant Angelina Mateja tucked her short, blond hair behind one ear and commented softly to her companion in Zakharan, "So *that* is the new RSO at the US embassy. He is younger than I thought for such an important position."

Captain Marek Zale smiled with amusement, turning his intense gaze toward her for a moment. "He is thirty-six. More than a year older than the king. Not so young."

"He appears younger." *And more handsome than I expected,* Angelina thought but didn't say. As one of the first female officers in the Zakharian National Forces, she was extremely careful about what she said to Captain Zale or anyone else she worked with.

Zakhar was fifty years behind the times in many ways, especially regarding women. The Zakharian National Forces had only opened to women after King Andre Alexei had ascended the throne of Zakhar four and a half years earlier. The men she worked with were just waiting for some sign she wasn't up to the job. Which meant she could never be anything less than the perfect professional officer.

Angelina towered over the petite queen she guarded so faithfully. Her five feet eleven inches without shoes made her nearly as tall as most of the men on the secu-

rity detail. And her skill with weapons of all sorts—
not to mention her skills without weapons—made her
perfectly qualified for her assignment as one of the
queen's bodyguards.

She was a formidable adversary with a hard-as-nails
reputation she'd worked diligently to earn. More than
one man on the queen's security detail had lost to her
during hand-to-hand combat training exercises. She'd
even taken down Captain Zale once, though that was
probably more from surprise than anything else. She'd
never managed to do it a second time, although she'd
tried. Repeatedly.

Now, watching the American heft a suitcase off the
baggage carousel, Angelina felt an unusual twinge of
physical attraction, a jolt of sexual desire in her belly…
and lower. It wasn't something she usually felt. Wasn't
something she usually *let* herself feel. But there it was.

Auburn-haired Alec Jones wasn't nearly as handsome as Princess Mara's husband, Trace McKinnon,
who was standing next to him. But he had a male attraction all his own, and was in superb fighting shape—
something that appealed to Angelina on the most basic
level. Even though he was covered with clothing, she
could see the muscles that pulled his jacket taut across
his broad shoulders.

She had an instant's vision of him naked—honed to
muscle, sinew and bone, much as she was—and wondered what it would be like to take *him* to her bed instead of the man she'd picked to rid her of her virginity
at the age of twenty. Curiosity had been followed by
disappointment nine years ago, but—Angelina's blue-
gray eyes gleamed momentarily—she didn't think sex
with this man would be disappointing. Far from it.

Just as quickly as the thought occurred to her she banished it, but not without regret. She'd long ago resolved that any kind of romantic involvement, not to mention sex, was incompatible with her job in the Zakharian National Forces. Especially given the patronizing attitude toward women held by most of the men in the rank and file as well as the officers. Sex with any man—even a non-Zakharian—was the *last* thing she should be thinking about. She wasn't about to risk her reputation, or her job, for a man. No matter how sexy and irresistible he was.

Alec turned abruptly and spotted a woman across the airport watching him. Intently. She was tall, blonde and slender, with a touch-me-and-die air about her. He didn't know why, but she pushed all his buttons without even trying, and he felt himself responding to her. Hard. Fast. He laughed under his breath and ordered his body to stand down. But he wasn't surprised when his body refused to obey.

The woman and the man with her were both dressed in the kind of clothes he usually wore when on duty— what he was wearing now, actually—including a jacket to hide his shoulder holster. And there was something about them that seemed eerily familiar, something that reminded him of his own expression when he unexpectedly spotted himself in a mirror in public. A watchfulness in their eyes. An alertness in the way they held themselves, as if ready for anything. *Bodyguards?* he wondered. He glanced around but didn't see anyone they might be guarding. Still…

"Five will get you ten, those two are bodyguards," he murmured to McKinnon as they walked in the direction of the pair, not even needing to indicate to his friend who he was talking about.

McKinnon laughed softly. "No bet," he said. "I made them as bodyguards, too, five minutes ago." He looked closer as they approached the couple, and his laughter faded. His mouth took on a grim cast and he cursed softly before adding, "I know them. Both of them. Which means they're not here by accident."

Since the eyes of the four had already met and held, the two Zakharians didn't bother trying to evade Alec and McKinnon as they came up to them.

The man read the expression on McKinnon's face, and said quickly, "Your wife, she was concerned for your safety. But she knew you would refuse protection, so she asked the queen what could be done…secretly. The queen asked us as a special favor if we would keep an eye on you when we were free to do so." He shrugged, and a small smile played over his lips. "So we are here. Have you ever tried to refuse your queen anything?"

Alec grinned, caught McKinnon's eye and tried but failed to stifle his smile. Substitute the words *your princess* for *your queen*, and he knew McKinnon wouldn't have been able to answer in the affirmative. He held out his hand. "Hi, I'm Alec Jones. I'm the new regional—"

"Regional security officer for the US embassy," the man completed the sentence for him. "Yes, we know. I am Captain Marek Zale," he added. "And this is Lieutenant Angelina Mateja. Queen's security detail."

Alec shook both their hands. "Pleased to meet you."

Angelina said abruptly, "You were once assigned to guard Princess Mara when she first went to Colorado, yes? You and your brother. She has spoken of you both with affection."

Alec was mesmerized by both her face and voice, not to mention her body. For once he didn't have to look down to talk with a woman—Lieutenant Mateja was only a couple inches shorter than he was, and somehow that was especially appealing. She didn't wear any makeup, not that he could see, but she didn't need it. Hers was an understated beauty of blue eyes so pale they were almost gray, baby-fine skin that begged for the caress of a man's fingers and good bone structure that would age well. All surrounded by a sassy cap of straight corn-silk blond hair.

And her voice? The slightly accented English and the word order to her sentences reminded him of Princess Mara, but she spoke in a deep, rich contralto that made him think of warm, gooey caramel melting on top of vanilla ice cream. As for her body, she was lithe and lean, but there were curves for a discerning man to appreciate. And Alec was a *very* discerning man.

"Yeah," Alec answered Lieutenant Mateja's question after a few seconds. "Liam—my younger brother, that is—and I, and this guy here," he said, indicating McKinnon with a tilt of his head, "we were all the princess's bodyguards the first six months she taught at the University of Colorado in Boulder." He slid a sideways glance at McKinnon. "Then she married McKinnon—" *there's no accounting for taste*, his bantering tone and expression conveyed "—and the State Department decided she no longer needed DSS protection, so Liam and I were pulled off the job."

Alec focused on Lieutenant Mateja again, wondering—as most men wondered when they encountered an attractive woman—what she'd be like in bed. He smiled inside as he imagined making love to someone he didn't have to bend down to kiss. Someone he could stretch out next to on the sheets. Someone as toned and taut as he was. But he was careful not to let his imaginings show on his face.

She already pushed his buttons, and now that he'd heard her voice, he was even more attracted to her than he had been earlier, and that was saying a lot.

It had been a while for him. His career with the DSS meant he was often posted outside the United States— DSS special agents had to be available for assignment anywhere in the world on short notice. And his last posting had been in the Middle East. *Look but don't touch* was the watchword for a prudent man in the Middle East where local women were concerned. As for Darla, the incident at the coffeehouse had put paid to any possibilities where she was concerned.

Then, when he'd been hustled out of the country, he hadn't been back in the States long enough to pick up the threads of his social life before being posted to Zakhar. So it had been a while. Longer than he cared to acknowledge.

But now that he'd met Angelina Mateja, Alec was suddenly looking forward to his new assignment with a renewed—and very male—interest.

Chapter 2

Alec woke well before dawn. Crossing several time zones in his flight from Washington, DC, to Zakhar meant that his sleep-wake pattern wasn't geared for local time. It would only take him a couple of days—three at the most—to adjust. But until then…he just had to suffer.

Despite the early hour, his body told him in no uncertain terms it had enough sleep. So he slipped from his decently comfortable bed, tugged on the appropriate clothes, tucked his spare SIG Sauer in the ankle holster he quickly strapped on and headed out for some much-needed exercise. Tiring his body out would help it adjust faster. Then all he had to do was force himself to stay awake until nightfall, and he was halfway there.

Alec was assuming the apartment lease held by the outgoing RSO—an apartment conveniently only five minutes away from the embassy—but until he officially took over the reins the day after tomorrow, the other guy was still in residence. The embassy had arranged for him to bunk temporarily at this little bed-and-breakfast near the center of Drago. The widow who ran it had given Alec his set of keys last night, and he quickly grabbed them off the nightstand before treading noiselessly down the stairs and out the front door.

This part of the city was mostly shrouded in darkness so early in the morning, with only an occasional street lamp to guide the way. There was light from the airport on the outskirts of town and the palace on the hill, but most of Drago was dark, its inhabitants quietly sleeping.

Alec wasn't overly concerned. Violent crime in Drago—in all of Zakhar, for that matter—was rare. The average tourist didn't have to worry about getting mugged.

He'd also studied a detailed map of Drago on the flight over, and had committed it to memory. It was one of the little knacks he had. His sister, Keira, called him the human Global Positioning System because, after studying a map, he could find his way just about anywhere and never got turned around or lost. *Helpful for someone who travels the world,* he reminded himself with a glimmer of a smile.

Now he turned left and headed toward the river, jogging at a steady pace. The air was cool, almost cold, and for a minute Alec regretted he hadn't dressed warmer. But then he dismissed the thought. His body would warm up quickly once he really got going.

Little threads of mist floated near the ground, and

the closer he got to the river the stronger and more eerie the mist became. He finally reached the embankment and turned left again. There was a wide walkway here that followed the river's meandering course for miles. What had obviously once been hard-packed dirt from centuries of use had been paved with porous asphalt to accommodate all-weather users. He held by his father's maxim with regard to running—go as far out as you possibly can, until your body calls it quits… Then turn around and head back. He figured this walkway would help him accomplish just that.

Alec had been jogging for roughly ten minutes when he heard the soft slap of running shoes on asphalt coming up behind him. He glanced over his shoulder but saw nothing. He slowed, then turned around and jogged in place for a few seconds until a figure materialized out of the mist and darkness, closing the gap between them quickly.

He smiled when he recognized the tall, slender woman on the footpath. "Lieutenant Mateja," he acknowledged.

She'd obviously been running for some time. Perspiration darkened the underarms of her gray sweatshirt, but her breathing wasn't even ragged when she briefly returned his smile and answered, "Good morning, Special Agent Jones."

Alec swung into step beside her. "The name's Alec."

She considered this for a moment and then nodded her assent to his implied offer. "Alec," she agreed. "I am Angelina to my friends." She hesitated for a moment, then added abruptly, "It is a good omen, your name. A good omen for the job you do. Defender of the People. That is what Alec means."

"How do you know that?"

"The meaning of names is a hobby of mine. Since I was a little girl, you understand. Names have always fascinated me. I remember when…" She hesitated.

"When…?" he prompted.

"When the king was a boy—he was the crown prince then, of course—his names caught my imagination. Andre Alexei. Manly Defender. That is what his names mean. A good omen for Zakhar, I thought, for a man who would be king someday, yes?"

"If you believe in that sort of thing."

"He has borne that out," Angelina insisted earnestly. "He is a man with strong convictions. He would lay down his life for what he believes. His example inspired me. His sister, too. If not for them, I would not be where I am today."

The conversation had gotten a little too intense a little too quickly for Alec, so he teased gently, "And what does Angelina mean? Angel-face?"

She flashed a startled glance in his direction, as if gauging the intent behind his compliment. Eventually an uncertain smile played over her lips, but something about her expression made Alec think she didn't often get personal compliments. Or maybe she didn't allow herself to *accept* personal compliments very often. *And isn't that curious?* he thought. *A beautiful woman like her?*

"So tell me," he coaxed as they ran companionably side by side. "If it doesn't mean Angel-face, what does Angelina mean?"

"Messenger of God." She looked uncomfortable, as if she thought he might think she was trying to lay claim to something she didn't deserve. "But my parents did not pick my name for that reason. They named me Angelina Zuzana because those were my grandmothers' names. Zuzana means lily."

"Angelina Zuzana. Beautiful names for a beautiful woman."

She didn't respond at first, and Alec could tell she was also uncomfortable being called beautiful. But then she said, "Thank you." Exactly like a woman who'd been raised to be polite…even if she didn't believe you.

A momentary silence hung between them until Alec asked casually, "If you're so into names, what does Liam mean? Liam's my younger broth—"

"Your brother, yes, I know. You are close?"

"Yeah. But I don't see him very often. We're usually on opposite sides of the world. Guarding Princess Mara together was a gift. I'm grateful for it but don't expect it to happen again. So do you know what his name means?"

"Strong-willed Warrior." Angelina laughed softly, clearly more at ease when the conversation didn't revolve around her. "Your parents, they named you well for the profession you chose, both of you." She considered this for a moment. "Or perhaps you chose the profession *because* of your names?"

Alec couldn't have cared less about good omens or bad where names were concerned, or why he and Liam had picked their line of work, but he did care about keeping Angelina talking to him in this friendly way. So after a moment he asked, "What about Keira? That's my baby sister's name."

Angelina darted a glance toward him, her eyes flickering over his hair. "Does she resemble you?"

He smiled ruefully. "You mean, does she have red hair, like me? Yeah. Sort of red-gold. Short and curly. Very pretty. Not really like my hair, thank goodness." He ruffled his short crop of auburn hair.

"Then your parents must not have known," she replied, breaking into a real smile without breaking stride. "I am not positive—it has been years since I studied the meaning of names—but I think Keira means Black-Haired."

Alec burst out laughing. "I guess they missed the boat on that one."

"Missed the boat?" Her forehead crinkled in question.

"That just means they made a mistake, that's all."

"Oh. Thank you for explaining."

"Other than her brown eyes, Keira doesn't really look like me or like Liam. She looks more like our older brothers...but don't tell them I said so."

"Why is that?" she asked swiftly.

"Well..." Alec considered the question. "Neither Shane nor Niall have red hair," he said, unable to hide that his own red hair was a sore spot with him, "and they have all the looks in the family—and Keira, of course. Shane and Niall look nothing alike, but Keira is like the best of both of them. In a feminine version, of course."

"Of course."

"I came along two years after Niall, and Liam followed not quite a year later. Everyone thinks we're twins 'cause we look so much like each other." His lips quirked ruefully. "Right down to our hair. Our mannerisms, and the way we talk, too. And of course, we both went into the US Marine Corps and the DSS.

So I guess it's natural people think we're twins." He paused for a moment. "Then two years after Liam, my mom had Keira." He chuckled. "My dad always kidded that my mom broke his perfect record—four boys and then one girl."

Angelina smiled perfunctorily at his little joke, but Alec could see she wasn't really amused. *Kind of like Keira,* he thought suddenly. Keira had never cared for the way their dad thought less of her because she was female. Wasn't that why Keira had always fought with brothers who were physically bigger and stronger than she was, to be respected as an equal? Wasn't that why she'd followed all four of her brothers into the Marine Corps? And wasn't that why she'd nearly died a few years back, because she was trying to prove to the agency she worked for that she was as good or better at her job than any man?

Alec suddenly realized they'd been jogging for a couple of miles, and Angelina had kept pace with him the entire way. She wasn't winded at all. Her feet kept time with his in a steady cadence, like the beat of a heart. His heart. The thought disturbed him in a way he'd never been disturbed before, but he didn't know why.

"What about you?" he asked after a minute's reflection, trying to bring his thoughts under control by making small talk. "Brothers? Sisters?"

She shook her head. "I had a brother who died when he was a baby. Then there was me. After that, my mother could have no more children. But I have a younger cousin—*had* a younger cousin—who was like a little sister to me. I have not seen her in many years."

She folded her lips together as if she had intended to say more but wouldn't.

Alec knew better than to ask her for an explanation. Not yet, anyway. Not with that closed, forbidding expression on her face. So he cast around in his mind for a new topic of conversation and settled on, "I know there's not much crime here, but aren't you—I don't know—a little worried about being out alone this early? I mean, you were obviously on your own in the dark and the mist for some time before we met up. Most women I know wouldn't risk it. Not in the States, anyway."

Angelina didn't say anything. She slowed slightly, and before Alec knew it, she had grabbed his arm, braced herself, and he found himself flat on his back on the grassy verge beside the path, with Angelina kneeling on his chest, one forearm against his throat.

Despite having the wind knocked out of him, the minute he caught his breath he began laughing. He couldn't help it. "Okay," he said, admiration leaching into his voice. "You've made your point."

She scrambled up and held out her hand to assist Alec in rising, and he took it. But instead of letting Angelina help him up as she expected, he tugged sharply, pulling her down on top of him again. He rolled over swiftly, taking her with him, until she was wedged tightly between his body and the ground. She squirmed, but he had her pinned neatly by his weight and the firm hold he had on her arms. "Never assume a man's no longer a threat," he warned her softly. "Unless he's dead."

She stopped struggling then. He gazed down into her face, watching the play of emotions that flickered over it, and was surprised. Chagrin—what he'd expected to see—wasn't followed by anger at how he'd turned the tables on her. Instead, it was quickly replaced by acceptance of a hard lesson learned. Alec had a feeling Angelina never forgot anything she learned, especially anything she learned the hard way.

Part of him wanted to stay like this, feeling her strong body beneath his the way he'd imagined the day before, but he was too much of a gentleman to take advantage of the situation. He jumped to his feet, pulling her up with him.

They dusted themselves off silently. Then, still without saying a word, they resumed their jogging. But something had changed between them. Alec couldn't put his finger on it, and he wasn't sure what it meant.

"You are good," she said finally, surprising him once again. Her tone was admiring, the compliment sincere, not grudging as he would have expected.

"So are you."

She shook her head. "With some men, yes. But not with you. You are like Captain Zale. I took you by surprise, that is all. I cannot expect to do that again."

The sun was rising over the mountains now, dispelling the river mist and painting the eastern sky with a rosy glow that reflected off both of them. Angelina was silent for a moment and then said softly, diffidently, "I do not believe your older brothers have all the looks in the family." Totally out of the blue. As if the subject had never been changed. Her serious blue-gray eyes met Alec's, and he could see what that admission meant to a woman like her.

He stopped so suddenly she didn't realize he was going to—*he* didn't realize he was going to—and she kept running for a few steps. Then she halted, turned and faced him. "What is wrong?" she asked. "Why have you stopped?"

Why did you say that? He wanted to ask, but didn't. For the first time since he'd been a callow teenager, he felt unsure of himself. Unsure of the woman he was with. Angelina was so different from all the women he'd known—except maybe his sister—that he didn't know what to make of her.

The blood was suddenly pulsing through his body. His fingers tingled, his breath ran ragged. Not from running. His body had never felt this way after running. This was an awareness. A sudden, urgent need to eliminate the distance between them. To make her tell him what she meant by that seemingly innocuous statement and the enigmatic expression in her eyes. To touch her. Ravage her. Leave his mark on her.

She didn't move when he did. Another woman would have quailed at the male intensity in his face. Another woman would have retreated. But Angelina wasn't like any other woman. She wouldn't back down. Ever. And something in Alec responded to that knowledge. Fiercely.

She was in his arms before he knew it. They were both damp, sweaty, both fighting for control of themselves, and each other. Her body was firm and hard against his, as he'd known it would be. But it was soft, too, a softness so totally unexpected it disarmed him.

Their lips met, but not in a kiss. No, definitely nothing as *tame* as a kiss. This was war between them, their mouths fused as if they were both firing shots over the bow in a take-no-prisoners stance. Hunger roared through his body, and an aching need to give her back just a tiny fraction of what she was giving him.

Then it was over. Angelina tore herself out of his embrace, and Alec watched as she wiped the back of her hand across her mouth, as if she was removing the taste of him from her lips. As if she could wipe out the memory the same way.

"Why did you do that?" she asked him finally.

"Because you wanted me to." It sounded arrogant put that way, so he added, "Because *I* wanted to."

"That is not true."

"Which? That I wanted to kiss you?" One corner of his mouth twitched upward into an engaging grin. "I wanted to. Oh, yeah, I definitely wanted to, since the first moment I saw you."

She shook her head. "Not that. You said I wanted you to kiss me. And that is not true."

His grin faded and he held her gaze with his steady one. "Yes, you did," he told her, accepting the truth even if she refused to acknowledge it. "You wanted to know what it would be like. We both did. And now we know." *And nothing will ever be the same again.*

Aleksandrov Vishenko sat in his luxurious pied-à-terre in the heart of Manhattan, sipping at his snifter of Courvoisier L'Essence, pondering ways and means. He'd been contacted—through secure channels—by Prince Nikolai Marianescu, the king of Zakhar's cousin. The cousin who'd failed so miserably eighteen months ago to dethrone the king and take his place, and who now resided in a prison cell.

The king's cousin had named most of his co-conspirators in the plot to kill the king—including two of Vishenko's henchmen—but he had not dared to name Vishenko himself. Now he was trying to use his previous silence—and the threat of disclosure—to force Vishenko to do his bidding. The prince wanted revenge on Zakhar's royal couple by assassinating their precious son who was not yet a month old—the heir all of Zakhar had prayed for.

Crown Prince Raoul was vulnerable, the prince insisted. There was a perfect window of opportunity coming up for him to die a very public, very gruesome death his parents would never recover from. The perfect revenge.

Vishenko smiled to himself, a smile that didn't reach his eyes, and reluctantly came to the same conclusion as the unfortunate prince who thought he still had leverage from within his prison cell. It was a false assumption, but Vishenko was not going to say so. Not yet.

He had his own reasons for wanting the child dead, and they had nothing to do with vengeance. Only expedience. A means to a desired end.

He didn't want Zakhar's king dead—not anymore—despite the ongoing risk of his illegal activities being exposed. Despite the fact that the Russian Brotherhood, the Bratva—a branch of which Vishenko headed in the US as well as Zakhar—cared nothing for the monarchy. Any monarchy. Or any government, for that matter.

The king was good for Zakhar, and therefore good for Vishenko—that was all he cared about. Stable governments meant stable economies, which were greatly beneficial to his various legitimate enterprises all over the world, including Zakhar. All his legitimate Zakharian enterprises had prospered these past few years under the king's rule. And he was nothing if not a pragmatist.

He just wanted the king…distracted for a time. Wanted the king's attention focused elsewhere, just long enough for Vishenko's men to wind down the operation that threatened to expose his identity.

The arrival of the American embassy's new regional security officer, Alec Jones—who the current RSO insisted was incorruptible—had prompted the Americans to suggest shutting things down immediately.

He couldn't do it. There were women in the pipeline, and the operation was just too profitable to bring it to a screeching halt. Especially when it had just been expanded six months ago. If the new RSO was truly not susceptible to bribery—and Vishenko was by no means convinced of that, since he believed every man had his price—then perhaps Alec Jones could be… nullified…in another fashion. The Americans would balk, of course. Corruption was one thing in their minds. Murder was something completely different.

So perhaps it would be better to do as the Americans wanted and shut things down…for now. A few more weeks—that's all his men needed to wrap things up and put the operation in Zakhar on the shelf. It could be dusted off later and reinstated if circumstances changed. If not…well, there were other European countries, after all. It would just be a matter of bribing the right officials.

Aleksandrov Vishenko had operated in the shadow world for years with few people the wiser, reaping the rewards that came to a man who had no scruples. No morals. It would not have been a bad thing if Prince Nikolai had dethroned the king of Zakhar and taken his place, for then Vishenko would have had the new king in his pocket.

Not to be, he thought with a fatalistic shrug. Prince Nikolai was in jail and would remain there. Which meant Vishenko was safe...for now. But that could change.

So the little crown prince had to die. Unfortunate but necessary. And when he did, Prince Nikolai would die, as well. Wrapping up that loose end, making it appear a suicide, would be tricky. But no more impossible than other deaths Vishenko had successfully arranged over the years, including deaths inside prisons. No more impossible than killing the crown prince.

There is one more loose end I must eliminate, he reminded himself coldly, clinically. This one would be harder to accomplish than killing the two princes— man and child—because he at least knew where they were. It was different with Caterina. She had run six years ago, vanishing into thin air, and had never been found despite the bounty he'd placed on her head. He'd agonized at first—unnecessarily, as it turned out— that Caterina would take the evidence she'd compiled against him to the feds, and he'd lived in fear for nearly two years, waiting for the ax to fall. Waiting to be arrested. Tried. Convicted. He'd finally relaxed...but not completely. His men had continued searching for her, to no avail.

Caterina had been a grievous error in judgment— two grievous errors, he admitted. Letting her into his life...and letting her live to tell. *I will not be secure until all three are dead,* he thought as he savored another sip of brandy. Prince Nikolai. Crown Prince Raoul. And Caterina Mateja.

Chapter 3

Alec sat quietly in a small conference room with only the secretary of state, the king of Zakhar and a man who'd been introduced as Colonel Marianescu, head of internal security. Though nothing more was said, Alec knew Colonel Marianescu was the king's cousin as well as his closest confidant and adviser. The fact that only four men were in the room was a dead give-away something extremely confidential was going to be discussed.

The king opened by thanking both Americans for being there. "I asked for this private meeting with you, Mr. Secretary," he said, his steely gaze fixing on the secretary of state before moving to Alec, "and with your embassy's new regional security officer, to tell you I had more than just a personal reason behind my request for a new RSO at the embassy in Zakhar. I

wanted to speak to you both in person—privately—
to explain."

The king's lips tightened. "We have heard rumors of
corruption and fraud at the US embassy here in Drago
related to trafficking in women." His flint-eyed expression left no doubt how he felt about this. "Prostitution,
Mr. Secretary. *Forced* prostitution. The queen is in-
censed, and rightfully so—any decent person would
feel the same. And the word is this corruption at your
embassy is occurring at high levels. Possibly even the
highest levels."

The secretary of state looked shocked. "I can assure
you, Your Majesty, that—"

The king cut him off. "I do not want assurances
from you, sir. I believe you are sincerely shocked by
this allegation. Nevertheless, if the rumors are to be
believed, Zakharians are involved...as both predator
and prey. And there are whispers the Bratva may have
a hand in this, as well."

Cold anger was coming off the king in waves. "I
want this crime syndicate stopped *now*. Not a year
from now, or two years from now, after an investigation finds proof that holds up in a US courtroom." He
glanced at Alec again. "The Drago police force is already on the case, but that investigation can only go so
far. By bringing in a new RSO, whatever is going on at
the US embassy *will* be stopped. Now. I am sure of it."

He drew a deep breath and forcibly relaxed. Then
he smiled faintly at Alec. "If I could trust you with my
sister's safety, Special Agent Jones—and I did—I believe I can trust you in this."

The allegations disturbed Alec, but he wasn't
shocked. This wouldn't be the first time someone in

a position of trust within a US embassy was accused of visa fraud, although he wouldn't have thought the embassy here in Zakhar was a likely target for people desperate enough to pay under the table to obtain a US visa to escape the conditions under which they lived.

But trafficking in women was different. Luring Zakharian girls and women to the United States for prostitution—and there was a premium paid for pretty blondes, of which Zakhar seemed to have more than its fair share—was a completely different prospect, and Alec could see all too easily how it could be true. Especially if the Russian Mafia—the Bratva, or Brotherhood, as it was euphemistically called—was involved.

If the king was right, that meant he was walking into a hornet's nest when he took over as RSO tomorrow, because he'd have to start an investigation without any idea how far the corruption went. Without any idea who could be trusted...and who couldn't.

That's just dandy, Alec thought but didn't say. He'd long ago learned the control diplomatic protocol demanded of his tongue. *Thanks ever so much, Your Majesty, for handing me an assignment right in the middle of a secret war zone.*

"Who knows of this?" he asked the king.

"Who knows that I know? Only my closest, most trusted advisers. The queen, of course, and my cousin," he said, indicating the man who sat so impassively next to him. "Two of my bodyguards, who were with me when I was first informed. And the three policemen who immediately brought this to Colonel Marianescu's attention, as they should have—this is a threat to Zakharian national security. And now you.

"To the best of my knowledge, no one at the embassy has any idea. That is why I allowed the world to think I was merely acceding to my sister's insistence I do something to help you, Special Agent Jones, after the unfortunate incident in the Middle East. If I had requested the US replace the current RSO for any other reason, suspicions would have been raised. Suspicions I had no intention of raising." The king smiled that faint smile again, a smile Alec was starting to understand. "Everything dovetailed nicely."

Alec nodded, following the logic, and his admiration for the king rose a notch. He'd heard a lot about him from Princess Mara—some of which was secret from most of the world—and of course he'd studied up on Zakhar, its politics and its king when he'd received his assignment here. But he hadn't expected such astute political awareness, such adroit handling of a situation that might have stymied a lesser man.

He thought about ways and means, his mind racing. Then he turned to the secretary of state. "Since we have no idea how far the corruption goes, I don't dare trust anyone currently at the embassy—not even the ambassador. Not yet. So I think the best approach is to ask the agency to lend a hand in the investigation."

"The agency?" The secretary of state looked doubtful, even though the agency had been created in secret after 9/11 to do what neither the FBI nor the CIA had been able to do before that tragedy, and had quickly established itself within the secret confines of the US government.

"It wouldn't be the first time the State Department and the Bureau of Diplomatic Security asked for their help," Alec reminded him. "The DSS borrowed Trace

McKinnon from them when Princess Mara started teaching in Colorado, remember?"

"Wouldn't the agency's presence raise the alarm? Isn't that exactly what you're trying to avoid?"

Alec shook his head. "Not if we ask the agency for McKinnon. I've worked with him before, and frankly, he's the best of the best. He's already in Zakhar, with a perfectly legitimate reason for being here totally unrelated to any kind of investigation." He nodded to himself, seeing the plan take shape in his mind. "We're friends. He's related to the king by marriage. It would lend credence to the rumor the king pulled strings to get me here for personal reasons. Suspicions would be lulled, not raised."

He looked at the king, almost excited at the prospect of working with McKinnon again, even on something as troubling as this. "I think that's it, Your Majesty. The perfect solution. The agency's the best at this kind of covert investigation. And they're authorized by Congress to act both within and outside US borders, so we wouldn't be overstepping any legal boundaries. That'll be critical when it comes time to prosecute these guys. I know that's secondary as far as you're concerned, but—"

"But it is of prime importance to your government," the king answered. "That I understand." He glanced over at the secretary of state. "I have no objections to this plan, Mr. Secretary. Do you?"

"Security in the cathedral must be tight," Captain Zale told the queen's security detail in the conference room on the third floor of the palace, where they had assembled. "I cannot stress this enough. Tight yet covert. The king's security detail will be there, of course, alongside us and the men newly assigned to guard the crown prince. But the eyes of Zakhar will be upon the christening—which is being broadcast on television for the first time—not to mention much of the rest of the world. The king wishes nothing to disrupt the ceremony or detract from the religious solemnity of the occasion."

He cleared his throat. "If possible, of course. To that end, silencers for all security participants was considered but rejected for a variety of reasons, including the difficulty of covert carry with a silencer, and the fact that it changes the balance of a gun—not something senior leadership wanted to risk. Questions?"

Angelina had questions, but she wasn't going to ask them yet. No matter how much she and the two other women on the team tried to fit in, the men still resented it if the women spoke first in group meetings like this. She'd learned to pick her battles. She glanced left and right, and wasn't disappointed.

"What precautions are being taken?" one man asked.

Another man threw out, "Who is responsible for advance security on the cathedral?"

"Will the guests have to pass through a metal detector as they enter the cathedral?" a third man queried. "And if so, who will be monitoring it?"

Captain Zale dealt with these questions and several others, explaining so everyone knew exactly who was responsible for what, and who would be stationed where.

There was a short silence. Then, "With so many security details there to guard the royal family, the potential exists for fractionalization instead of us operating as a cohesive whole," Angelina said quietly. "What is being done to prevent this?"

Captain Zale cast her a quick nod of approval. "Good question, Mateja." He faced the entire room. "There will be a dry run in the cathedral on Saturday," he said. "A dress rehearsal, as it were. Everyone who is not on duty that day is expected to be in attendance. This will help lay down clear lines of communication between all three security details."

His eyes narrowed. "Remember, this is not a pissing contest," he said crudely. "The king's men will be there, and naturally they think they are superior. That they are in command. We are the queen's men, lesser beings in their eyes. This is not true, and I have it on the best authority—the king himself. We have been handpicked by him to guard the queen against any and every threat. So do not let the attitude of the king's men distract you. Let them think they are superior. We know the truth. And *we*—not *they*—will ensure a successful outcome. Any further questions?" Silence held sway. "You are dismissed."

Angelina skimmed down the wide, marble stairs of the grand staircase, her feet barely touching the carpeted treads. When she was a little girl her father had complained that Angelina never walked anywhere, that she was always in a hurry to get where she was going, and it was still true. Very little had changed about Angelina since her childhood.

Today was actually an off-duty day for her— although like everyone else on the queen's security detail she'd been called in for the mandatory meeting just now—and she had plans. There was still time… if she didn't dawdle.

She had one thing she felt compelled to do first—

related to both her job and her growing friendship with Queen Juliana. A friendship that had quietly begun during the queen's recent pregnancy, when the queen had confided in Angelina her fears and worries about her pregnancy in a friendly, disarming way that invited Angelina's confidences in return. A way that made her love Queen Juliana as a true friend and not just her queen—not surprising, really, since the queen was only a year older than Angelina, and hadn't been born to her lofty position.

Their friendship was something Angelina didn't broadcast, though. She didn't want anyone saying her next promotion was due to anything other than pure merit. But until she personally checked things out at the cathedral and assured herself that Queen Juliana and her baby would be safe, Angelina wouldn't feel free to enjoy her day off.

She'd just turned down a side corridor that would take her to the vast parking lot behind the palace where her little Fiat—one of her few prized possessions— was parked, when someone called to her. "Lieutenant Mateja! Angelina, wait up!"

She turned, saw Alec Jones and was immediately torn. She hadn't expected to see him again today and wasn't prepared to deal with him—especially after this morning.

But courtesy had been instilled in Angelina since before she could walk, and she couldn't just slip away as if she hadn't heard him calling her name. As if she hadn't seen him coming after her. "Special Agent Jones," she acknowledged when he drew near.

"Alec," he reminded her. "Remember?"

Angelina tried but failed miserably to control the

slight flush that tinged her cheeks. Not at the reminder that she'd already agreed to call him Alec, but of the kiss they'd shared. The kiss she'd pretended she hadn't wanted. The kiss that had knocked her world off-kilter.

Alec had been right this morning—*damn him,* she thought now. She'd wondered what it would be like to kiss him. And in that moment she'd *wanted* him to kiss her. She just hadn't been prepared for it—hadn't been prepared for the way her body had responded to being in his arms, either. Not at all.

But she wasn't going to admit it to him. "Alec," she agreed coolly. "Yes, I remember. What are you doing here?"

"Meeting," was all he said. "Business. You?"

"Meeting." She was as terse as he was.

"So where are you headed now?"

She considered his question for a moment and realized there was no reason not to tell him. "I am heading to Saint Anne's Cathedral."

He nodded with evident admiration, and Angelina realized he understood why she was going there, even without her saying another word. "Smart," he said. "Very smart. Mind if I tag along?"

She raised her eyebrows in a question, and he added, "I've been invited to attend the christening." He gave a little huff of rueful laughter. "McKinnon told me the princess wrangled an invitation for me. It would be rude to decline, especially since I'm here at the—" He stopped abruptly, and Angelina wondered what he'd been going to say. "Anyway," he continued smoothly, as if this was what he'd intended to say from the start, "since I'll be there, it would make me feel better to know the lay of the land. Advance knowledge never hurts, does it?"

"No, it does not," she acceded. She hesitated, of two minds about letting Alec go with her. Then she remembered he was a highly trained professional who'd been in the bodyguard business longer than she had, and he might have insights she would find helpful. Just as he'd taught her a very important lesson this morning, there were other things she could learn from him. All at once her treacherous thoughts skittered down a path she refused to take—*he could teach you many things, yes!*—and though her body thrilled to that idea, she quickly brought both her body and her thoughts under control.

"How did you come to the palace?" she asked him.

"Taxi." He smiled at her. "One of those cute little Zakharian taxis that seem to be everywhere. I could have called for an embassy limo—the official dignity of the embassy's RSO must be maintained, I'm told—but it seemed kind of stuffy. Or I could have walked. The taxi was a reasonable compromise."

"I have my car here," she said. "If you do not mind being driven by a woman."

Alec grinned as if at a secret joke, and Angelina mentally chastised herself for the verbal slipup. She knew American men were not like Zakharian men. Most of them anyway. American men were used to American women doing—and doing well—just about everything a man could do. But all Alec said was, "You wouldn't ask me that if you knew Princess Mara used to drive herself to and from the university where she worked. That meant I was always in the passenger seat."

* * *

Fifteen minutes later they were in the vaulted main chapel of Saint Anne's Cathedral in Drago. After identifying herself and Alec to the custodian, they were allowed to wander at will.

Saint Anne's Cathedral was laid out like a giant cross, with a side chapel on each side of the main area, or nave, as it was called, facing the apse and the altar, effectively doubling the seating capacity. Angelina was mentally calculating sight lines—envisioning where the royal parents would stand near the baptismal font, where the two sets of godparents would stand, and where the archbishop and the other members of the ecclesiastical team would stand—when Alec spoke.

"What's up there?" he asked, pointing to the distant loft in the rear.

She glanced up, following the direction of his arm. "Choir loft," she answered absently, and pulled a notebook from her pocket to jot down a couple of questions she wanted to ask Captain Zale.

"How do you get up there?"

"Staircase. Access from the foyer."

"Will there be a choir present at the christening?"

"Of course. This is an incredibly important event for Zakhar," she informed him a little stiffly. "It is not just the baptism of a child, you understand. It is a celebration of the future of our country. Something like your Fourth of July, Thanksgiving and New Year's celebrations all rolled into one. A two-hundred-voice choir will be singing the 'Te Deum.' Just as they did at the king's coronation. Just as they did at his wedding to the queen."

Alec nodded his understanding, but all he said was,

"Then it's not likely an assassin would try to hide up there."

"There will be men posted there nevertheless," she assured him. "We are taking no chances."

Alec had wandered past the altar while she spoke, and now he asked, "What's behind these pipes?" indicating the organ pipes, some of which stretched from floor to ceiling, in a series of wooden cases. There were spaces between the pipes, some only an inch or two, some more.

"Nothing. Just space to allow the notes to resonate throughout the cathedral. No one could stand behind those pipes…not when the organ is playing," Angelina explained. "And the organ will be playing during much of the service. The sound waves…you have to understand the sound waves would cause such pain no one would risk it. It could rupture the eardrums. You would be writhing on the floor."

"Hmm." He slipped behind the pipes. Between the pipes and the wall was a large recess with access from both sides.

"What are you thinking?" she asked, following him, curious.

"What's to prevent an assassin from wearing high-tech noise-canceling headphones?"

Angelina opened her mouth to answer but closed it again, with her words unsaid, realizing he was right. She glanced at the notebook in her hand and quickly wrote Alec's question down—another thing to mention to Captain Zale—noting at the same time how much light the spaces between the pipes allowed into the shadowed recess. Enough light to write. Which meant plenty enough space to shoot between.

You were right to bring Alec with you, she told herself. *Perhaps someone else has thought of this, but
perhaps not.* She turned and faced the apse, peering
through one of the gaps, trying to think like an assassin. Despite the relatively narrow spaces between the
pipes, up close she could clearly see everything in front
of the altar. *A man could stand behind the organ pipes
and take aim between them. It would not be difficult.*

"It's not that hard a shot to make," Alec said softly
as he came to stand next to Angelina.

"You are correct," she told him. "Where they will
be during the ceremony—the entire royal family—I
could make that shot. In the pews. At the baptismal
font. At the altar. I could make it easily."

Her eyes met his. And just that quickly Angelina's
thoughts turned from the deadly serious business at
hand, to remembering what it had felt like when this
man had kissed her. Held her. Caressed her. The iron
hardness of his body when he'd pulled her down and
trapped her beneath him early this morning. The taste
of him on her lips.

So long. It had been so long since she'd let herself
even *think* of men as men. So long since she'd let herself remember she was a woman with a woman's heart,
a woman's needs. So long since she'd let herself relax
her guard enough to even consider the possibility of a
sexual relationship with a man.

But she was thinking of it now. Because *he* was
making her think of it. Because he'd kissed her this
morning as if it was a perfectly normal and natural
thing—which it was—but not for her.

She shuddered and caught her breath as a wave of
longing swept through her, longing for something she

knew she could never have. She started to turn away, but he stopped her, his hand warm and firm on her arm. And that intensified the ache.

His lips captured hers—or was it the other way around? Angelina didn't know who had moved first, but just like this morning, they were both aroused, both fighting for control, both trembling in the grip of a need that possessed them to the exclusion of all other thought.

"Angel," he whispered between incendiary kisses that set off sparks throughout her body. Holding her so tightly she knew she couldn't escape. Even if she'd wanted to escape...which she didn't. "Oh God, Angel."

No one had ever called her Angel. Not her parents, not her cousin, not her friends. No one. She didn't know why, but somehow, when Alec called her Angel, it made her feel special. Cherished. Unique. A name for him alone.

He pressed her against the organ pipes, then grasped one of her thighs and pulled it up, up, until he was holding her bent knee, stroking it through the slacks she wore. But she might as well not have been wearing anything for all the protection they afforded her. Because, with her knee raised and clasping his hip, the crux of her thighs was open to him. Vulnerable. And he pressed his erection against her mound until she moaned. Moaned, and melted.

She couldn't think. She tried, but thought was impossible. Her entire world had condensed into this moment in time, into desire that left her shaking and desperate. The only thing that let Angelina hold on to her sanity was the knowledge that Alec was as desperate as she was. That he was shaking, too. That she wasn't the only one vulnerable.

A sound impinged on her consciousness, the sound of footsteps echoing in the cathedral, then of someone calling her name in Zakharan. "Lieutenant Mateja?"

Angelina tore herself away from Alec, just as she had this morning. But this time she didn't try to pretend she hadn't wanted him as much as he'd wanted her. This time she didn't wipe the taste of him away.

"We cannot do this," she whispered to Alec. "*I* cannot do this." Putting on a calm face, she quickly moved out from behind the organ pipes. "I am here," she told the custodian in Zakharan, thankful she didn't wear lipstick that would now be smudged. She hoped the wizened little man wouldn't think to look behind the pipes, wouldn't ask where Alec was, or he'd wonder what the hell they were doing in that recessed space and put two and two together.

"You said you only needed a half hour," the custodian reminded her. "It has been almost twice that. It is nearly noon, and I must lock up so I can go to lunch. Are you finished here?"

"Five more minutes," she promised him. "I will be quick. I only have one more thing to check."

As soon as the custodian walked away, Alec came out from behind the pipes. She sensed his stare, but refused to meet his eyes, ashamed of what had taken place between them. Any kind of romantic entanglement was incompatible with the life she'd chosen. Every man she'd dated—and there hadn't been all that many since she'd joined the queen's security detail—automatically expected that once their relationship grew serious, Angelina would quit her dangerous job.

And that was *not* going to happen…until Angelina herself determined she could no longer do her job to her own satisfaction. As long as she stayed in peak physical condition, as long as her reaction time meant no one was better than she was at protecting the queen, her choice was clear.

She couldn't be soft and yielding, not for any man. She couldn't be anything other than what she was—tough and uncompromising. She couldn't even pretend…as other women she knew pretended. And that meant the life most Zakharian women took for granted was out of the realm of possibility for her.

Even if she didn't get involved romantically, even if this was only sex—*only sex*? she asked herself, remembering how things had exploded between Alec and her—she wasn't willing to risk her reputation. Things were difficult enough for a woman in the Zakharian National Forces. When sex reared its ugly head, men tended to look at women differently. *As if they didn't already.*

This was twice now she had surrendered to her body's insistent demands. Twice she had let Alec inside her defenses. Twice she had let herself forget who and what she was. And that was two times too many.

Chapter 4

Least said, soonest mended. Alec could hear the words in his head as clearly as if his mother were standing next to him reciting that old maxim. And he knew the wisest course of action was to say nothing to the outgoing RSO. What did you say to a man who was being bounced out of a coveted job to make room for you? Ostensibly because of political favoritism, but really because he was suspected of fraud and corruption?

No, it was better to say nothing at all, not even to commiserate with the guy over being displaced. So he listened politely as the outgoing RSO—a man he'd crossed paths with before—went through his calendar and case roster with Alec.

He noted that the guy had a hard time meeting Alec's eyes, and his laughter seemed forced—*signs of a guilty conscience?* Alec wondered. *Or just that he doesn't quite know what to say to me, too, especially since we know each other? It wasn't unheard of to be replaced on short notice. But it couldn't be easy. Still, it wasn't as if he was being demoted. Not exactly. And if he was clean, the DSS would soon place him as RSO somewhere else.*

"What's the ambassador like?" he asked, for something innocuous to say.

"Okay, I guess, for a political appointee."

Which didn't tell Alec much. He had an appointment with the ambassador this afternoon, and he was keeping an open mind. Even though the ambassador would also be a target in his upcoming investigation, that was just speculation at this point. The ambassador deserved respect from Alec in every way. At least until something was proved against him. As RSO, Alec was the personal adviser to the ambassador on all security issues, and was responsible for all aspects of the embassy's security. Conversely, Alec had every intention of using the ambassador as *his* adviser on all things Zakharian. At least until he got his feet wet.

"Well, I guess that's about it," the other man said. "You have the safe's combination already, but you'll change it, of course." He took a set of keys from his pocket and laid them on the desk in front of him. "You'll need these. Everything there opens a door somewhere in the embassy." The outgoing RSO smiled briefly, stood and offered his hand.

Alec didn't hesitate to shake it. He couldn't let the outgoing RSO suspect anything more than he might already suspect under the unusual circumstances.

* * *

Alec was run ragged over the next few days, but he loved every minute of it. This was work he was born to do, and he did it with style. With a flair all his own. Putting his personal stamp on the job without conscious effort.

In addition to his meeting with the ambassador, he held a meet-and-greet with the entire embassy staff, memorizing their names and matching faces to them. It was another little knack he had, a trick he'd learned back when he'd first joined the DSS—people loved being remembered. It cost him nothing and gained him willing cooperation when he least expected it.

He obtained a list of embassy employees from the ambassador on down, going back five years—including their work histories and whatever else was on file—and began going through the data meticulously. Alec had no idea how long the human trafficking might have been going on. He'd go back as far as necessary, but five years was a good start, and he'd work his way backward starting from the present. He put the current ambassador and his predecessor as RSO at the top of the list, because the king had specified the corruption could be occurring at the highest levels.

Related to the investigation, Alec met privately with Colonel Marianescu and the three policemen the king had specified were working the trafficking case from the Zakharian side of things. Zakhar's laws were stricter, their punishments more severe than in the United States, but crime existed everywhere, and Zakhar was no exception. The same rules of evidence didn't apply, though, and Alec couldn't help but feel a twinge of envy at how much easier it would be to make the case in Zakhar than it would be in the States, once all the evidence was assembled and indictments sought.

On Friday afternoon he met with Trace McKinnon at the palace to ensure complete privacy.

"The agency brought you up to speed?" Alec asked McKinnon when they were alone in the sitting room of the McKinnons' suite in the palace.

"Not really. All I was told was that the State Department asked for me again—something critical and urgent here in Zakhar—and that you would fill me in on everything."

Alec told him. It didn't take long—McKinnon didn't need all the *t*'s crossed and the *i*'s dotted. "I thought of you right off," Alec said. "Especially since you mentioned in the car from the airport that the princess took a year's leave of absence from the university after the twins were born. The plan wouldn't work if she had to rush home to get back to teaching, because it involves her, too."

"So you want Mara to stay on here in order to give me an ostensible reason for staying on, do I have that right?"

"Pretty much. And the job is right up the agency's alley. I wouldn't ask otherwise."

McKinnon nodded thoughtfully. "It tracks. And Mara did take a year's sabbatical." A smile crept across his face. "I'll have to check with her, but I know what she'll say."

"So, you're in?"

"Are you kidding? Making Mara happy by giving her a reason to stay here indefinitely? It's a no-brainer."

* * *

Angelina sat quietly in one corner of the queen's sitting room as Queen Juliana and Princess Mara drank tea and shared confidences about their husbands and their children in the way of longtime friends—which they were.

Angelina hadn't said anything when the queen had introduced her favorite bodyguard to her best friend a week ago, but she'd been thrilled to have finally met the princess who'd played such a pivotal role in her life. The princess was only a few months older than Angelina, but she'd been held up to Angelina as a role model by her mother since she was a little girl.

Angelina's mother hadn't realized Angelina wasn't patterning herself after the princess as a lady—she was inspired instead by the princess's scholastic achievements and steadfast determination to achieve her goals, despite the common Zakharian attitude toward women.

Angelina had been fired up to follow in the princess's footsteps. Not in mathematics—she'd known that wasn't her forte—but she'd pushed herself to excel scholastically just as the princess had done. She'd graduated from college a year early and followed that up immediately with law school and then a budding career as a prosecutor—as budding a career in the law as any woman could find in Zakhar—before joining the military.

Her original dream of being a prosecutor might have been supplanted by her current dream job as one of the queen's bodyguards, but that didn't mean her original dream was gone. Someday she'd go back to it. Just not anytime soon.

"Trace tells me you and Captain Zale met Alec at

the airport," Princess Mara said, and suddenly Angelina realized the princess was addressing her. "What did you think of him?"

Angelina wasn't about to admit she'd met Alec more than once—or that she'd kissed him twice—so she searched for something innocuous to say about a man the princess held in affection. "He seemed…nice, Your Highness."

"Mara, please," the princess said. "I am an American now, and I prefer the freedom of being just me." Her green eyes twinkled. "And Alec is many things, but *nice* is not a word I would have picked to describe him." She tilted her head to one side. "Liam, now, *he* is nice. Sweet, too. And idealistic. But Alec?" She shook her head. "No, Alec is not sweet. And he is not idealistic. But he is a man to contend with. I would not want to be on the wrong side of him, but I would trust him with my life."

Humming a tune under his breath, Alec left the McKinnons' suite and headed for the grand staircase. He was just about to go down when he saw a woman come out of another suite on the other side of the landing. A woman he recognized in a heartbeat. Recognized, and wanted to talk to. Urgently.

He'd thought of Angelina whenever he'd had a free moment. And even when he didn't really have a free moment, just a few seconds. Every night since he'd last seen her in the cathedral—since he'd kissed her until they were both trembling—he'd found himself thinking how lonely his bed was without her. As if they were already lovers. As if he knew what it would be like with her, so that her absence hurt. Physically. An ache that started—predictably—in his loins, but that spread throughout his body as he imagined her there next to him in bed.

"Angel." His voice wasn't loud, but it carried far enough.

She turned his way, startled. "Alec." She glanced around quickly and hurried over to where he stood at the top of the staircase. "You are not to call me that," she said in a hushed voice. When Alec tilted his head and gave her a questioning look, she explained, "You are not to call me Angel…in public."

"Why not?" Vivid in his memory was the moment he'd first used that name, and he could tell by her expression and the warm tide of color washing over her face she was remembering, too.

"It is…unprofessional."

"How is a nickname unprofessional?"

"Not any nickname, just that one." When Alec raised his brows in question, she added, "Because it is too…too feminine." Then she quickly changed the subject. "What are you doing here?"

"Visiting McKinnon. You?"

"I work here," she reminded him. "Queen's security detail, remember?"

"Right." He smiled at her, his most whimsical smile. Deliberately turning on the charm. "So when do you get off duty?"

She looked as if she wanted to smile back but wouldn't let herself. "Now, actually. I am done for the day."

Alec remembered Angelina saying, *"We cannot do this… I cannot do this,"* after they'd kissed in the cathedral. But she hadn't said why. Until she explained,

Alec wasn't about to just let it go. They *had* something together. Something good. Something explosive. Something worth fighting for. As long as he was in Zakhar—and he was here for at least a year, maybe more—he was going to pursue it. Unless she said no.

Alec wasn't a wolf. When a woman said no, that was it for him—he took her at her word. The trick was persuading her not to say no in the first place. To give her a damned good reason to say yes. "I cannot" wasn't the same thing as "no."

Now he said, "Dinner? I've got an apartment—I moved in two days ago—but I haven't had time to stock up the kitchen yet, so I've been eating out. I took the advice of somebody at the embassy last night—big mistake. Don't get me wrong, the food was okay. But a man on his own in a restaurant geared for couples gets shunted off to a table behind the service door, and the waiters act as if he's invisible."

Angelina made a valiant attempt to hold back her smile, but it was impossible. "I cannot see you allowing that to happen. Not you."

Alec grinned. "Okay, you're right. I didn't. But they tried. Believe me, they tried. It would've been easier if I'd had a date with me. Someone like you. A beautiful woman always gets great service."

She wasn't averse to the compliment—that was obvious. But just as obvious was the fact she wasn't expecting it—either the compliment or the flirtatious way it was delivered—and it took her off guard. Despite that, she came back quickly with, "Only if she is with a man. A woman dining out on her own in Zakhar is…unusual. Breakfast and lunch are not a problem. But dinner?" Her lips quirked into a hint of a smile.

"A woman alone is not considered a good tipper. But a man with a woman he is trying to impress—that is a different story."

He thought he knew the answer already, but he moved a step closer and asked, "So could I impress you…by being a big tipper?" His voice was husky with meaning.

She didn't back up, and he admired that about her. Most women would have…if a man invaded their personal space. But Angelina just shook her head. "You do not have to impress me that way," she said honestly, her blue-gray eyes meeting his. "I am already impressed."

She doesn't play games, Alec realized with a sense of shock. *But then you knew that.* It was refreshing. And at the same time disarming. *Tread cautiously,* a little voice in the back of his head warned him. But Alec—who was so good at trusting his instincts— ignored the warning.

His voice dropped a notch when he urged, "Have dinner with me, Angel. Pick a restaurant—any restaurant you want. Just have dinner with me." It wasn't his usual approach. He was good at charming a woman, an approach that had worked many times before. But somehow, his usual facile charm was absent this time around. And Alec had never held his breath as he waited for an answer. That was something new, and he wondered why her answer was suddenly so important.

Angelina tilted her chin up, staring at him so intently, so seriously, Alec was sure she was going to say no. The decision hung in the balance for a moment. Then she said, "Mischa's, in the central district, is probably the best choice. They have been there since before my mother was born." Her eyes smiled before her lips joined in. "They are not four-star, you understand. Casual dining, not formal. But the food is good, and at a reasonable price. You will like it, I think. Even the king enjoyed eating there with his fellow soldiers when he was in the Zakharian National Forces. There is a picture of him with his unit on one wall, with pictures of other famous diners."

"Sounds good. Where is it?"

"It is a little difficult to explain. Do you know the central district?"

"My apartment's there. And I should tell you my sister calls me the human GPS—I've never gotten lost yet, no matter where in the world I find myself."

Angelina's smile deepened. "Where exactly is your apartment?"

When Alec told her it was on Vasska Street near Jalena Lane, she said, "But that is very close to Mischa's. No more than five blocks away. You could walk to your apartment from the restaurant. And the market is on the way. I could help you shop—not everyone speaks English. Did you take a taxi?"

Alec shook his head. "Not this time, I'm afraid. One of the embassy cars brought me." He didn't tell her he wanted the embassy staff to know he was visiting his friend in the palace—adding fuel to the gossip he knew was already swirling about him. The best way to accomplish that was to have one of the embassy drivers bring him back and forth, casually-on-purpose mentioning the reason for his visit to the driver. If Alec and McKinnon met openly as friends, it was less likely someone would suspect McKinnon was involved in an investigation when he visited Alec at the embassy.

He also didn't tell Angelina that using an embassy

car and driver for ostensibly personal reasons was a violation of the rules—something he'd done deliberately. Not just to stress his friendship with McKinnon, but to spread the word he wasn't ethically a stickler. He was going to uncover whoever in the embassy was responsible for the fraud and corruption—that was a given, no matter how long it took—it would just be easier if *they* approached *him.* So the first step was making himself approachable. If he would bend the rules in one way, why not another?

Slippery slope, he reminded himself. Most people who trod the straight and narrow didn't realize just how true that was. Once you broke one rule, breaking the next wasn't quite so hard. Each successive infraction became easier to justify to yourself, until you found yourself at the bottom of the pit, with no way out.

He shook off his sudden introspective mood, and said, "The driver's waiting for me. I could have him drop us off at the restaurant instead of my apartment."

She thought about it for a few seconds and then shook her head decisively. "No, I cannot do that."

There's that "I cannot" again, Alec told himself. "Why not?"

Angelina hesitated. She glanced around nervously and blurted out, "It is one thing to talk to you here— although even that is… I do not want anyone to see me leaving the palace with you on a regular basis. We were already spotted the other day when we left for the cathedral together—it was mentioned to me by two men I work with."

Alec said the first thing that came to mind. "I wasn't aware US embassy employees were off-limits for the queen's security detail."

Now she seemed flustered. "It is not that…not exactly. I cannot explain…" She looked left and right, as if she feared they were being observed. But more than that—as if *she* was being observed…and judged. "Not here."

"At the restaurant, then?"

Again there was the strange hesitation that piqued Alec's interest. "All right," she said finally. "I will meet you there. Six o'clock?"

The assassination team didn't even have to break into Saint Anne's Cathedral. They walked in during vespers carrying rucksacks, joined the relatively large congregation gathered for a Friday evening service, and even made the proper responses during Mass—though neither of the men had been inside a church in years.

They lingered afterward, shuffling along with the exiting congregants and then slipping unnoticed into one of the side chapels when the rest of the crowd was making its way out the arched front doors. The christening wasn't until one o'clock Sunday afternoon, but the cathedral would be closed for security reasons after tonight's Mass, and the team had been warned they needed to get their weapons into place before the portable metal detectors were installed at all the cathedral's entrances tomorrow morning. Metal detectors that would remain in place until after the christening ceremony.

The men used the privacy of the confessionals to stash their Glock 18C selective fire pistols—other weapons options had been considered and discarded because the 18C was small enough to be concealed but could convert from semiautomatic to fully automatic at the flip of a switch. Not that they intended to use the fully automatic feature—they had one target and one target only. But if something happened and they needed to escape in a way they had not planned, full auto could come in handy. As for the confessionals, they would not be used between now and the ceremony on Sunday—and the weapons would be moved to a more secure location before the security teams conducted their extensive search early Sunday morning.

A large contingent of invited guests was expected Sunday afternoon, and certain rows would be roped off for them. Television cameras would be brought in Saturday afternoon, and set up for the broadcast to the nation on Sunday. But the king had also invited the citizens of Drago to attend the christening of his son and heir. Giant screens would be erected in the square outside the cathedral and the event would be projected on them, so whoever couldn't be squeezed into the pews or couldn't find standing room in the aisles would be able to watch the ceremony in the immense square.

A packed cathedral and a packed square—the security personnel would have their hands full trying to watch everyone, every minute. They would not notice the two inconspicuous men until it was too late. The assassins were counting on it.

Chapter 5

Angelina walked into the restaurant, her eyes quickly moving over all the diners, cataloging them. Then she breathed a sigh of relief. No one she knew was here tonight. Specifically, no one on the queen's security detail. There were two women she knew just in passing, and she recognized a third who'd been a friend of her cousin Caterina's in high school. The sight of Caterina's friend brought the mystery of her cousin's disappearance to the forefront of Angelina's consciousness.

Where are you, Caterina? Angelina thought now. A question she'd asked for more than eight years. A question that hurt just as much now as it had all those years ago, because Angelina felt responsible in some way.

Responsible...and guilty. Guilty she hadn't been able to prevent Caterina from leaving Zakhar in the first place, hadn't been able to talk her out of going.

Guilty she hadn't managed to track her cousin down when she'd vanished without a trace somewhere in the United States. *Why did you not stop her?* Angelina's conscience demanded now. *And why did you not find her when she disappeared? Even if only to bring her body home?*

The loss of the cousin who'd been like her little sister was a festering wound that would never heal unless Caterina miraculously reappeared, which Angelina no longer believed might happen. After all these years she knew in her heart her cousin was dead—but without a body there would never be closure.

"Hey," a warm deep voice said from behind her. "You're right on time." She turned around to see Alec's gaze flickering over her, masculine appreciation evident in his eyes. Angelina was glad she'd changed into a dress she'd pulled from the back of her closet—one of the few dresses in her wardrobe. She never wore dresses to work—slacks, a tailored blouse and a blazer to hide her ever-present shoulder holster were what she always wore on duty. Not just because a dress might be a distraction for whatever male team member she was working with that day, but because a dress would be a distraction for *her.* She just didn't feel *comfortable* in a dress. Not for work.

But it was different tonight. Or maybe it was who she was with that made the difference. Alec, whose eyes made her yearn for those very things she'd long ago decided weren't for her. Alec, whose kisses sparked a flame she'd been hard-pressed to quench...both times. Alec, who called her Angel in that strong, ardent way that demanded a response equally as ardent. As if he knew what they'd be like in bed, and it aroused him.

Now his eyes spoke volumes, and Angelina was fiercely glad she'd dressed up for him. The royal-blue color of her dress did something for her eyes, making them more blue than gray. The silky, blouson material clung discreetly in all the right places, making her aware of her femininity for the first time in a long time. The heels she'd unearthed from the bottom of her closet and decided to wear at the last minute made her as tall as Alec. She thanked her lucky stars he was so tall to begin with. Most men's egos were ridiculously fragile if their date was taller than they were, and on the few dates she'd allowed herself in the past, she'd always been careful to wear flats so she wouldn't tower over the man she was with. She didn't have to worry about that tonight.

"They're holding a table for us," Alec told her. He placed a warm hand on the small of Angelina's back to guide her, and a little thrill shot through her. She tried to tell herself not to respond to him—his eyes, his smile, his touch. But her body was telling her that— unlike her totally disappointing, one and only sexual encounter—sex with Alec would be far from disappointing. Something she'd already realized the first time she saw him.

Just for a moment she let herself fantasize about what it would be like with Alec, before she shut down her errant thoughts with a firm resolve. Regret stabbed through her. If her job weren't so important to her… if Zakharian men—especially the men in her line of work—weren't so judgmental of women they saw as *women*…if she dared risk exploring this attraction between Alec and her…

Angelina sighed to herself, but made sure nothing of what she was feeling showed on her face.

Alec declined a menu when they were seated at their table, telling Angelina, "Order for me, please. You know what's good here, I don't."

She laughed a little at the unexpected offer—so different from most men she'd dated, who always wanted to order for her. "But I do not know what you like," she demurred.

"Meat and potatoes," he said with a smile. "Isn't that what most men prefer? And no zucchini. I can eat any vegetable except zucchini. Other than that, I'm easy." His voice dropped a notch. "I'm putting myself in your hands, Angel," he said softly. And just that easily, her control over her body's reactions was shattered as she imagined the alternate meaning that could be applied to his words. A sexual meaning.

He did that to her throughout their leisurely meal, from the bacon-wrapped Mediterranean dates stuffed with almonds, all the way through the dessert she usually didn't eat but ordered especially for him: mini chocolate éclairs that were a specialty of the house. There was nothing she could call him on outright. He just had a way of saying something totally innocuous that could be taken more than one way if your mind was looking for a double entendre. And hers most definitely was.

Over dessert, he asked, "So explain to me again why I'm not supposed to call you Angel. Not that Angelina isn't a beautiful name, but—" his eyes sought hers "—it seems so...I don't know...distant. Formal."

Angelina sighed. "You do not understand. I cannot allow myself to appear weak to the men I work with. Which means I cannot allow myself to appear feminine. Angel—" She glanced down at her plate, then back up at Alec, struggling to overcome her hard-won reserve. "I loved it when you called me Angel," she admitted in a low voice. "But—"

"But not in public. I get it."

She hesitated, unsure if he really understood. "If anyone heard you call me Angel, they might think that you…that I…" She cleared her throat. "I cannot allow the men I work with to think of me as a woman. Can you understand that? It is different for you. Where you come from, women no longer have to worry about being taken seriously. Especially women doing what used to be a man's job."

Alec shook his head. "My sister, Keira, could tell you that's not true."

"What do you mean?"

"My dad—he's been dead for a long time now, but—" Alec grimaced. "Remember how I told you my dad always kidded that my mom broke his perfect record—four boys and then one girl?" She nodded. "He wasn't really kidding. Keira always had to fight for respect from my dad growing up. Not because of anything she did or didn't do. Just because she was a girl."

It shamed him to remember. "All of us—my brothers and I—we kind of took our dad's attitude. Don't get me wrong, we loved Keira, just as our dad did. But we didn't give her a lot of respect. Not then. It wasn't until she followed us into the Marine Corps that we started seeing her as…well…as someone who deserved our respect.

"Then she went to work for the agency—the same agency McKinnon works for. And a few years back, she stepped in front of a man to take a bullet meant for him. Saved his life…but almost lost her own." His face contracted in pain, the pain he still felt over almost losing his only sister.

Angelina reached across the table and touched Alec's hand in silent comfort. "Why did you tell me this?" she asked softly.

"Because I didn't want you to have any illusions about how easy women have it in the American culture." His eyes held hers. "And because I didn't want you to have any illusions about me, either. I'm not the man you think I am."

"That is not true," she contradicted. "Perhaps you do not see yourself as I do. Just telling me what you have told me, admitting it to me and to yourself—no Zakharian man I know would do this. That makes you unique, Alec. Unique to me."

They walked afterward, both needing the exercise after the meal they'd eaten. From time to time Angelina pointed out some landmark of note, though mostly they just wandered through the central district in companionable silence.

"Drago is a beautiful city," Alec said finally. "Unspoiled. I like that. It's different from most European capitals."

"Where else have you been posted?" she asked, unable to keep a touch of wistfulness from her voice. She loved her country, loved her city, but she had dreamed of traveling someday, dreams that hadn't yet materialized. Except for her trip to the United States searching for Caterina. But that had hardly been a pleasure trip.

"I was in The Hague a few years back. The Netherlands. The International Criminal Court is headquartered there. That was an experience, let me tell you."

"How so?"

He expounded for a few minutes, then said, "When I was in The Hague, Liam was stationed in Rome, which is about the closest we've ever worked to each other except for the six months when we were assigned to guard Princess Mara together."

"But you are still close to your brother. That is what you said, yes?"

Alec laughed. "Yeah. Even though we've rarely seen each other since we left home, except for the occasional Christmas holiday."

"My cousin was—" She broke off.

"You said the other day you had a cousin who was like a little sister to you," Alec reminded her. "What happened to her?"

Angelina thought about it for a moment before answering, choosing her words carefully. "She disappeared more than eight years ago. She was only sixteen."

Alec stopped walking, tugging her back toward him. "Oh, Angel, I'm so sorry." He cupped her cheek with his hand, his dark brown eyes full of sympathy. "She just vanished? Did she run away, or...?"

Angelina shook her head. "She went to America to model—she was so excited about it. But from the moment she stepped on the plane, I never heard from her again."

Alec saw Angelina safely home, his mind working furiously. He performed a quick electronic sweep as soon as he entered the privacy of his apartment, then got on the phone with Trace McKinnon. "Angelina Mateja," he said abruptly. "Lieutenant Mateja. Queen's security detail."

"What about her?"

"She had a cousin who disappeared roughly eight years ago. A cousin who supposedly went to the US to model but was never heard from again."

McKinnon cursed softly, making the connection. "You think this trafficking ring has been going on for that long?"

"I don't know, but I'm going to find out. Can you see what you can uncover on the cousin?"

"You got a name?"

"Nope. I don't even know if she has the same last name as Angelina. All I know is she was sixteen when she vanished, so she'd be around twenty-four now."

"I'm on it. I'll let you know what I learn."

"Thanks. And McKinnon?"

"Yeah?"

"I didn't tell Angelina anything. I could have pumped her for more information, but she's too intelligent, too savvy. I didn't want to raise her suspicions."

"Among other things."

Alec bristled. "What the hell does that mean?"

McKinnon laughed, not unkindly. "Nothing. Nothing at all."

Even before they hung up, Alec knew McKinnon had been lying, and wondered if his attraction to Angelina was obvious to everyone…or if McKinnon was just more astute than most. *Probably the latter,* he consoled himself. McKinnon was a damned good special agent. He hadn't gotten where he was with merely run-of-the-mill powers of observation and an average ability to assemble disparate clues. But that didn't make it any easier to accept.

* * *

Sunday dawned, a bright and beautiful fall day with clear skies and a gentle breeze. A perfect day for the christening of Crown Prince Raoul Theodore Alexei Stepan. *As if God himself is smiling on the occasion,* Alec thought whimsically as he arrived in the Drago town square just as the sun peeked over the mountaintops to the east.

He wasn't supposed to be here this early. In fact, he was supposed to arrive with the McKinnons, whose guest he was. But Alec had cried off, telling McKinnon he'd make his own way to the christening and meet them there because he wanted to experience the whole event as a spectator, not just as a guest. But that meant he was already dressed for the occasion in the formal morning suit he wore for official embassy events, right down to a carnation in his lapel.

Alec wasn't the first to arrive, though. A crowd had already begun to assemble, lines forming to enter the cathedral when the doors opened at noon. Members of the Drago police department and the Zakharian National Forces were on hand to keep things orderly, but they were hardly necessary with the friendly crowd.

Smiles and jests were the order of the day—no pushing or shoving. As he watched the crowd—so different from American crowds—Alec theorized people must have come from miles around, not just from Drago. But everyone seemed to be in a jubilant mood. He struck up a conversation with an elderly couple near the front of one line, grateful his knowledge of Zakharan was up to the task, and his theory was quickly confirmed.

"We are from Timon, near the eastern border," the

husband said. "We left home at midnight to be here today."

"Why?"

"To witness the christening, of course," the man told him, as if it should be obvious. "And the official royal acknowledgment that the baby is the true heir of Zakhar's king. I was right here when the king himself was christened almost thirty-five years ago." His wrinkled face became animated. "I was almost the same age then that the king is now, and I remember that day as if it were yesterday."

In his head Alec heard Angelina say, *"It is not just the baptism of a child, you understand. It is a celebration of the future of our country..."*

Alec smiled, beginning to understand why these two elderly Zakharians were willing to subject themselves to this ordeal along with the rest of the crowd. "We don't have ceremonies like this in the US."

"That is your country's misfortune," the man said with a touch of superiority, before his wife chimed in.

"This is a historical event," she explained. "This ceremony—it is more than five hundred years old, you understand. The line of direct descent from father to son has *never* been broken. God willing, it never will be."

"Were you here the last time, too?"

"But of course. My husband and I, we were both here. That is why we are here today." She beamed at Alec and went on to explain that it wasn't just a historical event for Zakhar, it was a good omen. Not that the Zakharians were any more superstitious than citizens of other European countries, as a general rule, but they had come to believe the good fortune and prosperity

Zakhar had experienced throughout the centuries was somehow tied in with the House of Marianescu. Zakhar had never had a truly bad king in all those years of the monarchy's direct descent. Was this cause and effect? "No Zakharian is willing to put it to the test," she added in all seriousness. "And now we will not have to." She took her elderly husband's hand. "Not in our lifetime."

After a little more conversation, Alec thanked them both and excused himself to wander around the square outside the cathedral, taking everything in.

Large screens were being erected to project the ancient ritual from inside the cathedral, one performed by every Zakharian king except the first Andre Alexei— his heir had been born in captivity, far away from Drago. But his successor, his son Raoul, had begun the ritual when *his* first son was born.

The clock tower in the square had just proclaimed the time as nine o'clock when cars began arriving, disgorging a phalanx of steely-eyed men with the distinct look of bodyguards about them. They swarmed up the cathedral steps and disappeared inside. "Security teams," Alec murmured to himself. A couple of women dressed just like the men were also there, and he remembered Angelina saying Queen Juliana had requested a certain number of female bodyguards, although the vast majority of her security detail were men.

Neither Captain Zale nor Lieutenant Mateja were with them, and though Angelina hadn't mentioned it to him, it didn't take much to figure out they would arrive with the royal family. Which meant Angelina was highly thought of by her superiors.

As if he were inside the cathedral with them, Alec

knew the security teams were taking up their assigned positions, fanning out throughout the cathedral, making sure security was tight. Everything that could be done to ensure the safety of the royals would be done, but none of the members of the various security details would breathe easy until the christening was safely over. *Been there, done that.*

More cars arrived at ten, but Alec noted all these arrivals were moving in through a side door. His eagle eyes spotted the photo-ID badges that were being flashed to the security team monitoring the entrance and the portable metal detector set up there. *Not guests,* he figured. *Must be participants in the ceremony— musicians, choir members, people like that.*

As he walked around the square for the umpteenth time, Alec still couldn't get over how vast the crowd was—there had to be close to a quarter-million people here—and they remained orderly. Many had been there for hours, but the overall celebratory atmosphere engendered good-natured camaraderie.

Whoever had organized this event had thought of just about everything that might be needed by those in attendance, including portable latrines set up discreetly just out of view. And—surprising to Alec—when someone had to step out of line to use the facilities, no one moved up. That person's place in line was there when he or she returned.

Just after eleven, the personally invited guests started arriving, limousines pulling up at the foot of the shallow stairway leading to the cathedral's main doorway.

Internationally famous movie star Dirk DeWinter received one of the loudest and longest ovations when he arrived alone. Alec, as well as the crowd, knew him as the actor who'd portrayed King Andre Alexei the First—the king's illustrious ancestor and the founder of the House of Marianescu—in the movie *King's Ransom*, opposite the actress who was now queen. Dirk smiled briefly for the crowd and acknowledged their cheers with a wave of his hand before he, too, disappeared through the cathedral's main entrance.

DeWinter was followed by the US secretary of state, who Alec had known would be in attendance representing the president, accompanied by his DSS bodyguards; the prime ministers of England and several European countries, who Alec also immediately recognized; and a world-renowned duke and duchess of England, the birth of whose children had created a media frenzy in their own country and around the globe, much like the one accompanying the birth of Zakhar's Crown Prince Raoul.

The invited guests had all arrived and been seated by the time the clock tower in the square chimed the noon hour, and the lines to enter the cathedral perked up. Everyone who could would be squeezed into the cathedral, even if it meant standing room only.

Alec saw that what was going on inside the cathedral was already being broadcast outside on the giant screens. And by the expressions on the faces of those near the end of the lines, he figured they were consoling themselves they'd probably have a better view of the christening out here than those who managed to find space inside.

At twelve-thirty, the lines of people were politely turned away, and the remaining crowd quickly moved to find seats in the square. At a quarter to one, the extended members of the royal family arrived—distant cousins, maternal aunts and uncles. Alec knew that was his cue. He politely made his way through the shifting crowd to the foot of the cathedral stairs, waiting for the McKinnons' limousine.

Prince Xavier, the king's first cousin on his father's side, arrived alone to a mixed reception from the crowd. No one wanted to believe the prince been part of his younger brother's attempts on the life of the king and queen, but a shadow of a doubt remained in the minds of many, despite the king's vehement assertions to the contrary.

Alec was convinced of the prince's innocence, and had been almost from the moment he'd met him. But a gut feeling wasn't evidence, and he didn't really blame the crowd for its ambivalence.

Princess Mara and her husband arrived last of all, and as the huge sea of people in the square raised a cheer for them, Alec moved forward. By way of greeting, he said sotto voce to McKinnon, "This is a security nightmare."

"Don't I know it." McKinnon smiled coldly. "I hope you're strapped." He tapped his right hand lightly over the breast of his formal suit. "I am."

"Since you told me to come prepared, you shouldn't even have to ask." Alec moved to the princess's left side, knowing McKinnon wouldn't yield the right side to anyone, king or commoner. Alec was right-handed, too, and his shoulder holster was rigged for a right-handed draw, same as McKinnon's. But the princess was McKinnon's wife—that was the bottom line. Anyone trying to hurt her would have to go through McKinnon first.

The metal detector would have gone crazy on either of them—in addition to the gun in his shoulder holster, Alec was wearing his ankle holster with his backup gun—except McKinnon stepped to one side and spoke quietly to one of the guards there. "Yes, sir, it is all arranged," the guard said respectfully in Zakharan, and he opened the velvet rope to let the three of them pass through to the right of the metal detector.

An usher was waiting on the other side and led them down the center aisle, all the way to the front. He removed the ribbon blocking off the aisle to the front pew and seated them on the left side. Alec didn't know who else was going to be seated after them, so he moved nearly all the way to the left, figuring that would leave plenty of room remaining for whoever would sit there—the king, the queen, their infant son and any security guards who would be accompanying them.

Through the open door of the cathedral came a roar from the crowd, and Alec knew the royal family had arrived, right on time. *Let's get this show on the road,* he told himself with a touch of humor. Movement to the left of the altar had his gaze sliding in that direction, his hand never far from the unbuttoned jacket of his morning suit. But it was only the archbishop, dressed in his ecclesiastical robes, with two bishops and a handful of acolytes coming from the sacristy, moving into place near the altar and the ancient marble baptismal font off to the right.

The organist, who'd been playing for the past fifteen minutes, came to the end of Henry Purcell's *Trumpet Tune.* He paused, waited for a signal, then nodded to the string quartet and moved right into Jeremiah Clarke's *Trumpet Voluntary*.

The stately music filled the cathedral with sound, and Alec realized Angelina had been right. No assassin could stand behind the organ pipes while the music was playing, unless—and he'd been just as right about this—that person was wearing some kind of noise-canceling headgear. He'd already spotted plainclothes security guards stationed on both sides of the recessed area, so apparently she'd passed along his concern to whoever was in charge of security. But he couldn't get it out of his mind that anything might happen. *And wasn't that what McKinnon was worried about when he asked me to come armed?*

When everyone in the cathedral stood and turned toward the rear, Alec stood, too. But even as he faced the rear, his gaze was sweeping left and right, taking in every detail. Plainclothes security guards were everywhere, earpieces in place, looking for all the world like the Secret Service protecting the president of the United States, except none of them were wearing sunglasses—not inside the cathedral.

Then he spotted Angelina coming up the already crowded far-right aisle—her left, his right—and his heart leaped at the sight of her. She was so beautiful as she slowly advanced, keeping pace with Zakhar's king and his queen. The queen was carrying their infant son in her arms as she and the king made their stately way up the center aisle.

Angelina's eyes were constantly looking left and right, just as he'd done earlier. Guarding the queen as best she could without being right beside her. So tall, so straight, so intensely focused. Like a Norse Valkyrie.

Or a guardian angel, he thought. *Yeah, that's more appropriate for church. So determined nothing will happen on her watch.*

   Just like me.

Chapter 6

For no reason he could think of, Alec suddenly remembered the scene in the coffeehouse. Remembered the two bearded young men who'd entered so innocuously but who bore hatred in their hearts and carried death in their minds and hands. His sixth sense—the one he always trusted, which had never let him down—told him there was danger here. He didn't know from where or from whom, just that it was here…somewhere.

His hand was already reaching for his SIG Sauer, but then he stopped, cursing internally. If he drew his gun, he could trigger an international incident, and he already had one black mark against him with the State Department for taking down those terrorists—even though it had been necessary. One of the security guards here was bound to see his drawn gun, think he was a threat to the royal family, shoot first and ask questions later. Even if he wasn't killed, the State Department would have a hell of a lot of explaining to do. And so would he.

Angelina spotted Alec immediately in the front pew as the royal family took their seats next to the McKinnons, though she shunted him to the back of her mind because she had to focus on doing her job. Her eyes scoured the vast room, but she saw nothing that warranted alarm. So far so good.

As the archbishop began the sacred rite of baptism, the organ began playing, and after a few bars, the choir burst into song. She tuned everything out as she kept her focus on the royal family.

She moved slightly so she could have a clearer view of them as they stood and approached the archbishop at the baptismal font, accompanied by the McKinnons and the other set of godparents. Seeing the archbishop's mouth moving but not hearing the words. Watching as the baby's head was bared and holy water was sprinkled on top of it. Casting out original sin, if you believed the church. *But a baby has no sin in his heart,* a small part of her brain insisted.

Then her eyes zeroed in on the man directly in her line of sight on the right, stationed behind the altar. And suddenly she *knew.* Knew the royal family was in imminent danger. Because at this angle, with the light hitting the large television camera just right, she could see the gun half hidden within easy reach of his hand, artfully concealed as part of his equipment. The setup was beautiful—no one would suspect him…until it was too late.

She couldn't just draw her weapon and shoot

to kill—not only did she not have a clear shot, she couldn't just open fire. All the security details here—so many men, all of them armed—and someone innocent was sure to be wounded, perhaps killed. Maybe more than one. She couldn't start a bloodbath. And there was no guarantee the royal family would be immune from harm, which was the only thing she cared about at this moment.

Don't look at him, she warned herself. *Don't let him suspect you know...anything.* She had to get closer. Close enough to take him down without firing her weapon—if she could.

Suddenly a cold feeling gripped her. If there was one assassin, there could be more, disguised exactly like him. If one man had smuggled a weapon into the cathedral, what was to prevent a second? Or a third? Or a whole contingent?

She moved again, as if merely shifting position restlessly, but really to bring another man clearly into focus, this time on the left side behind the altar. Confirming her suspicion. He, too, had a lethal weapon close to hand.

Her gaze darted left and right, searching for other would-be assassins, but then she remembered yesterday's security briefing and the practice run-through. Those two television cameras were the only cameras not operated remotely from the control center set up in one of the cathedral's offices. So maybe—*maybe*—the two cameramen were the only potential assassins she needed to worry about.

When? her brain was frantically trying to reason out. *When will they attack? And who is their target?* When the answer came to her, she marveled that no one had thought of it before. *The baby. The crown prince. He is their target. Of course.* If the king or queen was their target, the assassins would have had a clear shot at either or both of them long before this. So it could not be them. That meant it had to be the baby. And that meant there was only one moment when the assassins would have a clear shot at the baby.

The ancient ritual unique to Zakhar. Everyone knew what it was. Everyone knew it was coming soon. Everyone knew the king would raise his eyes to heaven as he raised the baby above his head in both hands—one hand supporting the baby's head, the other beneath the little posterior—as he turned toward the people assembled in the cathedral and presented the baby to God and his subjects, reciting the ancient words acknowledging his son and heir before God and man. The assassins would have a perfect opportunity in that moment. The baby would be completely vulnerable. No one could protect him. Not his father. Not his mother. No one could protect the baby…except her. If she could get there in time.

But she couldn't do it alone. Not with two—or more—assassins. Angelina tapped her earpiece and uttered Captain Zale's name in an urgent undertone. "Yes?" came the reply in a voice that told her this had better be important.

"Sir, the two cameramen. One is stationed on the left side, behind the altar, the other on the right. They are armed. Repeat, they are armed. They should not be, but they are. Look closely at the steering ring beneath each camera. That is not auxiliary camera equipment, sir, those are weapons."

Two seconds passed, then three. Then four. Finally,

"I see them," came the calm reply. "You have good eyes, Lieutenant."

"The baby is their target," she continued in that same intense undertone. "Why wait otherwise? Why not open fire immediately? That is the only thing that makes sense. They are waiting for—"

"The ancient ritual," agreed Captain Zale. "Good thinking, Lieutenant. I will notify the heads of the other two security details, but we cannot wait for that. Move in…quietly. I will take the one on the right, closest to me. You take the one on the left."

"The king wishes nothing to disrupt the ceremony or detract from the religious solemnity of the occasion," Angelina heard Captain Zale say in her mind. And she knew she had to do her best to comply with the king's wishes…if possible. Not at the risk to the royal family, but…

"Yes, sir." She was already moving before he finished, knowing she had only one chance to get this right. Only one chance to slip around and behind the cameraman unnoticed. Only one chance to quietly disarm the assassin-in-waiting and remove him from the apse without causing a stir.

Alec saw Angelina speaking quietly into her earpiece before slipping nearly unnoticed behind the people standing in the aisle watching the ceremony unfold. He glanced over to the right and recognized Captain Zale doing the same thing on the other side. Something was up.

He'd been watching Angelina for most of the time, not the ceremony, and now he cast his mind back quickly. What had she seen that he hadn't? Then he remembered the moment she'd stiffened as she watched the royal family in front of the baptismal font. But then she'd relaxed, or seemed to. He surreptitiously slid a little to the left on the pew to get a better angle, and that's when he noticed the cameraman behind and to the right of the altar.

Cameraman, he told himself. *That has to be it. She saw something. Nothing else makes sense.*

And though he didn't have a clear view of the cameraman on the left, it didn't take much for him to figure both cameramen were in on the conspiracy. And Angelina was attempting to take the one on the left down by stealth while Captain Zale did the same on the right.

The McKinnons were just taking their seats again, their role as godparents in the baptism finished, when Alec caught McKinnon's eye and mouthed one word. *Cameramen.*

McKinnon unhurriedly took his seat, his gaze sliding away, but Alec saw him make the connection. Saw him bend and whisper in Princess Mara's ear. Heard the princess's slightly indrawn breath, but was inordinately proud of her when nothing showed on her face at the warning she'd just been given by her husband.

She turned toward Alec—a seemingly casual move—and whispered, "My brother will die before he lets anything happen to his son. Or his wife. Please, Alec. Please do what you must to protect him."

"I'm on it," he assured her. He slid slowly all the way to his left on the wooden pew, holding his breath, and muttered, "Excuse me," to the people standing there as he slipped from the pew. Alec was shielded from the cameramen's view by the people standing in the aisle—much as Angelina had been—and he quietly made his way behind them.

In his mind, as plain as if a map of the entire cathedral were laid out before him, he knew there was a side chapel ahead of him, knew taking that circuitous route was the only way someone would be able to sneak up behind the cameraman stationed on the left side of the apse behind the altar. Angelina would know that, too.

When he came to the entryway, Alec took it. People were seated in the side chapel, of course, and standing in the aisles. The side chapels were just as packed as the rest of the cathedral, even though the view of the proceedings from there would be limited. But that meant neither cameraman would be able to see him, either, especially since their cameras and their attention would be riveted on the royal family standing at the baptismal font.

Angelina was already on the far side from him; she must have quickly made her way all around the back of the side chapel and up to the front again. Alec saw her lips moving and knew she had to be communicating with someone else on the security team, but the distance was too great for him to hear what she was saying. He ignored the startled glances that came his way from the people in the pews and standing in the aisles as he followed the same path she must have followed.

He was still too far away when Angelina disappeared from view.

Angelina had drawn her gun, but her hand was half hidden in the sleeve of her blazer and her arm was down by her side to ensure as few people as possible spotted the gun she carried. All she needed was a few more seconds. *Let no one raise the alarm,* she prayed as she quietly moved along the back wall behind the cameraman.

The king turned with the baby in his hands, and the cameraman reached surreptitiously for the weapon half camouflaged by the steering ring to which it was affixed. But before his hand could grasp it, Angelina had her left forearm around his throat. Her gun was pressed against the right side of his neck, beneath his ear. "Do not move," she said softly in Zakharan, for his ears alone. "Do not make a sound. Remove your hand—ah—slowly. Very slowly. Leave the gun where it is." When he complied, she said, "Now back away from the camera."

He was an inch or so taller than she was and a good forty pounds heavier, but she controlled him easily. She drew him backward from the camera's stationary position in the apse to the back wall, thankful the camera provided some camouflage for what she was doing from the people in the main chapel. And the angle hid the back wall—and the two of them—from the side chapel's view.

At first, Angelina was afraid she would have to take the cameraman out by way of the side chapel, where people would see what she was doing, and perhaps cause a panic. *The king wishes nothing to disrupt the ceremony or detract from the religious solemnity of the occasion* flashed into her mind again.

The door to the sacristy appeared in her side vision, and Angelina gratefully steered her captive toward it. *Perfect,* she thought. The door had scarcely closed behind them when it opened again, and Angelina whirled around, dragging the cameraman backward with her to confront this new threat. She breathed a quick sigh of relief when she recognized Alec, until the idea occurred to her he might think she wasn't capable of handling this on her own.

"What are you doing here?" she demanded fiercely, while at the same time making sure she didn't raise her voice loud enough to be heard outside the sacristy. "This is not your responsibility! I do *not* need your assistance!"

Alec's eyes narrowed, but the flash of admiration in them mollified her. He turned, locked the door, and faced Angelina again. "I know you don't need me— you've got everything under control," he said in the same low voice. "But Princess Mara recruited my help in saving her brother and his family—that makes it my responsibility." He indicated her captive. "And shouldn't this discussion wait for a more opportune moment? Like after this man is secured and interrogated?"

Angelina realized he was right. She needed to contact Captain Zale immediately to let him know her status, that this would-be assassin was no longer a threat to the royal family. But with both hands occupied, that was impossible. Not to mention she could use some help tying him up.

She glanced around for something, anything, they could use. She hated to use any of the priestly vestments for this very unpriestly requirement, but the sacristy was woefully lacking anything else that might substitute for the handcuffs a policeman would carry but a bodyguard didn't. Alec made it easy for her, grabbing a pure white stole—the long, narrow strip of cloth priests and bishops wore draped around their necks—

from a hanger, and approaching Angelina and her captive, careful not to interfere with the control she still maintained over the man.

"Hands behind you," he told the cameraman in Zakharan.

The man hesitated, and Angelina pressed her weapon even tighter against his neck. "Do it!" she commanded.

It wasn't easy. Since she still held the man in a chokehold, Alec had to maneuver between her body and the cameraman's in order to bind the man's hands behind his back. Despite the adrenaline still coursing through her body, or perhaps because of it, Angelina was acutely conscious of everywhere Alec accidentally touched her. When he was finally finished and the cameraman was securely trussed, she released the iron hold she'd had on the man's neck and swiftly holstered her SIG Sauer P320. She gave the man a little push in Alec's direction.

"Watch him, please. I must contact Captain Zale." She moved a short distance away, tapping her earpiece and uttering Captain Zale's name but still keeping her gaze glued on Alec and their prisoner.

"Yes, Lieutenant?"

"All secure here, sir. We are in the sacristy. But I was forced to leave the gun he was going to use—" She stopped abruptly as Alec shook his head and opened his coat, showing the would-be assassin's Glock 18C tucked neatly into his belt. Her eyes met Alec's, and this time it was *her* admiration for *him* glowing there. She smiled her appreciation of his quick thinking. "Cancel that, sir. Alec Jones, the US RSO is with me. He secured the weapon and has it with him."

"Good job, Lieutenant." Just three little words of praise, but the tone they were uttered in meant the world to her. She'd done her job. She'd saved the crown prince. And she'd managed to do it without disrupting the religious ceremony, just as the king had wished. A flush of pride rose to her cheeks, despite her best efforts to contain it.

"The other cameraman is already in custody, also without incident," Captain Zale continued. "And the christening ceremony is nearly over. Stay there for the time being. I will send someone to retrieve your prisoner so you can accompany the queen back to the palace. With this attempt on the royal family, their security is paramount, and I want *you* guarding the queen. I must stay to interrogate the prisoners, so I am counting on you and the other man I assign to ensure the queen's safety. You are not relieved of that duty until *I* say you are relieved. Understood?"

"Yes, sir."

When they disconnected, Alec raised his eyebrows in a question, and Angelina quickly relayed the conversation to him. Not the few words of praise or her reaction to them, but that Captain Zale wanted her to accompany the queen back to the palace and was sending someone to relieve her here.

Only a minute later they heard the rattle of the doorknob on the locked sacristy door, followed by a sharp knock. "Lieutenant Mateja?" said a muffled voice.

Angelina drew her gun before she stood off to one side, reached out and unlocked the door quickly, so if someone tried to burst through the door she wouldn't be taken unaware. She relaxed her guard when she peered out and recognized the man as a fellow body-guard.

"Sorry, Sasha," she said, letting him in, then locking the door behind him and turning to follow him into the room. "I did not want to take a ch—"

A gunshot reverberated through the sacristy, and the cameraman Alec was guarding dropped to the ground without a sound. Angelina didn't hesitate. Sasha's arm had already shifted in Alec's direction, but before he could get off another shot, she fired. He crumpled.

With her P320 still pointed at Sasha, she approached his body cautiously and then kicked the gun that had fallen from his hand into the far corner of the room. She went down on one knee to check his pulse behind his ear, but she knew even before she did it that it wasn't necessary. He was dead.

She glanced over at Alec, whose own SIG Sauer was now drawn but who was also on one knee, checking the pulse on the cameraman. Their eyes met and Alec shook his head. "No chance," he said.

Guilt slammed into her. "My fault."

"Are you crazy?" Alec stood, quickly holstered his weapon and approached her. He grasped her arms with his strong hands and shook her slightly. "How the hell is this your fault?"

She swallowed hard and fought the shakes that suddenly threatened to overwhelm her as the realization sank in—she'd killed a man. She'd never killed a man before. She'd always known she might have to in her line of work. Had tried to prepare herself for the possibility…the eventuality. Had told herself she could handle it, especially if the man deserved to die, as Sasha most certainly had.

But *thinking* and *doing* were two completely different things. A man had lost his life at her hands. A man she knew. What she was feeling now was nothing like she'd imagined she'd feel.

"I let down my guard," she whispered. "I should not have, but I did." She tore herself from Alec's hands and backed away. She glanced down at the SIG Sauer in her right hand, almost as if she was surprised to see it still there, and she holstered it automatically.

Just as automatically, she tapped her earpiece. "Captain Zale?" When he answered, she said in a wooden voice, "My prisoner is dead, sir. The man you sent to retrieve him, Lieutenant Tcholek, must have been part of the conspiracy, because he shot the cameraman. Lieutenant Tcholek is also dead, sir. I shot—"

"I did not send Tcholek. I sent Liev Arkady. But I *just* sent him—he should be there shortly. What the hell is going on?"

Angelina was startled out of her autonomic state. She glanced at Alec and mouthed the words *He did not send Sasha.* And knew from his expression he'd made the same connection she just had. Sasha must have seen her go into the sacristy with her prisoner. Must have seen Alec enter shortly thereafter. Must have been involved in the conspiracy. Part of her had already known he had to be, but she hadn't really focused on it before. Now she did.

Was he the one who'd retrieved the guns for the would-be assassins? she wondered now. She couldn't remember Sasha's assigned post in the cathedral—there were so many on the various security teams here, it would be impossible to remember who was posted where. But it made sense he was instrumental in getting the weapons into the hands of the would-be assassins. What else had he been involved in? And was anyone else she knew, anyone else on one of the security details, involved in the assassination conspiracy? It made her sick just to think of it, but the question *had* to be asked.

Another knock sounded on the sacristy door. "Lieutenant Mateja? It is Lieutenant Arkady. I am here to collect your prisoner." This time when Angelina unlocked the door, she was taking absolutely no chances. One man too late.

Chapter 7

It was very, very late—almost midnight—when Angelina returned to her apartment. She unlocked the door, secured it behind her and headed for her bedroom. But the blinking light on the answering machine stopped her. She almost ignored it, not really up to dealing with anything else tonight, but what if it was important? She hesitated for only a moment and then hit the play button. Her mother's voice, with its plaintive tone, floated out of the speaker.

"Angelina, darling, where are you? Why did you not call us tonight? We have been waiting, wondering where you could be. We did not see you at the christening ceremony this afternoon, but then we were forced to join the crowd in the square outside—we were not able to get into the cathedral. The lines were too long, and your father complained his feet hurt too much to stand all that time. He said a better daughter would have arranged invitations for us—a better daughter would make sure her parents would not have to stand in line with everyone else. But you know his way. He did not really mean it."

Angelina closed her suddenly aching eyes and took several deep breaths, trying to calm the turmoil inside caused by her mother's careless words.

"Still," her mother continued, "with such an important job, as you are constantly telling us—so important you do not have time to find a husband and give us the grandchildren that would make our remaining years worthwhile—it should not have been too difficult to arrange. A word to the queen, perhaps, and we could have… But then, you do not mean to be so thoughtless, I know. Your father says it is all my fault, that I should have raised you better, that you do not think of the sacrifices we have made for you all these years. But I told him—"

Angelina clicked the delete button without waiting for her mother to finish. She didn't need to hear the rest because it would be more of the same thing. On and on. The constant criticism. The "we do not mean to complain" complaints. Always managing to throw into any conversation Angelina's lack of a husband. Lack of children. Never understanding the choices she'd made for her life. *Her* life. Not theirs.

As for asking the queen for an invitation for her parents, she should never have mentioned the queen's friendship to them. It had slipped out one day in conversation, and she'd known it was a mistake almost immediately, but it was too late. How many times since then had she told her parents she would never presume on her friendship with the queen? Not even for them. But they'd refused to believe her. Refused to understand. *They will never understand,* she thought, a band of pain tightening around her heart. *Just as they will never understand me.*

She pushed those thoughts aside with an effort and went directly to her bedroom. She stripped off her clothes and left them in a little pile on the floor, but carefully hung her shoulder holster containing her SIG Sauer P320 on its designated hook inside her closet door for easy access. She'd been surprised her interrogators had allowed her to take her gun home with her, but they had, after they'd performed ballistics tests on it.

A hot shower beckoned. With the steaming-hot water streaming over her head, she could finally let herself cry. Cry the way she'd been wanting to cry since the moment she'd killed Sasha. Cry the way she hadn't cried since she'd finally admitted she wasn't going to be able to find her cousin, no matter how hard she tried.

She sagged against the tiles, the fingers of one hand splayed against the water-slick wall as sobs tore through her—her regret over taking a man's life all mixed up with her remorse over Caterina, her inability to make her parents proud of her no matter how she tried and everything else she'd failed to do right in her life. She cried until the hot water turned lukewarm, until she cried herself out, and then wiped her eyes. She stepped tiredly from the shower and toweled herself off. She used a separate towel for her hair, rubbing it briskly until it was barely damp, then grabbed a comb off the small counter beside the washbasin and quickly combed her hair, forcing herself to look in the mirror.

She scarcely recognized the woman who stared back at her. Her eyes were red and swollen, her face puffy. She remembered the pride she'd felt earlier when Captain Zale had told her, "Good job, Lieutenant." *Proud. You were so proud, and now what?* A proverb from the Bible came to her, one her mother had often quoted. *Pride goeth before destruction, and an haughty spirit before a fall.*

She'd been so proud she'd helped save the crown prince. So proud she hadn't interrupted the christening in doing so. But now her pride was humbled. In ashes. The questions her interrogators had thrown at her made it very clear they'd suspected her—as if she'd killed Sasha to cover up her own involvement. Crazy as that idea was, it had made a kind of illogical sense to her when her interrogators had raised the possibility.

Even Captain Zale had not defended her, and that hurt most of all. Everything she'd done since joining the queen's security detail, all the sacrifices she'd made, and no one stood up for her.

The doorbell rang, startling her from her sad reverie. Who could possibly be calling on her at this hour of the night? She'd already spent hours being thoroughly interrogated by Captain Zale and the heads of the other two security details. They'd finally let her go when they were convinced she had nothing more to tell them and the crime scene reconstruction and preliminary ballistics tests had corroborated her story that Sasha had shot the cameraman to cover up *his* involvement in the plot, and that she'd shot Sasha in self-defense.

Even if she were completely cleared of suspicion, as seemed likely, given the strong evidence, would she ever be trusted—*really* trusted—again? Or would they insist on believing a *man* would not have let down his guard? That a *man* would have acted differently in the same situation?

She pulled her full-length ice-blue chenille robe on, firmly tying the belt as she walked barefoot to the front door. "Yes?" she asked in a voice that said whoever was on the other side had better have a damned good reason for being there.

"It's Alec, Angel. Open the door."

Angelina hesitated for a moment and realized she probably owed Alec thanks. If he hadn't been a witness to what had occurred in the sacristy, she might not be a free woman now. She might still be suspected of being part of the assassination attempt.

She unlocked the door and pulled it open, then just stood there staring at Alec. He looked good, given it was past midnight after a long, adrenaline-packed day. *A hell of a lot better than I do.*

"I thought so," Alec said, taking in her still-swollen eyes. "I thought you'd be beating yourself up over this."

She breathed sharply, and then said mechanically, "Come in." She turned around and led the way into her small living room. She faced Alec again, good manners dictating she say, "Please be seated," as she indicated the couch.

But Alec was having none of that. He moved to stand right in front of her, his hands grasping her arms. "You're not thinking straight," he told her roughly. "You did what you had to do. You're not responsible—not for any of it."

"I am," she replied, her words just a breath of sound. "I killed a man. And I caused the death of another man because I let down my guard."

Alec shook his head. "You can't second-guess yourself like this. Not now. Not ever. You saved a life today, and that has to count for something."

"Yes," she said. "I prevented that man from trying to kill the crown prince, but you cannot say with certainty I saved a—"

His hands tightened on her arms as he pulled her flush with his body. His rock-hard body. "I'm not talking about the king's son. I'm talking about me. You saved my life, Angel. I saw it in Tcholek's eyes when he shot the cameraman. I was next. I was dead in the water, caught without my own gun drawn. It was my own damn fault, there was no way I wasn't going to die—except you prevented it. You shot first. If your reflexes had been just a half second slower, I'd be dead now."

She breathed deeply as the truth of his words sank in. So maybe she *had* done something right, after all, even if she'd been forced to take a man's life to do it.

If only she could roll back the clock to yesterday. Or even to the moment before Sasha had entered the sacristy. *But I cannot,* she reminded herself with brutal candor. *I cannot turn back the clock any more than I can forget killing Sasha.*

If she couldn't change what had happened, could she distract herself from remembering that moment when she'd touched Sasha's still-warm body and had known he was dead? Could she focus instead on Alec? Alive, whole, uncompromisingly male…

Out of the jumble of her thoughts and emotions, one thing stood out—she wanted him. Now more than ever. She'd wanted him from the beginning, although she'd told herself it was impossible. But was it really?

Would it be wrong to use Alec to forget what she didn't want to remember, just for tonight? How many times had she dreamed of what it would be like to take Alec to her bed? How many ways would she regret this lost opportunity if she let it pass her by?

He wanted her, too. Now. This very minute. His body didn't lie, and she knew he wanted her just as much as she wanted him. "Alec…" That's all she said. Just his name. Would it be enough? They seemed to operate on the same wavelength in so many different ways, would he understand the invitation she couldn't put into words?

His brown eyes darkened as his whole body tightened. Then he was kissing her the way he'd kissed her on the jogging path. The way he'd kissed her in the cathedral. With a man's whole purpose behind it. A man's ardent desire.

He was so *strong*! She couldn't get over how powerfully he held her as he covered her face with kisses, whispering his name for her: "Angel, oh God, Angel!" Intoxicating kisses that sapped her strength and made her tremble with longing. Longing to feel his bare skin beneath her hands, to finally know what his muscles felt like with nothing covering them.

From thought to deed. "I want you naked," she breathed, tugging at the morning coat he still wore, and he obliged, stripping it off and dropping it on the floor. His shoulder holster came next, and when he shrugged out of it, she took it from him and carefully placed it on the end table beside the sofa. He surprised her when he bent and removed his ankle holster, which she also took from him and put down beside his primary gun. When she turned back, he'd already stripped off his tie and was unbuttoning his shirt from the top down, but he wasn't going fast enough for Angelina. She tugged his shirttails out and began unbuttoning from the bottom up. When their hands met in the middle, Alec laughed softly, and after a second, she did, too.

His shirt disappeared, and for some reason, Angelina couldn't seem to catch her breath. Unlike her one and only other lover, Alec's chest was smooth, nearly hairless, but tanned. She'd already noted he didn't have the milky complexion and freckles that usually accompanied red hair, and now she saw his tan extended… everywhere. At least, everywhere she could see so far.

She flexed her hands and placed them on his chest. Tentatively at first, but gaining courage for a bolder approach, she stroked and kneaded, feeling his muscles bunch and tighten under her ministrations. "You have a beautiful chest," she told him, laughing a little under her breath. "I cannot seem to stop touching it."

Her words—or was it her touch?—seemed to have a powerful effect on him, because he tensed and his nipples beaded. Then his hands were on the belt of her robe, tugging impatiently at the knot she'd tied so securely. "You have no idea what you do to me," he told her, the hard edge to his tone letting her know *exactly* what she was doing to him. It was a heady feeling.

The knot gave way finally. Her robe fell open and he pushed it off her completely, letting it drop to the floor in an untidy heap. Then his hands were doing to her what she was doing to him, and—*Oh God,* she thought as she tried to drag in enough air to survive, because his caresses were robbing her of every normal function. Desperate for more—more of everything, more of *Alec*—she fumbled with his belt, but he forestalled her there, too, unbuckling, unzipping, heeling off his shoes, stripping off his pants until he stood naked before her. Strong. Erect. Impossibly aroused.

The throbbing between Angelina's legs grew more intense, making her fully aware of her own needs for the first time in nearly forever. She tried to drag Alec down onto the sofa with her, but he shook his head. "I'll be damned if our first time is going to be on a sofa," he said roughly. "And it's not going to be quick." He cupped her face in his hands and captured her lips, luring her tongue with his. He finally let her go when she whimpered with need, and he whispered, "Hell no, Angel. This is going to take all night."

All night. The words swirled in her mind, one word chasing after the other. *All. Night. All. Night. All. Night.* Wasn't that what she wanted? One night to forget not only what she didn't want to remember, but that she wasn't free the way most women were free? One night to let herself experience everything Alec offered? Every touch. Every taste. Every sensation. One whole night—or what was left of it—to live the fantasy.

"Yes, please." Was that her voice? That soft, yielding, *feminine* sound?

She'd thought her meek acquiescence would make him happy, but she was wrong. His face hardened until the bones stood out, and the sudden intensity in his expression made her eyes shift under his. He caught her chin with one hand and forced her to look at him. "I'm going to please you, Angel," he said softly but implacably. "I'm going to please you until you scream my name. And you're going to please me...until *I* scream *your* name. That's the only way this is going to work between us. You're going to tell me what you like...

every step of the way. You're going to tell me what you want. And I'll do the same for you. And when we're done, we'll start all over again. And again. And again. Until neither of us can take any more."

Angelina shivered and her nipples tightened unbearably as she realized Alec wasn't like any other man she'd known in her life. He was…unique. He didn't want soft and yielding. He seemed to want her just as she was. Tough. Uncompromising. Determined. Strong. He respected those qualities in her, because…because he was the same way.

She searched his eyes, his face, and knew it was the truth. He wanted *exactly* those things from her she'd been afraid would always prevent her from having what most other women had. She would never have to hide her true self from Alec. Never have to pretend to be someone else. It was a freeing revelation.

Then sudden fear whipped through her. Not fear of Alec, but of herself. Fear she wouldn't be satisfied with one night. That she'd want more. That one night with Alec would only make her crave him like an addict craved a drug. That she would want forever.

But she couldn't let fear rule her. She never had. She never would. She would take this night with Alec because she wanted it…wanted him. That was all. And she wanted what Alec had promised her—she wanted him to make her scream his name.

Even more, she desperately wanted to make him scream her name. That thought was an aphrodisiac all its own, that a man like him—so strong, so powerful—would surrender control to her, mind and body. Her eyes gleamed at the thought. "Yes," she promised, running her short, unvarnished nails over his taut muscles, accepting everything he offered…for one night only. "I *will* make you scream."

Angelina couldn't bear it. Not one more minute. She writhed beneath Alec's tongue, her hands fisted in the cotton sheets, her body arching, arching, as if she could dislodge his hold on her and escape that way. But he held her hips firm, his tongue making forays into her core, then back up to tease and torment the little nub that throbbed and swelled and threatened to overwhelm her desire to hold back, to not let him—

Then she exploded, crying his name, wanting it to be over but also wanting it to last forever. *La petite mort*—the little death—as the French called it. And it was. It *was*.

Alec refused to stop until she was shaking and trembling, until she collapsed boneless and sobbing for breath, unable to do anything else. Then he slid up her body, grabbed a condom from the handful he'd placed on the nightstand, rolled it on and thrust deep. Angelina came again almost immediately, her nails digging into his buttocks, pulling him tightly into her body as he flexed and thrust, flexed and thrust. Again. Then again. She came one last time seconds before he came, too—a powerful orgasmic explosion that tore her name from his throat.

Alec lay there for a few seconds, his eyes closed as he dragged one shuddering breath after another into his body. Then he withdrew carefully, disposed of the condom and settled back onto the bed. He tugged gently until she lay with her back against him, one of his strong arms curved around her waist to anchor her in place.

She thought he was dozing because his breathing was deep and even, but then he whispered in her ear in Zakharan. Sexy words. Incredibly intimate words. At first, her body reacted as if he'd caressed her—nipples tightening, a throbbing in her loins—but then she suddenly wondered how many other Zakharian women he'd slept with since his arrival…and which one had taught him those words.

He must have noticed her slight stiffening, must have read her mind, because he said intently—still in Zakharan—"I've never used those words in bed, Angel. You're my first…in that way."

She believed him. Just as she believed him when he said, "It's been a long time for me. Longer than a man likes to admit, even to himself." His hand slid down until it was nestled at the crux of her thighs, fingers brushing lightly. Reminding her of what they'd just shared numerous times. "But that's not why I'm here," he told her, his deep voice quiet in the stillness of the night. "I'm here because you're the only one I want. Tell me you feel the same way."

She sighed—an acknowledgment and an acceptance of his explanation—and let herself relax back against him. "I do," she admitted.

"Good."

Before she realized it, he drifted off. She didn't mind. She loved having Alec hold her this way, even in sleep, his semi-arousal pressed up against her backside. *Although,* she thought with a quick flare of humor, *he should not be capable of being aroused at all. Not after all the times we…*

Stamina. Alec had unbelievable stamina, and apparently, so did she. But now she was exhausted, although she was still too wired to sleep. They'd slept like the dead between bouts of intense sexual pleasure, but never more than an hour at a time. And each time they'd awakened, Alec had given her two or three orgasms for each one of his. Her body was sated—more than sated.

This last time had been the worst—or the best— *depends on how you look at it,* she reminded herself with a satisfied smile. He'd used his fingers, watching her face and deriving pleasure from making her come despite herself. Then, when she'd grasped him firmly, wanting to torment him in return, he'd escaped her hold and slid down her body. Starting with her toes, he'd slowly worked his way up her ankles, her calves, the backs of her knees, her thighs. All this before he really got to work with his tongue at the apex of her thighs.

She sighed deeply at the memories. All good. *If I never have sex again, I'll die a happy woman,* she thought dreamily.

"Come for me," he'd told her, coaxing her into letting go with the deep voice that never failed to thrill her—his voice alone had made her shudder. "That's right, Angel. That's right. Come for me." And she had. She'd been embarrassed at how easily he'd been able to entice her first climax out of her with just his fingers. Not to mention how embarrassed she'd felt admitting to him this was only her second time with a man. And the first time she'd enjoyed it.

But he hadn't let her be embarrassed. Not that first time. Not any time. He'd encouraged her to touch him everywhere. She'd used her hands. Lips. Tongue. Teeth. And just as he said he would, he'd told her what he liked, how he liked it. How long he liked it. And he'd coaxed her into telling him what she liked, how she liked it. How long she liked it. Until they knew each other intimately. Until they no longer had to say a word. Until everything just meshed…every time.

Angelina sighed drowsily again, a sound of pure joy. Pure contentment. She wanted to stay like this forever…remembering. But before she knew it, she'd fallen asleep.

Alec woke first. He eased himself away, then lay on his side, his head propped up on one hand, watching Angelina sleep. Loving the sight of her, so sleep- and sex-tousled. Her face rosy and satisfied. She'd been perturbed at first that he'd brought condoms with him. As if he'd known they would become lovers tonight. As if he'd *planned* it.

But then he'd told her in all honesty, "I've been carrying condoms with me since the first day I kissed you. Not because I planned to seduce you, but because I would never put you at risk. I wanted to be ready if you ever said yes." Then he'd laughed softly, deep in his throat. "Not that I didn't want to make love to you—even before I kissed you. Remember when we met at the airport?"

She'd nodded and he'd told her, "I saw you watching me. There was just something about you, something that said, 'Touch me and die.'" He'd laughed again. "Okay, so you were a challenge, and I could never re-sist a challenge. But it wasn't just that. Everything you said, everything you did—even taking me down the day we went jogging—told me, 'This woman is unique. She would understand.'"

She hadn't asked him, "Understand what?" But if

she had, he'd have told her at least some of what he was thinking. Even if she wasn't ready to hear it yet.

He and Angelina were dynamite together in bed. He'd imagined they would be, but the reality put even his dreams to shame. She was so giving. Not just in what she was willing to do to and for him—although that had been an eye-opening revelation—but the trust she'd given him. Letting go of her inhibitions. Letting him know how vulnerable she was—but only with him. Letting him see how much she enjoyed everything he did to her.

It was an incredible turn-on to know he was the one giving her so much unbearable pleasure, and making her cry out his name. Knowing, too, he was the first man to tap the vein of intense sexuality that ran so deep in her, so carefully hidden from the rest of the world. God, would he ever get enough of her?

She still pushes all your buttons, Jones. She always will. Just admit it.

That was certainly true. But even as he acknowledged the truth of that statement, he acknowledged another truth—an unpalatable one. Unless he figured out a way to keep Angelina without destroying either her career or his—something that would destroy *them*—any button pushing in the future would have to be done long-distance.

Chapter 8

Angelina woke late—too late to go for her normal morning run—having had maybe four hours of sleep total. But the lack of sleep didn't bother her; she'd never felt better in her life, despite the lingering awareness between her legs that made walking to the bathroom a gingery effort after she slipped quietly from the bed so as not to waken Alec.

The shower tempted her. She needed one after last night...and this morning. She wasn't even going to count how many times she'd climaxed, although the number ten stood out in big bold letters in her mind for some reason. Not every time had been cataclysmic— but even when she'd told Alec, "I cannot," they'd both known she could...and did.

She no sooner stepped under the hot spray when the shower curtain was jerked open and a big male body joined hers, taking up more than his share of the available space, crowding her deliberately. Taking possession of her body as if he had the right. *Which he does*, she acknowledged to herself. She'd given him that right. Just as he'd given her the right to take possession of his body, which she was quick to do now. Stroking. Fondling. Then standing on tiptoe to fit him at the apex of her thighs.

"Don't, Angel," he said at last, but his refusal was halfhearted. "I need to be at the embassy in less than an hour, and I still have to go back to my apartment and change. I can't show up at work wearing—" She tightened her legs deliberately and he groaned deep in his throat. "Oh God, Angel. Not now. I—"

A tiny corner of her mind told her she shouldn't, but she couldn't resist. She slid to her knees in front of him, holding his erection in her hands and taking him into her mouth. Alec managed to turn the water off and brace himself against the shower tiles, but that was the last conscious movement he made until she'd wrung a shuddering orgasm from him.

When she finally let him go, stood and turned the water back on to wash both of them, he growled, "You're a witch, you know that?"

Angelina smiled, for the first time understanding completely the expression *like a cat at the cream pot*. "Five minutes," she said, soaping his body briskly and moving so the shower spray would rinse him off. "You could spare five minutes."

"Yeah, but now I need to return the favor, and that will take a hell of a lot longer than five minutes."

She shook her head. "No time. You must get to the embassy, remember? Besides…" She laughed softly.

"I am way ahead of you already. Even after this." She was out of the shower before he could stop her, and she handed him the towel she'd used on her hair last night. They dried off in silence, but when she wrapped her towel around her and tried to slip past him into her bedroom, he stopped her with one hand on her arm, all banter gone from his expression. "This doesn't end here, Angel."

Part of her wanted to tell him it had to. That this was a one-time thing. But another part of her yearned to believe in the fairy-tale ending. And because she knew neither of them had time for the kind of discussion Alec was obviously intending, she compromised. "I must get to work, too," she told him. "Now is not the time."

"When?"

He wanted to pin her down. "Tonight?" she offered. "I am off at five. You could meet me here after that. Or I could come to your apartment."

He hesitated for only a second. "I'll come here. Five-thirty okay? I'll take you to dinner, and we can talk."

She would have agreed to anything that got Alec out of her apartment now. She'd worry about tonight later. "Fine."

When Angelina arrived at the palace for her regular duty guarding the queen, she was stopped outside the queen's suite by Captain Zale and Lieutenant Arkady before she could knock and gain admittance.

"The king wishes to see you, Lieutenant Mateja," Captain Zale said without preamble. "Lieutenant Arkady will take your duty today."

This cannot be good. A sinking feeling swept through her, but she stiffened her spine and asked coolly, "The entire day? Or just until my audience with the king is finished?" She caught her breath as another thought occurred to her, one with devastating impact. "Or am I being relieved of duty permanently?"

"Let us say until further notice. Until we hear what the king has to say."

Angelina followed Captain Zale down the long corridor, but instead of taking the grand staircase down to the king's public office suite on the first floor, he stopped abruptly at the door to the king's secluded private office off his personal suite of rooms and knocked. She didn't know if this was a good sign or bad—she'd rarely spoken to the king, and never in his private office.

The door was opened by one of the king's bodyguards, Major Lukas Branko, a man she'd known only by sight until yesterday's interrogation. The expression on his face wasn't encouraging, and Angelina's heart sank further. But she wasn't about to betray how she felt to anyone. No one would know it would kill her to be relieved of duty. No one would know she would never be able to hold her head up again if that happened.

"Captain Zale and Lieutenant Mateja to see you, Sire," he announced without letting them enter.

"Thank you, Lukas," came the deep voice she recognized as belonging to the king. "Please leave us. And take Captain Zale with you." The king moved into her line of sight. "Come in, Lieutenant." He waited for Angelina to enter and the two men to leave. Then he closed the door behind them. "Please have a seat," the king said, indicating one of the chairs in front of his massive desk.

"I would prefer to stand, Sire," she said, speaking nothing more than the truth. If the ax was going to fall, she'd rather receive it standing than sitting.

"As you wish." The king seated himself behind the desk, silently observing Angelina standing ramrod straight in front of him, then smiled his faint smile. "It has just occurred to me you might have misinterpreted my invitation," he said finally.

She was startled into blurting out, "Invitation, Sire? Captain Zale presented it as a command."

"Ah," he said, his smile deepening as the little mystery was explained to him. "Let me apologize, Lieutenant. I have not called you here to relieve you of duty. Nor have I called you here to reprimand you. I merely wanted to thank you in person for saving my son's life."

Monumental relief flooded her at the king's words. She wasn't being relieved of her commission. She wasn't even being removed from the queen's security detail, the two things she'd feared most. She closed her eyes and thanked God. Fervently. Then she opened her eyes again and looked at the king. "No need to thank me, Your Majesty. Keeping your family safe is my duty...and my honor."

The smile that had faded from the king's face at Angelina's initial reaction to hearing she wasn't being relieved of duty—the relief she'd found impossible to keep from her expression—returned. "Very good, Lieutenant," he said softly, his vivid green eyes gleaming with approval. "That kind of devotion is what I like to see in all my men. Especially those who are assigned to guard the queen. The queen," he amended, "and now the prince."

Like every Zakharian, Angelina knew the king

would gladly sacrifice his own life to keep his wife and son safe. And like every loyal Zakharian on the three security details, love for their king made them fiercely protective of the entire royal family.

But the king was still speaking, and Angelina forced herself to focus on his words. "I heard everything yesterday from Captain Zale and others. I even had the US embassy's regional security officer here—at his request."

Alec? Alec talked to the king about what happened? Why did he not tell me? "I did not know that, Sire."

"The US embassy's RSO was my sister's guest at the christening yesterday—you probably know he was once her bodyguard. When her husband told her of the danger, she apparently asked Special Agent Jones to assist in any way he could, which is why he... I think *intervened* was the word he used. But his involvement was after the fact. *After* you had spotted the would-be assassins. *After* you had accurately deduced their target and informed Captain Zale of the threat." The king's voice hardened. "*After* you had realized exactly what the would-be assassins were waiting for—the precise moment my son would be most vulnerable."

Angelina suppressed a tiny shiver at the coldness in the voice uttering that last sentence. The king had gone from friendly and approachable to hard and implacable in seconds. "And *after* you had taken one of the would-be assassins prisoner," he continued without pause, "ensuring he would no longer be a threat to my son."

It was exactly what Angelina needed to hear. But she didn't want the king to praise her for something that had been an accident. "I was not looking for threats at that precise moment, Sire," she confessed. "I was watching the baptism...like most people in the cathedral. Thinking about the religious meaning of the ceremony. One of the cameramen happened to be in my line of sight. That is when I saw the gun half hidden in his camera. And I knew..."

She trailed off and took a deep breath. "When I looked at the other cameraman and saw he also had a weapon in his possession, it all fell into place, and I knew the crown prince had to be the target. Once I realized that—"

"You realized what they were waiting for. Yes, Lieutenant, I had already deduced that." She watched as the king made a visible effort to relax the tension in his muscles at the thought of what had nearly happened yesterday. "Who can say what guides our thoughts, our actions? Divine intervention? Perhaps. But I have learned to my sorrow that God does not always intervene to save the innocent. He relies on us. And in this case, on you, Lieutenant. You did not fail God. You did not fail me." He smiled his faint smile again. "So. How do I reward you for saving my son's life?"

This is why every loyal Zakharian loves the king, Angelina realized as emotion welled up in her throat, threatening to overwhelm her. She swallowed hard. "That your family is safe is reward enough, Your Majesty."

"Hmm." He leaned back in his chair, observing her, and Angelina knew he was seeing more than she really wanted him to see. "I will have to think about this. In the meantime, Lieutenant, please accept my heartfelt thanks for a job well done." He stood and held out his hand, and when she tentatively offered hers, he shook it firmly, decisively, giving her his trust so completely that she swore to herself she would never let him down.

* * *

Angelina had no sooner exited the king's private office when Major Branko stopped her. "Colonel Marianescu wishes to see you, Lieutenant," he said.

"But the king—" she began, almost blurting out
that the king had cleared her of wrongdoing. Then,
"Yes, sir."

She headed down the corridor without another word,
stopping at the door to Colonel Marianescu's office.
She drew a deep breath, tapped on the door and pushed
it open at the strong command to enter.

"You wished to see me, Colonel?" she asked from
the doorway.

"Come in and shut the door, Lieutenant." When
she did, the king's cousin crossed the room to where
she stood nervously by the door and offered his hand.
"Thank you, Lieutenant, from the bottom of my heart."

She took the hand but couldn't help asking, "Sir?"
Not really understanding. She knew the colonel and the
king were close, almost like brothers, but…

"If anything had happened to the crown prince," he
explained, "there are those who would firmly believe
I had a hand in it somehow." His expression was even
more austere than normal. "The way many still believe
I had a hand in my brother's schemes eighteen months
ago. Or at least knowledge of them."

Angelina didn't know what to say. Like the king,
she didn't believe it. No one who'd ever served under
Colonel Marianescu—including all those on the security details—believed it, either, but she knew many
Zakharians still harbored the question in their minds.

She didn't have to say anything, though, because
the colonel added, "I owe you a debt of gratitude,

Lieutenant. Know that you can call upon me anytime, anywhere, should you ever need anything. This is not coming from the head of internal security. This is coming from me, personally."

But that wasn't the end of her incredible day. No sooner had she returned to duty in the queen's suite, when diminutive Queen Juliana threw herself at Angelina, her long dark hair curling around a face flushed with gratitude, her violet eyes sparkling with unshed tears. "Thank you, Angelina," she uttered in a fervent voice as she hugged her fiercely. "I can never thank you enough. Oh, I knew if anyone tried to hurt Raoul or me, you would prevent it. And I was right." Then she burst into tears.

Angelina quickly seated the queen in an armchair in the sitting room, and knelt on one knee in front of her. "I'm sorry," the queen said, using the heels of her hands to wipe the tears from her eyes like a little girl. "I wasn't going to cry. Honestly, I wasn't. But I can't seem to help it. If anything had happened to Raoul…" A fresh upwelling of tears overwhelmed the queen's efforts to hold them back.

A touch of humor speared through Angelina as she acknowledged the queen was one of those few women who looked beautiful even when they were crying, her tear-stained eyes like damp pansies, the delicate color in her cheeks unaffected. *Unlike me,* she thought with an inner smile, remembering her red, swollen eyes and puffy face last night.

But Alec did not care how I looked. The thought hit her like an avalanche, and hard on the heels of that thought came another one. *All he cared about was con-*

vincing me I did the right thing yesterday. All he cared about was making me accept the truth. Not just about killing Sasha, but about the two of us—Alec and me. About how we feel. Not only how we feel physically, but all the things we share...like what motivates us.

She wasn't going to be able to walk away from him. Not after he'd abolished every sexual inhibition she'd ever had—wiped them right off the map. Not after he'd taught her it was perfectly acceptable to be demanding in bed. Not after he'd taught her just how demanding she could be with the right man. A man who could fulfill every sexual fantasy she'd ever had and then some.

But it wasn't just the sex. If that were all, she could take her fill and walk away. No, what she couldn't walk away from was the way she felt when she was with him. The way he made her feel even when she *wasn't* with him. As if she were more when he was in her life. As if she could accomplish anything...when he was in her life.

She was strong, but so was he. Bigger, more muscular, yes. But also strong inside, where it counted most. She was determined, but so was he. And that appealed to her. She couldn't respect a man who wasn't at least as strong and determined as she was.

She'd killed a man, *but so had he.* No one who hadn't lived through that experience could really understand. But Alec could. He did. And he hadn't let her fall into despair over it. *"You did what you had to do,"* he'd told her, and he'd been right. Why hadn't she seen that on her own?

Alec had never seen his job as a nine-to-five that he could put away at the end of the day. He never "closed up shop," never stopped working if he was on something that needed to be finished.

Except today. Come hell or high water, he would be at Angelina's apartment at five-thirty. Waiting for her. Because he couldn't *not* be there. Because he knew— even if she didn't—that yesterday's events weren't over. Whoever had arranged the assassination attempt was still out there. Still a danger. Not just to the royal family, but to Angelina, too. He shuddered when he thought about how close she'd come to dying. Not just in the sacristy, but when she'd confronted the cameraman and dragged him away. A second here, a second there, and things could have had a very different outcome.

And yet, he'd been so proud of her. He hadn't been close enough to hear what she'd said to the cameraman, but he'd seen every move she made, could almost have predicted everything she'd do because he would have done exactly the same thing under the circumstances. He'd grabbed the Glock from the camera that she'd been forced to leave behind, and had joined her in the sacristy as soon as he could. *Not* because he didn't think she could handle things—he hadn't been lying yesterday when he told her she had everything under control. But because he'd wanted to be with her for whatever happened.

The clock's minute hand, the one that had seemed frozen in place for the past half hour, finally clicked onto the twelve. Five o'clock. Time to go.

He said good-night to his administrative assistant and was gone before she could reply, and then he made the five-minute walk to his apartment in less than four minutes. He showered, shaved and dressed swiftly— jeans, a long-sleeved polo shirt in a deep shade of forest green and a brown tweed blazer. He was out the door again in ten minutes, which left him plenty of time to walk to Angelina's apartment.

He passed the flower shop almost without seeing it, but then backtracked quickly. The flower arrangement that had caught his eye in the window seemed to have been made just for her. *Lilies,* he thought, remembering her middle name. *Perfect.* Lilies of the valley—with their small, white choral bells hanging upside down from their stalks—tiny blue forget-me-nots and jasmine. Sweet-smelling jasmine. He paid for his purchase and waited impatiently while the florist wrapped the arrangement in tissue paper and placed it carefully in a box.

He was a minute late when he finally arrived, but it was worth it when she promptly opened the door, as if she'd been waiting for him. She wore jeans and an ice-blue sweater that matched her blue-gray eyes and reminded him of the robe she'd been wearing last night. As if he needed a reminder.

The complete surprise on her face when she unwrapped his floral offering touched something deep inside him. Had no one ever given her flowers before? Was he the first in this way, too?

"They are beautiful," she told him with just a hint of shyness. "Thank you."

"When I saw them in the shop window, they whispered your names to me—Angelina Zuzana. I had to stop, even if it meant being late." He touched one tiny bell on a stalk of lilies of the valley. "My mom loves these, and always has them in her garden. They're a perennial, you know. And when they bloom, she goes around singing that children's song about lilies of the valley." He smiled at the memory. "My mom was always singing to us when we were kids. She still does to my niece, Alyssa, and she still has her garden."

"My mother loves flowers, too," Angelina confessed. "But her garden is a bower of roses she tends as if they are her children."

"She's still alive?"

"Oh, yes. Both my parents. I see them every week, if I can. She is not so old—just fifty-four. My father is much older—almost sixty-six. But I..." She trailed off.

Alec wanted to know what she'd been going to say. "But you...?"

"But I am not close to them. They do not...that is... they are very old-fashioned, even for Zakhar. They wanted me to marry young. To give them grandchildren. Especially since my brother died when he was a baby, and I am my parents' only remaining child. They do not like that I am still unmarried at twenty-nine. And they especially do not like that I am on the queen's security detail. The danger, you see. If I were to die without giving them grandchildren..."

Alec correctly interpreted this, and stated flatly, "So they don't know about yesterday, do they? They don't know you were involved."

Angelina shook her head. Not sadly, just with acceptance of something she could never change. "I cannot tell them. They would not understand. Not just because it would be a reminder of the danger to me, but...to have killed a man...that is a... It goes against tradition, you understand. Not a womanly thing to do."

Alec cursed under his breath, but he was starting to understand Angelina a little better. Not just the woman she was, but the forces that had shaped her, and how she'd had to fight to overcome those prejudices. How she'd had to fight for *everything* she was.

In many ways she reminded him of his younger sister. Keira had always fought for acceptance—as the only girl in their family, in the Marine Corps, in the agency she worked for. Had always fought for respect. As he'd told Angelina, when he was younger he hadn't seen it, hadn't realized he was perpetrating a stereotype with regard to his sister. But that didn't mean that was how he saw things now. He'd learned in the years since then, and was still learning.

Yesterday had rocked his world. Shaken it off its foundations. Before yesterday, if someone had asked him whether a woman should sacrifice her career for a man's, he'd have had no hesitation in saying, "Absolutely!" Not just because he was a man, but because that was the way his father had raised him. Because that's the way things had been for years and still were for the most part, despite some relatively recent changes in the United States.

What had happened yesterday had clearly shown him how wrong he'd been. Why should Angelina give up a job that meant everything to her, the culmination of a lifetime of sacrifices on her part? A job she was damned good at? But if he wanted a future with her— and right now, he couldn't imagine *not* having a future with Angelina—what other choice did they have? He wouldn't be staying in Zakhar. Not permanently. He couldn't even if he wanted to, because he'd eventually be reassigned. That was the nature of his work. And if he wanted to be promoted, it was almost guaranteed he'd have to relocate to wherever that promotion was— that's how the federal government operated.

It wasn't until he'd convinced himself he'd never ask Angelina to make that kind of sacrifice for him that he realized just how devastating a blow it would be to him if he asked her and she *didn't* choose him.

Chapter 9

They had dinner at Mischa's in the central district again. Afterward they walked as they'd done the first time, although this time they were able to walk much farther afield since Angelina wasn't wearing heels. Conversation at dinner had been restricted by their surroundings—neither had wanted to discuss anything related to yesterday since it might be overheard by other diners. But as they walked, they talked freely.

"Where does the investigation go from here?" Alec asked.

Angelina shook her head. "I am not involved in that," she said softly. "Captain Zale and the heads of the other two security details are in charge of the investigation from this point on." She started to say something more but changed her mind at the last minute.

"And you're just going to let them push you aside

like that? You're not even involved in the interrogation of the remaining cameraman?"

"I would like to be," she said, unable to keep a trace of wistfulness from her voice.

"You should be."

It seemed a criticism, and Angelina was quick to defend herself. "You do not understand. I am in no position to insist on anything. I am fortunate to still have my job. I am fortunate not to still be under investigation myself."

He stopped walking to look at her. "For *what*?" His expression of incredulity was a welcome sight. At least Alec thought it an impossibility she was involved in the conspiracy. When she explained, he snorted. "Idiots."

"No, they are—"

"Yes, idiots, if they think there's even the slightest chance you had anything to do with the assassination attempt. Don't they know you at all? I haven't known you very long, but even I know that much about you."

"It is not just that," she continued. "When they finally let me leave last night, the king's men—Majors Kostya and Branko—implied that even if I was not involved, I was somehow at fault because—" She couldn't finish her sentence.

"Because you're a woman?" Again there was that note of incredulity in Alec's voice, and it warmed her heart. "No man could have done better, Angel. I know I couldn't."

"The king agrees with you," she added quickly. "I think it is only because of him that I was allowed to return to my post guarding the queen."

Alec took her hand in his, stared at it for a moment and then pressed a kiss in the palm. Angelina had never had her palm kissed, and she felt it tingle all through her. Then he said, "I'm glad you told me about the king. I like him. And I respect him more than most men I know. If I thought that he—but he doesn't, and that's good."

He hesitated but then seemed to reach a decision. "I'm going to tell you something, something you can't tell a soul. But I know you won't."

"Tell me what?"

"Let's walk." He tucked her hand in the crook of his elbow. After a minute, he said, "I don't know what you might have heard about why I'm here." She opened her mouth but then decided it was better not to say anything. "Yeah," he said, glancing at her, humor in his eyes. "I'll bet you've heard rumors."

"It is not a reflection on you," she rushed to say. "Princess Mara…she is well liked in Zakhar. Everyone knows you were one of her bodyguards when she went to Colorado—it is not a secret."

"So no one was surprised when strings were pulled to get me here as RSO at the embassy," he finished for her.

Angelina's eyes crinkled in embarrassment. "That is how the world works sometimes. Princess Mara made no secret of her indignation over how you were treated at your last posting. The king—he is a great king for Zakhar, you understand. But he is like clay where the women he loves are concerned. His wife and his sister. He will do anything for them."

"I'll bet," Alec said dryly. "Especially if what they ask for falls nicely in line with what he wants."

Angelina cast him a quizzical look. "What do you mean by that?"

He smiled, but his smile had more than a touch of cynicism in it. "What if I told you the king had another—entirely different—reason for bringing me here? And what if I told you the real reason I'm here could involve you…indirectly?"

This time she was the one who stopped. "How?"

"Let's keep walking and I'll explain." He turned left, bringing them to the river embankment walkway. The sun had already set, but the lights of Zakhar were reflected in the slowly moving water, making for a romantic setting—if either of them cared about that at this moment. "You told me your cousin disappeared about eight years ago, right?"

A little pang shot through her, as it always did when her missing cousin was mentioned. "Caterina," she said softly, regretfully. "Her name is Caterina."

"Yeah, I know."

Puzzled, she asked, "How do you know that? I did not think I—"

"McKinnon found out for me."

Even more puzzled than before, Angelina said, "Princess Mara's husband? Why? I do not understand."

"The king brought me here because there's a human-trafficking ring operating between Zakhar and the US, for purposes of prostitution. And we suspect certain people at the US embassy might be involved. Including the previous RSOs."

Everything fell into place and Angelina felt herself go cold despite the warm jacket she was wearing. "Oh my God," she said, coming to a complete halt, her eyes riveted on Alec's face. "Modeling. Caterina received a work visa from the embassy to do modeling in the US." Her eyes narrowed and her lips tightened. "But when

I went to the embassy after she disappeared without a word, no one there would speak to me. No one would help me try to find her. Oh my God."

Alec's eyes were full of sympathy. "Yeah. We had no idea about your cousin. Didn't know the trafficking ring had been in operation that long—and we still don't, not for sure. But it all fits neatly. McKinnon works for a secret US agency—I can't tell you any more than that, other than the agency is authorized to operate both within and outside the US, which is important for legal reasons. I recruited him to help me in this investigation for that, and because he's got a legitimate excuse for being here in Zakhar totally unrelated to anything happening at the embassy. And we're friends—that's well known."

He drew a deep breath and let it out. "So the cover story is the king caved to pressure from his sister and pulled strings with the State Department to get me here. McKinnon's here because of his wife. And together we're secretly investigating the embassy's involvement in trafficking in women. Including your missing cousin."

Emotions she thought she'd long ago buried rose up suddenly, and she frantically tried to hold them back, biting her lip until it bled. Then she knew she couldn't do it, and she buried her face in her hands as the sobs she couldn't repress tore through her. Nearly silent sobs—at least she had enough control for that—but Alec put his arms around her, holding her tight as she wept for the cousin she still loved and missed so dreadfully.

"Shh," he soothed. "I'm sorry, Angel."

She choked out her cousin's name and hid her face

against Alec's shoulder, struggling to regain control. "I never cry," she insisted. "I do not. I really do not." Despite the fact that she'd cried last night. Despite the fact that she was crying now.

"It's okay to cry," he reassured her. "If it was my little sister—if this had happened to Keira—I'd be crying, too."

"Help! Help! Someone help!" The voice reverberated down the long, echoing hallway of the old prison on the outskirts of Drago, and two guards came running. Dinnertime for the prisoners was over, and it wasn't yet time for bed check. But the loud voice could be heard at the guard station and beyond, and the alarm in its tone was real, not feigned, as it called out repeatedly.

"What is it, Toussaint?" one of the guards said brusquely when the two men reached the cell. One hand grasped the key ring on his belt that would unlock the cell door, the other grasped the baton that would subdue the prisoner if this was some kind of ruse.

"Not me," Toussaint said quickly. "*Him.* The one in the next cell over. The king's cousin." The man bent his head and covered his ears. "I could hear him. Horrible. Horrible!"

Both guards moved one cell to the left, and the sight that met their eyes had both men cursing. One man fumbled for the key while the other grabbed his radio. "We need an emergency medical team in cell block D. Now. Now!"

Angelina and Alec walked back to her apartment with their arms wrapped around each other, as if they didn't dare let go. When they finally stood in her bedroom, Alec kissed her slowly. Thoroughly. "No rush tonight," he said softly as he tilted her head back, running his hands through her short, straight hair as if the silky texture pleased him immensely. "I want to take my sweet time. I want to seduce you, Angel. Is that okay?"

Her eyes met his. Those brown eyes so open, so honest. So beautiful to her. "I would like that, I think." She felt unexpectedly shy. Why she would feel so after last night, when they'd writhed naked in each other's arms, when they'd taken each other to unbelievable heights was a mystery. But she did.

He gently pressed her shoulders down so she was sitting on the bed, and he went down on one knee in front of her. He untied her shoes slowly, drawing one off, then the other. Her socks followed, and he caressed her bare ankles with his strong hands until she shivered, her nipples tightening uncontrollably, a sudden throbbing in her womanhood telling her his seduction was having an effect. A totally expected effect, after last night.

He reached for the fastening of her jeans and she tried to help him, but he gently pushed her hands away. "No, Angel. This is my seduction. Let me do it my way."

She acquiesced, wondering where the demanding lover of last night had gone, and who this stranger was who'd taken his place. But then she stopped wondering, because she no longer cared.

Alec removed her clothing piece by piece. Maddeningly, achingly slowly. Pausing each time to kiss the flesh he'd exposed, telling her without words how beautiful she was to him. Making her sigh at how gentle, how tender he could be.

She closed her eyes and floated on a cloud of blissful sensation, letting him do whatever he wanted with her body, because everything he did was exactly what she needed when she needed it.

When he slipped her underwear down her legs and off, placing a kiss on the silky, golden curls he'd exposed, she suddenly realized she was completely naked and he was still fully clothed. A tiny dart of panic went through her, but Alec was prepared for that. "No," he soothed, calming her fears with a kiss as he moved up and lay beside her on the bed. "Be patient, Angel. Trust me." His voice dropped until it was barely a whisper. "Just close your eyes again and let yourself feel."

She closed her eyes. *Trust me,* he'd said. And she did. She would.

She felt the bed respond as his weight was removed, and she heard a rustling sound she imagined was Alec removing his clothes. Then he was back next to her, his hard, naked body warm against hers.

He nuzzled her breasts, cupping them with his hands, and used his tongue to tease the nipples into tight little peaks. Angelina shivered, but not from the cold. She wanted…she wanted… She didn't know how he knew, but he did. *He must.* Because his hand moved down, down, over her belly, to the curls guarding her womanhood. He toyed with them for just a moment and then slid his fingers between the petals, making her gasp. Then a second finger joined the first. Stroking deep. Deeper, his thumb finding the little nub at the same time, flicking over it until she moaned and her legs thrashed restlessly.

She almost opened her eyes then, because she wanted to see his face. Wanted to know if what he was feeling was anything approaching what she felt. But...*trust me,* he'd said. *Just close your eyes...let yourself feel...*

His fingers continued working their magic until she knew she couldn't hold back any longer. Until she arched and cried out Alec's name—not the screams of the night before, but a soft moan of exquisite pleasure as she throbbed around his fingers. Endlessly. When he finally removed his fingers, she felt such a sense of loss a whimper escaped her. But then Alec moved between her legs and she felt a blunt probing as his shielded flesh teased the entrance to her body. Teased, then withdrew. Pushed a little deeper, then withdrew again. Never enough. Never deep enough.

The next time he entered her, she arched, trying to pull him deeper, but he held back. His muscles were trembling—she could feel it. But he still refused to complete his possession of her for some reason she couldn't fathom. "Please, Alec," she begged as a sigh of longing rippled through her. "Please."

"Look at me, Angel." His voice was deep and husky with desire held on a tight leash. And when her eyes flew open, she found him staring down at her with such emotional intensity she caught her breath. He surged into her, so deep she knew he couldn't go any deeper.

Then he began a rhythm. Slow. Measured. Tortuous. Making sweet love to her, but taking his time. The first climax had been nothing compared to the one that was building now. Just as last night—as wondrous as it had been—was nothing compared to what she was feeling now.

Then she couldn't think anymore. Didn't want to. She was on fire, burning up from the inside out. Aching. Needing. But he wasn't going to let her go...wasn't going to let her find her release...until they found it together.

"Why?" she asked him when she could finally breathe again.

He propped up his head on one hand, idly running the fingers of his other hand over the swell of her breast, the curve of her hip. As if he just had to touch her. "Why what?"

"Tonight...last night...do not misunderstand, I loved last night. It was..." She tried to think of a word that would describe last night, but all she could come up with was, "Incredible. I had not imagined there were so many ways to..." She felt herself flushing. "But tonight was different. So very different. Incredible, too, but different."

She didn't know how to tell him the two nights appealed to different aspects of her character. There would be times she wanted him as he was last night—the fierce, demanding lover who would accept no less from her in return. Warrior heart calling to warrior heart. And there would be other times she wanted him as he was tonight—the sweet, tender lover. The seducer, who made her feel cherished. Adored.

But he seemed to understand anyway. "If I'd made love to you last night the way I did tonight, it wouldn't have been what you needed. Last night you needed to erase the self-doubt. Needed to remember just how strong you really are. All I did was remind you." He smiled lazily. "All I did was let loose a woman who met me halfway and demanded everything I had to give. And yeah, it was incredible. Mind blowing."

He toyed with her hair. "But tonight…tonight you needed tenderness. You still needed everything I had to give, but emotionally, not sexually." He rolled onto his back, tugging her until she sprawled across his naked body. "I want to be the one who gives you what you need, Angel," he said seriously, holding her gaze with his. "No matter what. No matter when. And I want the same from you."

She didn't know what to say. Everything was still too new. Too unexpected. She'd denied this side of herself for so long, rationalizing she could never have her career and a man, too, that the two things seemed incompatible. And she'd been content with the choice she'd made. More than content—she'd been reasonably happy with her life exactly as it had been.

Until she met Alec. Until she realized she'd never really had to make a choice at all before now. She now realized how much she'd be giving up if she made the same choice this time around.

But she had to tell him something. "I… I have been alone for a long time, Alec. I have made a life for myself that was enough…until I met you. And now that life is no longer enough. I was not expecting it. And to be honest, I did not want my life to change."

She caught a fleeting glimpse of pain in his eyes before he hid it. Both hurt her—that she'd caused him pain, and that he felt he had to hide his pain from her. "But now there is you," she continued. "I am not so easily changeable, I think. I need time to come to terms with everything that has happened. The reality of you is so much more than my secret fantasies." She touched his face with fingers that weren't quite steady, then bent to brush her lips over his.

"But one thing I must tell you," she continued when she finally raised her head. "You have given me more joy in two nights than I ever thought to have in my entire life." She knew he could see the smile in her eyes before it spread slowly over her face. "That is your gift to me. Joy. I did not know how much I needed it. But you did, and you gave it to me. I want to give that same gift to you."

Her words affected him powerfully—his face betrayed him. The same for the hard male flesh that responded as if she'd caressed him. "You do, Angel," he said softly, his tone husky with emotion. "What we have is enough for now. You need time? Time you shall have. That, and anything else you need. As I said, I want to be the one who gives you what you need. Just ask."

She hesitated, torn because she was afraid he wouldn't understand. "There is one other thing I need," she said finally. "Please do not take this the wrong way, but I do not want the men with whom I work to know about us. Not yet. Not that I am ashamed of what I feel for you," she rushed to add as his eyes darkened. "It is not that. Please do not think that. You are a man any woman would be proud to call her own."

"Then why?"

"I am judged by the men on the queen's security detail, and within the Zakharian National Forces. You must see how I cannot let my personal life be a distraction. 'Emotional.' That is what the men say. 'Women are too emotional to do a man's job.'"

"I never said that." His words rang with sincerity. "I never would."

"I know you would not, but it is not you I must work with. I am already looked at differently by Captain Zale and others than I was before yesterday. You know this."

His voice was hard when he said, "I already told you, no man could have done better."

"But what if Captain Zale thinks I was distracted from my duty, let us say, because you were there? Because of how I feel about you?"

"You weren't." Decisive. Sure.

His faith in her—so absolute—made her blink back sudden tears. She'd cried more in the past two days than she'd cried in the past eight years since Caterina disappeared. Tears no one but Alec had seen. She wanted him to always believe in her, but she had to be honest. "I will never know for sure," she said softly. Words it hurt her to admit, but words she had to say to him.

"*I* know," he said, still in that same implacable tone.

"How can you *know* when I do not?"

His voice gentled. "Because I know you, Angel, like I know myself. Trust me on this." He pulled her head down and cradled it against his shoulder, a gesture that comforted her more than she would ever have believed possible. Or necessary. "*Nothing* will ever distract you from your duty."

Chapter 10

Eleven men and one woman sat around the conference table in what was called the war room. Zakhar had not fought in a war that required this size of a room since the Second World War, when the king's grandfather sat on the throne, and it was rarely used. But relics of Zakhar's illustrious military history were everywhere on the walls, including an authenticated copy of the portrait of the first Andre Alexei, the original of which hung in the portrait gallery downstairs. Angelina fixed her eyes on the portrait, wondering for the thousandth time how such a fearsome warrior could have been the same man who said, "It is her…or no one," referring to Queen Eleonora. The same man whose fierce love for his queen was legendary.

Everyone rose when the king entered, the wooden chairs making no sound on the large carpet beneath the conference table, and Angelina put her musings aside to consider another day, wondering instead why she'd been included in this high-level meeting. Captain Zale hadn't told her. He'd merely said the king had commanded her presence.

"Please be seated," the king said curtly before taking the chair at the head of the table next to his cousin, the head of internal security. "You all know why you are here," he told them. "But I will say it anyway. Prince Nikolai is dead." The king shot one glance at his cousin, who was Prince Nikolai's older brother, but Colonel Marianescu betrayed not a flicker of emotion.

The king continued, "My cousin supposedly hanged himself in his prison cell last night." She could have heard a pin drop. "I say supposedly, because there are indications it was not by his choice." The king folded his lips tightly together, as if keeping his temper by the slimmest of threads.

"I also find it convenient—too convenient—that the interrogation of the surviving would-be assassin from Sunday's attempt has yielded a confession so quickly." He glanced around the table, his gaze moving from one face to the next, ending on Angelina's. "Far too convenient, because he named my cousin Niko as the instigator of the plot to assassinate my son."

Angelina had never heard a harder, colder voice than the king's. Then he said softly, "I do not believe it. It is too neat. Too pat." A couple of voices were raised in objection, but the king held up his hand to silence them. "Do I believe my cousin wanted my son dead? Absolutely. Do not waste your breath on that. But do I believe he could have arranged this from his prison cell? All on his own? Without access to money? Accomplices? No. I would be a fool to believe that." *And I am not a fool.* He didn't say it, but everyone at the table heard him anyway.

He looked around the table again, and his gaze ended up on Angelina's face. "Do not forget the cameramen were not the only ones involved. Lieutenant Sasha Tcholek, who was trusted to guard the queen and was then transferred to guard the crown prince, was part of the conspiracy."

She knew—all Zakhar knew—the king loved his wife. But even though she'd been a witness on occasion to intimate moments between the king and the queen she guarded, even though she knew their devotion to each other, seeing the king like this startled her. And—she caught her breath at the realization—it made her think of Alec. Alec, who'd been angry on her behalf. Alec, who she sensed could be just as ruthless as the king.

She quickly pushed thoughts of Alec to one side, because the king was speaking again. "I want three things," he told them, his tone reminding those gathered around the conference table he was one of the last absolute monarchs on earth—at the Zakharians' insistence. "First, I want further interrogation of the prisoner with the aim of learning the *entire* truth behind the assassination attempt. Second, I want an investigation into the backgrounds of both would-be assassins. Find the connection between them, my cousin, Lieutenant Tcholek and whoever else is involved. Do the same for Lieutenant Tcholek."

He paused, poured water from the carafe in front of him into a glass and took a sip. "Third, I want a complete investigation of *every* man on the crown prince's security detail. The same goes for the queen's security detail." He paused, and added softly, "And mine. We are fortunate Lieutenant Mateja was quick-witted enough to take Tcholek down, but we cannot rely on her every time. No stone unturned, is that understood? What nearly happened *never* happens again."

The chorus of assent seemed to please the king, and he stood. "Thank you, gentlemen. You are dismissed." Everyone rose and headed for the door, Angelina among them, but the king called out, "Captain Zale. Lieutenant Mateja. A moment, please. No, Zax," he told his cousin. "You stay too, please."

The king waited until only the four of them remained and then ordered, "Shut the door, please."

Angelina obeyed, wondering what this was all about. She didn't have long to wonder. "It has come to my attention, Captain, there still exists doubt and suspicion in some quarters regarding Lieutenant Mateja's actions on Sunday." Captain Zale shot a sharp glance at Angelina. "No, Captain. Lieutenant Mateja has said nothing to me. Nor did she say anything to the queen. Admirable, perhaps, on her part. She is completely loyal to you. But know this. Of every man on the security details, including my own, the *only* officers above suspicion in my mind at this moment are Lieutenant Mateja and Colonel Marianescu," he said, using his cousin's military title. "Lieutenant Mateja will be investigated—as every officer will be investigated— but that is a formality, Captain. Keep that in mind. You are dismissed."

When Angelina turned to follow Colonel Marianescu and Captain Zale from the room, the king stopped her. "One more moment, Lieutenant, if you please."

When they were alone, the king said, "Something else has come to my attention, Lieutenant, regarding the killing of Lieutenant Tcholek."

"Yes, Sire?"

"You did what you had to do, Lieutenant." His voice was soft but seriously intent. "You are a fighting man—a woman, yes, but a fighting man nevertheless. You cannot let this killing weigh on your conscience. Nor the death of the other man. These things happened, and you must live with them. Take solace that they deserved to die, although not, perhaps, by your hand. But you cannot second-guess yourself. Not now. Not ever."

Suddenly Angelina knew the source of the king's information. *Alec,* a little voice whispered in her mind. *Alec talked to the king again.*

The king wasn't finished. "For a fighting man, instinct is everything. Reflexes rely on instinct. If you doubt yourself, doubt your instincts, this could be fatal. To you and the person you are guarding. You cannot afford to doubt. I have entrusted the most precious thing in my world to you, but I must know you are able to put the killing behind you and move forward with the same certainty of purpose you had before. You may be called upon to kill again someday in the line of duty. I *must* know you will not hesitate…if necessary."

Angelina stiffened. "Yes, Sire."

The king assessed her in that disconcerting way he had. "Good," he said finally. "Very good." He smiled his faint smile. "And Lieutenant, for what it is worth, I would have done exactly what you did under the circumstances. No more, no less. Exactly what you did."

* * *

She pounced on Alec the minute he walked through her door. "You traitor," she accused him, her eyes narrowing, but playfully. "You talked to the king again."

He didn't even try to deny it. "Yeah, I did."

"But why?"

"Because you didn't deserve to be looked at with suspicion, or have anyone second-guess what you did on Sunday. And the only one who could fix that was the king. You told me the king was the reason your captain let you return to work so soon, right?"

"Yes, but—"

"So I talked to the king. Man-to-man. I respected the hell out of him before this, but now...now I totally get why you Zakharians love him so fiercely. The loyalty he gives his men is incredible. Unbelievable, even. And unexpected. No wonder you give him your complete loyalty in return."

He smiled suddenly, as if at a memory. "You know, McKinnon told me the king sent men to spy on him when he was falling in love with the princess. Men with orders to kill him, if necessary, to protect her."

"I do not see what there is to smile about that," she said, puzzled.

"Then the king kidnapped McKinnon—although he already had a plane ticket to come here—and brought him by stealth to Zakhar, to ask him one question," Alec continued. "And to force him to see what he'd done to the princess by lying to her. By telling her he didn't love her."

"I still do not see—"

"Ruthless. The king is ruthless where someone he cares about is concerned," Alec said in the deep voice that never failed to thrill her. Still smiling, but the smile was a little crooked now. "I am, too, Angel. I'm ruthless where you're concerned." He put his arms around her and drew her close. "Don't ask me to change, because I can't change who I am any more than you can change who you are. I told you I want to be the one who gives you everything you need, and I do. I always will. Even if you don't think you need it."

Aleksandrov Vishenko eyed his minions coldly. "And how is it the Zakharian prince is still alive? I thought the plan was foolproof. Were there not two assassins? And was there not a backup? Someone on the inside?"

The first man started to say no plan was foolproof, but one look at Vishenko's face and he decided discretion was the better part of valor. The second man was apparently made of sterner stuff. "Two men are dead," he said practically. "At least they cannot talk. One is a prisoner but, as previously arranged, he named Prince Nikolai as the instigator of the assassination plot. And with Prince Nikolai dead—" he shrugged "—nothing can be traced to you."

The first man jumped in eagerly. "And word is that even though the little prince is not dead, the king is now focused exclusively on rooting out any other conspirators on their security teams. So he has been distracted...exactly as you wished."

"*Exactly* as I wished?" Vishenko asked in a rumbling volcano of a voice that made the two men quail. "If it had been *exactly* as I wished, the king's son would be dead." He let that sink in for a minute. "And what of your other assignment?"

The first man cleared his throat. "There has been some progress there," he said cautiously. "We sent out the word on the woman…and the increased reward. The higher reward may have done the trick. An informant thinks he may have spotted her in—" He glanced at the other man, a frantic question on his face.

"Denver, Colorado," the second man supplied smoothly. "Why she would be there we don't know, but we have sent a man to investigate."

Vishenko nodded his approval. "Good. Very good. Let me know what he learns."

The phone rang, waking Alec from a sound sleep. He'd long ago learned how to wake immediately—you couldn't function effectively as a bodyguard if your brain was groggy when you first woke up, not even for a few minutes—so he was sharp and alert when he grabbed the phone. "Hello?"

"Did I wake you? Sorry," his sister, Keira, said, but the perfunctory way the apology was offered told Alec she wasn't sincere.

Keira wouldn't be calling him at this hour of the night if it wasn't important, so he didn't bother with small talk. "What's up?"

"Trace asked me to check on a name last week, and Cody authorized it," she said, referring to her husband, McKinnon's boss in the agency. "He wanted anything I could uncover, including any work visas, tourist visas, et cetera, that might have been issued in that name— and let him know what I found."

Keira had tracked down a work visa that had been issued just over eight years ago in Caterina Mateja's name, but it had never been renewed. And since the original visa had expired long since, the holder of the visa should have returned to her home country. But there was no record of her on any flight or boat leaving the United States. Nothing Keira could find, and she had access to just about every data file.

Lots of people overstayed their US visas, dropping off the grid and becoming illegal immigrants. The federal government wasn't all that good about tracking people who overstayed their welcome, even after 9/11.

"Caterina Mateja just resurfaced in a totally different case."

Angelina stood at attention in Captain Zale's tiny office in the palace, off a small, out-of-the-way corridor. She was worried the king's intervention on her behalf only made things worse where her commanding officer was concerned, but she was determined to make her request anyway.

"Yes, Lieutenant?" Captain Zale's tone wasn't unfriendly, but it wasn't the warm, approving tone she'd grown to expect from him.

"I would like to be involved in the interrogation of the prisoner, sir," she said, not beating around the bush. "On my own time, of course. I am not asking to be relieved of duty for this."

Captain Zale made a sound of impatience and said curtly, "Sit down, Mateja." When she was seated, he said abruptly, "I owe you an apology."

"Sir?" This was the last thing she'd expected.

"No one appreciates being reprimanded. And especially not by one's supreme commander," he added dryly, referring to the king. "But I deserved the reprimand."

"Sir?"

"Do not keep saying 'sir' as if you do not follow what I am saying," he said testily. "I know you understand." He grimaced. "Perhaps I was hard on you because I blamed myself."

"Si—" She stopped herself before she could say it. "Blame yourself for what, sir?"

"For not telling you the name of the person I was sending to relieve you." One corner of his mouth twitched into the beginning of a rueful smile. "I should have told you. Easy to see that now, of course. If I had, you would never have dropped your guard with Tcholek. You would have been suspicious of him from the first. Then we would have three to interrogate instead of only one."

"I do blame myself for that, sir," she said quietly. "For dropping my guard. Or I did, until—" She caught herself before she could blurt out Alec's name, and changed what she was going to say. "Until the king told me I could not let it affect me. I must put the killing behind me and move forward with the same certainty of purpose I have always had. He said I must trust my instincts. Always."

"He is right. He is always right. That is why he is the king." His expression held nothing but an absolute belief in the truth of his statement. "Your request is approved, Lieutenant."

Alec hand-delivered the message Keira had sent to McKinnon via the embassy's encrypted fax. He'd decrypted it himself and read what Keira had uncovered before he picked up the phone to request a meeting with McKinnon. The two men met on the embankment overlooking the river.

"She very carefully says there's only a possibility what she just uncovered is connected to the human-trafficking case," McKinnon said slowly, "but knowing what we know…"

Alec just looked at him. "You know something I don't, obviously. You and Keira."

"Yeah." McKinnon was quiet for a moment and then seemed to reach a decision. "I wouldn't normally say anything about an ongoing case, but I think you need to know this isn't the first time Keira and I have run into Aleksandrov Vishenko. But I hope to God it's the last."

"Tell me."

McKinnon leaned on the guardrail, staring out at a slow-moving barge on the river, but Alec could see his eyes weren't focused outward, they were looking inward. "Remember when Keira was shot?"

"Of course."

"That case revolved around Vishenko's nephew, Michael Vishenko, aka Michael Pennington, and an organization called the New World Militia." He made a movement of frustration. "Christ, this goes back *years*."

"I've got nothing but time." Alec's voice was calm, but he had an urgent feeling inside, the one that told him he was on the right track, on the brink of something big.

"I wasn't working for the agency when this whole thing started—the agency didn't even exist. I was a US marshal back then. I was assigned to guard a witness testifying in a trial against a man named David Pennington, Michael Pennington's father. We didn't know it at the time, but Pennington was working hand in glove with Aleksandrov Vishenko. It's a long, involved story, and I don't need to tell you all of it, but what you *do* need to know is that Alexei Vishenko—as he's more commonly known to law enforcement—is the head of a particularly vicious branch of the Bratva, aka—"

"The Brotherhood," Alec broke in. "The Russian Mafia." He nodded slowly as things started to connect. "The king told me up front he'd heard rumors the Bratva was involved in this operation, remember?" He cursed under his breath. "Now Keira's message makes sense to me."

"Drugs. Gunrunning. Prostitution. Money laundering. You name it—if it's illegal, Vishenko has a hand in it. And those are just his illegal activities. He's plowed his money into legitimate enterprises, as well. Not as profitable, but profitable enough. And completely aboveboard. He even pays his taxes on his legitimate earnings."

McKinnon's eyes narrowed. "The FBI has been after him for years. So has the IRS. And so has the agency—ever since we learned of Vishenko's connection with the two Penningtons, father and son. We've never managed to make anything stick, and neither have the Fibbies—no one will testify against Vishenko. The two times the FBI managed to scrape up witnesses against him early on, the witnesses ended up dead. Gruesomely dead. And the US marshals guarding them were also killed."

He breathed deeply. "You can forget the IRS—Vishenko's too smart for them to make a case based on imputed income. Don't get me wrong, he lives like a king. But his income from his legitimate businesses accounts for his lifestyle, and he's been extremely careful not to exceed that. The FBI is still trying to make a racketeering case—RICO could bring him down and the government could confiscate everything—but the Fibbies can't convince anyone to flip on Vishenko, not anymore—men would rather go to jail themselves than risk certain death…and can you blame them?"

"Apparently not. And the agency hasn't had any luck, either?"

McKinnon made a sound of disgust. "Much as I hate to admit it, no. We're in the same boat as the FBI. The old Sicilian law of *omerta* is nothing compared to the cone of silence surrounding Vishenko—no one will roll on him. Until someone does…"

"Great. Just great."

"Yeah, but the agency hasn't given up. And if he's involved in this case…" McKinnon smiled, but his eyes were like blue ice. "God, what wouldn't I give to be instrumental in putting him away for good," he said softly.

Alec nodded. "Me, too. So let's recap what we know so far. As I see it, there are three legs involved in the human trafficking of Zakharian women for prostitution purposes."

"Knock out one, and the other legs will probably collapse. That's the theory," McKinnon said, a real smile starting. "So this tracks. A criminal element here in Zakhar—and there *is* a criminal element, no matter how draconian the laws are—lures the women with promises of modeling contracts, acting contracts, anything that will convince young, impressionable women to willingly agree to go to the US. The US embassy in Drago issues the visas for a price. Vishenko's Bratva takes delivery of the women once they arrive in the States, and either sells them to gangs across the country—and there's more of a market for that than you'd believe—or he pimps them out through his own organization."

Alec closed his eyes briefly as he thought about telling all this to Angelina. "God," he said, fixing his burning gaze on McKinnon, not realizing how much he was betraying his personal feelings toward Angelina. "Angelina's cousin…"

"Yeah. If she was part of this, it had to be a nightmare for her. But the one good thing is, if Keira's right, Caterina Mateja's still alive."

"But for how long?" Alec asked fiercely. "If Keira's right, Vishenko has a million-dollar price tag on her head." He stopped suddenly as an idea occurred to him. An idea that should have occurred to him right away, as soon as he read Keira's message. An idea that could have monumental repercussions. "She knows something," he said softly, almost to himself. "Caterina knows something." Adrenaline surged through him, and he grasped McKinnon's arm. "That's why Vishenko wants her dead. That's why the price is so high. She knows something—or she has evidence that can put him away—and he knows it."

McKinnon shook his head regretfully. "Don't jump to conclusions—the case is a long way from being made. Okay, so maybe she knows something. Or maybe she has evidence. But what makes you think—even if you can find her—she'll testify against Vishenko?"

"Angelina would do it," Alec said, the absolute certainty in his head and his heart reflected in his voice. "She'd do it because it's the right thing to do, no matter the risk. If Caterina's anything like her cousin, she'll do it. She'll testify."

"Say you're right. Say she'd be willing to testify. Say you can keep her safe long enough to get her in front of a jury so she *can* testify. How are you going to find her before Vishenko does? You can't match the bounty he placed on her. Not even close. Plus, he's got a head start."

"I'll find her," Alec said grimly. "I'll find her. I've got two secret weapons—Keira and Angelina." His face hardened and his eyes went cold. "And when I find her, I'll keep her safe if it's the last thing I do."

Chapter 11

Angelina watched the handcuffed prisoner—whose name was Boris Tabor—through the two-way mirror looking into the interview room, trying to understand the mind of a would-be assassin and what approach would get him to talk. She glanced at Captain Zale standing by the two-way mirror next to her.

"We know a lot about him," the captain said in his blunt way. "And yet we know next to nothing."

"He really *was* a cameraman," Angelina said, glancing at her notes. "He worked in the newsroom of ZTV here in Drago for twenty-one years, until he was replaced by a remotely controlled robotic camera. The other man—the one I captured, the one Sasha killed—was not. Apparently he was coached in what to do by Boris Tabor."

She didn't need to add that Tabor was deeply in debt

and strapped for cash—or he had been until two weeks ago, when he'd deposited an unusually large sum of money in his bank account. Source unknown. So far.

Like her, Captain Zale knew Tabor had already been in debt before he'd lost his job—preliminary reports placed the blame for this squarely on his wife's shoulders, a beautiful woman who wanted more of the finer things in life than her husband could afford. But he'd been desperate to keep her, so he'd gone into debt to buy her whatever her heart desired. And when he'd lost his job, he'd lost his home and lost his ability to borrow. Shortly thereafter—unusual for Zakhar—his wife had divorced him. Divorce was still a shameful thing to many Zakharians, and word was, Tabor had sworn to get his wife back—no one knew how.

"He has no children," Angelina murmured to herself, trying to get a handle on Tabor's mind-set. Again, this was unusual for Zakhar. Most couples had three or more children.

"He was willing to kill a child," Captain Zale reminded her. "Even if he had children of his own, I doubt we could have appealed to him on those grounds."

She shook her head with regret. "You are right. That appeal would not have worked. And he has no incentive to talk." Tabor had to know the most likely sentence would be life in prison. Although unlike in the States, life in prison in Zakhar literally meant *life*. The actual sentence read, "life plus one day," as if the meaning needed to be hammered home.

Captain Zale snorted. "His previous interrogators reminded him of the gruesome sentence still on the books regarding an assassination attempt on a member of Zakhar's royal family, successful or not. Unfortunately he knows the king commuted that punishment in the case of Prince Nikolai and those who conspired with him eighteen months ago. So that threat was worthless."

Angelina could tell by the captain's tone he wished otherwise, but it wasn't their call to make. She could see the king invoking the ancient punishment the law allowed—Tabor had tried to kill the king's son, after all—but the queen had influenced the king to leniency before. Angelina knew it was likely the queen would again, no matter how tempted the king might be.

"Whoever orchestrated the assassination attempt must have dangled a carrot in front of Tabor he could not resist—"

"Money," Angelina said quickly. "A lot of money. It is the only thing that makes sense. Enough to wipe out his debt. To win back his wife and regain his pride." An idea was forming, but it was still nebulous. Still just a niggling in the back of her brain.

Instead of trying to force the idea to take shape—something she knew was unlikely to be successful—Angelina let her mind wander to the others involved in the assassination attempt. Since they hadn't yet been able to identify the other cameraman, they hadn't established a paper trail on him, and his motive remained unclear. Except for his fake identification badge, which rivaled the real thing, complete with his picture—not surprising, given Tcholek's involvement in the conspiracy—no identification at all had been found on his body, and his fingerprints weren't on file in Zakhar. A request had been submitted to Interpol through channels, but so far they hadn't heard anything.

Tabor had also been provided with a fake identification badge, but in his real name, and Angelina wondered about that now. Was it because he really was a TV cameraman? Or was there another reason?

She glanced down at her notes again. Neither Tabor nor the other man had been assigned to cover the christening—the bodies of the real cameramen had been found the next day by hikers in the mountains surrounding Drago. Ballistics tests proved they'd been killed with Tcholek's gun, so he'd obviously been instrumental in effecting the substitution. The team investigating the assassination attempt had already surmised that, but it was good to have proof. She wished she knew why Sasha had betrayed them.

As if their thoughts had followed the same path, Captain Zale said abruptly, "I would give a year of my life to know why Tcholek did it." Self-recrimination was evident in his voice. Sasha had once been part of his team, and Angelina knew the knowledge that he had harbored a traitor in the ranks was eating at her captain.

"So you do not believe—as the other investigators insist—that the motive was money?"

The captain shook his head. "His bank accounts show nothing out of the ordinary. Knowing that, and knowing him, I find it hard to believe."

Angelina agreed with Captain Zale. She remembered Sasha from working with him on the queen's security detail. He'd even asked her out a couple of times, and had taken her refusals in good part. He'd seemed no different from anyone else she'd worked with. Which meant money *couldn't* have been the motivating factor. There had to be another reason.

She sighed softly. It wasn't absolutely necessary to

know why. She just needed to know who. *Who* might lead to *why*. And in order to know who, she had to find the key to breaking Boris Tabor. Somehow. *What makes you think you will succeed where others have failed?* she asked herself derisively, and for just a moment she felt defeated even before she started. Then she took a deep breath and squared her shoulders. Alec thought she could do this. She had to try.

Angelina put down the clipboard containing her notes, when all at once the idea she'd tried not to force suddenly coalesced in her brain. Her eyes widened in sudden excitement, and she nodded to herself as everything came together. She picked the clipboard up again, removed her notes, and on a blank piece of paper quickly jotted down some questions to use as a prop. Then she glanced at Captain Zale again.

"Tag team?" he asked.

She shook her head, trying not to let her enthusiasm for her idea overwhelm her common sense. "That has been tried several times," she said, "with no success. I would like to try on my own. Look at him," she told her captain. "He is tired, both physically and of being questioned by men who have tried to intimidate him. I have an approach I think might work."

"It cannot hurt," he agreed.

The door to the viewing room opened and two senior members of the king's security detail entered the room—men Angelina recognized—and her heart sank. If Majors Kostya and Branko were here to question the prisoner, her chance would be lost.

But Captain Zale surprised her. "Go ahead, Lieutenant," he ordered. "The prisoner is yours to question. The video camera will be running, of course."

"Of course." She opened the door and walked into the room before the majors could stop her.

"Good morning, Mr. Tabor," she said pleasantly, holding out her hand. "I am Angelina Mateja." She deliberately didn't use her professional rank, having already figured he would react negatively to a woman in a position of power. Then she pretended to be surprised he was handcuffed. "Oh, I am *so* sorry. Let me undo those for you." She quickly unlocked the handcuffs, pushed them to the other side of the table and held out her hand again.

He looked at her a little uncertainly, rubbing his wrists, but then the good manners he'd probably been raised with came to the fore, and he shook her hand. "Good morning."

"May I sit down?" He waved a hand at the other three chairs, and Angelina seated herself in the chair closest to him rather than across the table. "Thank you."

She smiled sweetly at him, winning a brief smile in return. But then he said truculently, "I have nothing further to say, Miss Mateja. I have said all I know."

She kept her smile in place, tilting her head to one side. "Now, you see, Mr. Tabor, I find that difficult to believe."

"I am not lying! I told those other investigators and I am telling you. Prince Nikolai was the mastermind of the plot. The king's own cousin. And that is all I have to say!"

She forced understanding onto her face, nodding as if she believed him. "And yet, Mr. Tabor, I think perhaps you know more than you are saying—not that I think you are lying. No, not that. Not *you*. But sometimes we may hear things that do not make sense to us…until the right question is asked. Is that not true?"

Obviously mollified that Angelina had admitted he wasn't lying, he agreed, although reluctantly. "Yes, that is true sometimes."

"Then will you just bear with me as I ask my questions?" She put a little submissiveness into her voice, playing up to him, and indicated her list attached to a clipboard, as if she—a mere woman—was just following orders.

After a moment, he nodded slowly. "Ask your questions, Miss Mateja. I know nothing more than I have said, but…ask your questions."

"Thank you." She smiled gently. "First, Mr. Tabor, will you tell me in your own words how a man like you came to be involved? Someone must have approached you. It could not have been Prince Nikolai—he is in prison." She wasn't about to reveal that Prince Nikolai was dead…under suspicious circumstances. She didn't want to alarm this man.

"It was Tcholek. Sasha Tcholek. He…"

Angelina looked up from her clipboard. "Yes?"

Boris Tabor licked his dry lips. "May I have a glass of water?"

"Of course." She got up from her chair, deliberately leaving her clipboard on the table, and walked out. While Captain Zale fetched a pitcher of water and a glass, she stood silently with Majors Kostya and Branko, watching as Boris Tabor quickly, furtively, read the questions on her list. It was a made-up list of innocuous questions, not the questions she intended to ask. But he would not know that until it was too late.

When Captain Zale returned with the water, Angelina took the pitcher and the glass from him, waited for him to open the door for her and backed into the room. "Here you are, Mr. Tabor," she said, placing the glass on the table and serving him from the pitcher rather than letting him do it himself, putting herself into a subservient role. As he drank, she reseated herself at the table.

"Sasha Tcholek," she prompted, making a meaningless notation on her clipboard, as if she was ticking off another question.

"I have said this before. Many times."

"Humor me?" She smiled at him. "I do not want to be reprimanded for not asking my list of questions."

He sighed deeply but did as she asked. "Tcholek supplied the badges and the guns. He even told us where to secret the guns in the cathedral, and he is the one who retrieved them for us. He said Prince Nikolai would pay a fortune to be revenged on his cousin."

When he stopped, Angelina raised her eyebrows, innocently curious. "A fortune?"

"Yes," he said curtly. "A fortune." He didn't say anything more, and Angelina waited patiently. Finally he added in a rough voice, "I…I lost my job two years ago. I could not find another."

"And a man has his pride," she said softly, nodding her comprehension of the quandary he'd been in. "You could not take charity, not a man like you."

"Yes," he agreed quickly. "I am glad you understand."

A half hour came and went. Then an hour. And still they danced around and around the edges of knowledge. After establishing a rapport, with Boris Tabor seemingly in command, Angelina finally asked, "Tell

me about the other man. He was not a professional cameraman like you, yes?" Admiration was in her voice,
as if she was impressed by his former job as a professional cameraman in the television industry.

"He was not," Tabor said with a little huff of superiority. "I had to show him what to do. How to handle
the camera. Something as simple as panning in and
out, how to control the steering ring, how to lock the
wheels—everything! He knew nothing about television
cameras. He did not even know how to turn one on!"

"If he was not a cameraman, then what was he?
What was his profession?"

Tabor hesitated. "He never said."

"But a smart man like you…you guessed. Yes?"

"He and Tcholek talked together alone sometimes,
you understand. Almost in whispers. I did not always
hear them."

"But you knew."

"I…suspected. I did not know."

Angelina propped an elbow on the table and leaned
her chin on her hand, as if the story fascinated her.
"What did you suspect?"

The long silence that followed Angelina's question was finally broken when Boris Tabor admitted,
"Some kind of criminal activity. Drugs, perhaps. Perhaps women. I did not really want to know."

"Of course," she agreed seriously. She glanced down
at her clipboard, but only to give herself something to
do. She already knew the next question she would ask.
"When the other man…what was his name? I forget."

"Yuri Ivanovitch. He was Russian," Tabor said with
a touch of contempt. "Not Zakharian."

"Right, Yuri," she said, snapping her fingers, as if

she'd known it all along but it had just slipped her mind. "When Yuri Ivanovitch and Sasha Tcholek were talking in whispers, did they ever mention another name?"

Tabor's eyes fell under hers. "Yes, but I...I did not know who they were talking about."

"So it could not have been Prince Nikolai."

"No."

"If you heard the name again, would you recognize it?"

He hesitated for several seconds. "Perhaps."

Angelina sensed she was close. "Would you try something for me, Mr. Tabor?"

"If I can."

She leaned her chin on her hand again. "Close your eyes. Sometimes, when we close our eyes, our other senses take over. Would you do that for me?" He eyed her suspiciously at first, but Angelina smiled her most innocent smile, and he eventually closed his eyes. "Thank you, Mr. Tabor. You are so good to help me like this."

His chest swelled with pride, and Angelina quickly lowered her eyes to mask the gleam of satisfaction at how easily he could be manipulated. "Now, with your eyes closed, Mr. Tabor," she said, keeping her voice guileless, "think about Yuri and Sasha whispering together." She used their first names deliberately, stressing the difference between them and the formal way she called him "*Mr.* Tabor," as if he were more important than they were, more respectable. "Think about how they thought they were keeping secrets from you but you were too smart for them. You could hear them sometimes, but you did not let on. You did not trust them, so you listened. Not to spy on them—you are too honorable a man for that—but to protect yourself, yes?"

"Yes. That is exactly what I thought."

Her voice was soft and deliberately feminine, but low and mesmerizing. Not putting the man in a trance—not exactly. But lulling him into a cocoon of security. "They are talking together. Whispering, perhaps. But you can hear them. You pretend you do not, but you can hear them. They speak a name, a name you do not recognize, but you know it is important somehow. You know you must remember this name in case they try to deprive you of your fair share of the money. The money Prince Nikolai offered through Sasha. The money you need to regain your pride as a man. The money you need to win back your wife."

Mentioning his wife was a calculated risk, but Angelina took it. And it didn't draw a protest from Boris Tabor. "No, you will not let them trick you out of the money you have earned," she continued, still with that soft, hypnotic cadence. "So you remember the name. The name. You say it to yourself over and over so you will never forget. You repeat it when they are not around. It is burned in your memory now. You know it, yes? The name they whispered together. The name you *must* remember."

"Yes," Tabor said in a near trance. "Vishenko. Alexei Vishenko. Another Russian, like Yuri. I did not recognize the name, but I knew it was important. Prince Nikolai—Tcholek said Prince Nikolai would pay, but he was in prison. How could he pay? I needed the money. A fortune I was promised. I could not trust Tcholek because he lied when he said Prince Nikolai would pay. So I listened. And then I knew the money came from the other Russian, from Alexei Vishenko."

Tabor came to the end of his recitation and there was a long silence. Then he opened his eyes and stared at her, almost transfixed, as if he couldn't believe he'd told her the name he'd denied even existed.

"Thank you, Mr. Tabor," Angelina said with a disarming smile. "I am glad you remembered the name. Glad you told me. The king will be grateful, too."

"You…" Boris Tabor shouted. "You tricked me!" He was out of his seat almost before Angelina could react, reaching for her throat. She blocked his hands with an upraised forearm and twisted one of his arms behind his back, immobilizing him and pushing him facedown onto the table. Captain Zale and the two majors rushed into the interview room and quickly reattached the handcuffs Angelina had undone, cuffing Tabor's arms behind his back.

"Come, Mr. Tabor," Captain Zale said pleasantly. "Let me return you to your cell." He glanced at Angelina, his eyes warm with respect and admiration. "I will return shortly, Lieutenant."

She picked up her clipboard, which had been knocked to the floor in the scuffle, and faced Majors Kostya and Branko.

They were staring at her, not exactly in amazement, but with nearly identical expressions that said they couldn't believe Angelina had been successful where they, and all the other male interrogators, had failed.

She drew herself up to her full five feet eleven inches. She was still shorter than the majors, but she wouldn't back down to them. She couldn't let them intimidate her, either. Her dream was to someday attain their exalted rank, and she knew that would never happen if she didn't stand up for herself. "Yes, Major Branko?" she asked coolly, looking from one to the other. "Major Kostya? You had a question?"

Major Kostya glanced at Major Branko, then back at Angelina. "Do you know what you have done, Lieutenant?"

"I think so," she answered cautiously.

Major Branko spoke then. "Do you know who Alexei Vishenko is?"

She wished she did. The name obviously meant something to these men, but not to her. All she knew was that Alexei Vishenko—whoever he was—was the real mastermind behind the plot to assassinate the crown prince. Might even be involved in the death of Prince Nikolai, but she wouldn't know that until further investigation. "No, sir," she said finally. "I do not know who he is."

"You have heard of the Bratva, yes?" said Major Kostya.

Startled, she said, "Yes, sir. It means the Brotherhood, does it not? The Russian mob. But they do not operate in Zak—" She broke off, shaking her head in disbelief at the carefully blank expressions on their faces. "Not here in Zakhar?"

"Yes, here," Major Kostya confirmed. "The king did not know this until recently. But yes, the Bratva's tentacles have even reached into Zakhar."

"So who is Alexei Vishenko?"

"His real name is Aleksandrov Vishenko," Major Branko explained. "Interpol knows him by both names. He is the head of a branch of the Bratva that operates in the US…as well as Zakhar." His face was impassive. "He deals in drugs. Money laundering. Prostitution."

When she heard the word *prostitution*, Angelina suddenly remembered what Alec had told her about why he was here. About why the king had requested him and only him as the US embassy's RSO. *"The king brought me here because there's a human-trafficking ring operating between Zakhar and the US, for purposes of prostitution."*

Was it possible? Could Alexei Vishenko—the Russian mobster behind the assassination attempt—be the same man who was responsible for the human-trafficking ring that had ensnared Caterina? And if he was, what could she do about it? How could she use this information to help find her cousin…if she was even still alive?

"You will keep that information to yourself, Lieutenant," Major Kostya ordered, casting a reproving glance at his colleague, as if he'd said too much.

"Captain Zale—"

"Not even Captain Zale," insisted Major Kostya coldly. "Unless and until the king himself authorizes the release of that information."

"But the investigation," she began. "The attempted assassination… Captain Zale needs to know there could be a connection."

"We will take the investigation from here, and will inform His Majesty."

Resentment flared through her. How dare these men—majors who far outranked her, yes, but still *men*—pat her on the head, in effect, and tell her to run along? They weren't the ones who'd tricked Boris Tabor into giving up Alexei Vishenko's name. They weren't the ones who'd saved Crown Prince Raoul, either, despite their air of superiority. It was the *queen's* security detail—she and Captain Zale—not the *king's* who'd accomplished those things.

As Captain Zale had said just over a week ago, the king's men thought they were in command. But Captain Zale had also said, *"Let them think they are superior. We know the truth. And we—not they—will ensure a successful outcome."*

Military law wasn't the same as civilian law, but ever since she'd joined the Zakharian National Forces, Angelina had made it a point to add a detailed understanding of military law to her résumé in addition to her civil law degree. In the normal course of things—if they were all just members of the military—the majors, who outranked Captain Zale as well as herself—could give her an order she had to obey.

But while she was still a member of the Zakharian National Forces, she was on detached status. That meant the normal code of military law didn't apply. Captain Zale answered directly to Colonel Marianescu, who answered directly to the king—and she answered to Captain Zale.

Angelina knew the majors had no legal authority to give her an order in violation of the chain of command. She would not tell them this, however, but would let them think they'd intimidated her into silence while she ignored their *illegal* order and informed Captain Zale at the first opportunity.

Chapter 12

Angelina's first thought as soon as she left the jail was to call Alec and share the good news with him. Then she quashed that impulse. *Do not get into the habit of relying on him,* she warned herself. *Not even to celebrate.* A warning that would be difficult to remember, especially since she didn't want to.

If she couldn't tell Alec, she couldn't tell anyone. Certainly not her parents. And none of her friends, either. This was an ongoing investigation, and until all the guilty parties had been arrested, she had to keep what she knew confidential. Except from Alec. Alec, who was here at the king's instigation. Who'd *intervened*, as he'd explained to the king, to help break up the assassination attempt. Who'd discussed her with the king—man-to-man, as he'd worded it—to get him to intercede on her behalf with Captain Zale.

Using that as an excuse to do what she wanted anyway, she pulled out her cell phone and hit the speed-dial button for Alec's office in the embassy. He'd keyed all his numbers into her cell phone last night over her perfunctory objections.

He wasn't in his office. Or at least that's what his administrative assistant told Angelina when the American woman picked up the phone. "No, no message," she said abruptly. "I will call back, thank you."

She called his cell phone, but it went right to voice mail. She didn't leave a message.

She was disappointed beyond belief, because she'd wanted to hear his voice. Wanted to hear him call her "Angel" the way no one else did. He'd be proud of what she'd managed to accomplish. Alec had believed in her when she'd been at her lowest point emotionally. Now she wanted to share this emotional high with him, as well.

But she didn't call back. She told herself she was too busy, and she was. She made sure of it, even though it was an off-duty day for her. She stopped to see her parents and listened to their carping with as much patience as she could muster. She went to the gym, working out with weights as she did religiously three times a week, as well as sparring with her tae kwon do instructor, and having the satisfaction of taking him down twice. She practiced for an hour at the gun range—she was sharp and intended to stay sharp.

Grocery shopping really had been a necessity— she was out of milk and eggs and several other items she used every day. She returned books to the library. She ran every errand she could think of, even laying flowers on the graves of Caterina's parents—

something she'd neglected to do lately, she realized as guilt washed through her. She tried to make it to the cemetery once a month, doing what her cousin would have done if she could.

She found herself loitering near the US embassy for no reason she could fathom, gazing longingly at the windows, wondering which one was Alec's office. *This must stop,* she told herself sternly, forcing herself to turn around and head toward her apartment with her firm stride. *You are acting like...*

Like most of the women of her acquaintance, whose men took precedence in their lives. They had stimulating, fulfilling careers but would gladly trade them for the traditional Zakharian role of wife and mother. Only a handful of women would choose otherwise.

The more Angelina thought about it, the more wound up she became. Back at her apartment, she quickly changed into her jogging clothes and headed out for the run she'd skipped this morning because she'd wanted to get to the jail as early as possible to interrogate the prisoner after Captain Zale told her she could.

She jogged for miles, looping through the central district, then out to the palace on the hill and back again before heading to the walkway that followed the meandering path of the river. She ran until she was drenched with sweat and the sun was setting. With a stitch in her side, she forced herself to walk back to her apartment through the chill of the evening.

Alec was waiting for her by her front door when she got off the elevator. The smile that broke over his face when he saw her would have gladdened the heart of most women if they hadn't been working themselves into a frenzy the way Angelina had.

His smile faded when she didn't return his smile, just stared at him with a distant, uncompromising expression she knew held no welcome. "What's wrong?" he asked, walking toward her, too perceptive not to know immediately something wasn't right, and too direct not to question it.

"Nothing." Angelina wasn't about to tell him. But when he went to kiss her, she shied away, and his face hardened with understanding.

"You didn't call back." He almost bit off the words. Accusing.

"How did you know I—" she began, and then grew angry at herself for the betrayal. "You were busy," she told him tightly. "As was I."

"Not too busy to go jogging," he said, indicating her sweaty clothes that were a dead giveaway. "If you'd told me, we could have gone together. If you'd waited for me..."

"I did not need a man to jog with me."

Comprehension dawned on his face, and his eyes narrowed. "So that's what this is all about." His sudden anger took her by surprise. "Did it ever occur to you that *I* might need *you*?" he asked tightly. "That I might have had a hell of a day? That I might have needed the stress relief jogging brings? That I might have needed your company—not to soothe me, not to minister to me, but just to *be* with me? To be with someone who *understands*? Or don't you give a damn about me?"

Her anger rose to match his. "*I* am not the one who was unavailable. If you needed me, why did you not call? You have my phone numbers—you insisted I give them to you. But you did not call, not even when you suspected I had called you. You think I have nothing better to do than wait around in case you have a free moment? That my work is not important, too?"

She pushed past him to get to her apartment, but he caught her arm and swung her around. "Damn it, Angel," he said gratingly. "Don't walk away from me when we're fighting."

She jerked her arm away from his hand. "Touch me again and die," she hissed at him. They stared at each other for a few seconds, both of them breathing heavily. Then Alec did something Angelina never expected. He laughed.

At first, his laughter merely fueled her anger, but then he said, "Touch me and die. Christ, Angel, do you have any idea how much that makes me want you? How much that makes me want to ravage you? Force you to admit you want me as much as I want you? You have no clue, do you?"

Alec and Angelina barely made it inside her front door before they were tearing each other's clothes off. Frantic kisses. Random words of need and desire. He managed to get a condom on just in the nick of time before she enveloped him, meeting his fierce thrusts with demands of her own—now, now, *now*! He plastered her against the wall, riding her fast and hard until she came in a shuddering wave of desire unlike anything she'd ever known.

She sagged against his shoulder and realized he wasn't done. He was still rock hard inside her body, but waiting. Waiting for her to be ready for him to continue. "Alec," she moaned, unable to prevent that *needy* catch in her voice. Her breasts were crushed against his chest, her nipples still aching from contact with him and from an orgasm that had shredded her self-control.

Then he moved again. Slower this time. Tantalizing both of them. But less than a minute later, his tempo increased. As if even Alec's iron self-control had limits and they'd reached them. His mouth found hers and took possession of it. Demanding, not coaxing. And Angelina gave him everything. Willingly. Then he grasped her hips, holding her in place as his thrusts grew wild. Frenzied. And the world spun out of focus as she came again just as he did, arching into her one last time, throwing back his head in a wordless cry.

She would have slumped to the floor when her knees gave way, except he held her in place against the wall. His eyes were closed, his throat working soundlessly, and he was breathing as if he'd been running flat out. When she made a little sound and attempted to free herself, he managed to say, "Give me a minute, Angel," so she did.

When he finally withdrew from her body, she thought he'd let her go, but he didn't. He still held her hips, but then his hands slid up, over the curve of her waist, the sides of her breasts, grasping her shoulders so she couldn't escape when he demanded, "Why?"

"Why?" She was too dazed to understand what he was asking.

"Why were you avoiding me?"

"I was not—" she began. Then she admitted, "You are right. I *was* avoiding you."

"Did I do something? Did I *not* do something?"

"That is not why…" She shook her head, unable to explain the convoluted thought process that had led to their confrontation. This time when she pulled away from him he let her go.

"Then why?" As if she owed him an answer.

And I do owe him an answer, she admitted to herself. And though her answer was just as logical as his question, there were layers of complexity to it. Layers he probably wouldn't understand. "Shower first," she deferred. "I needed a shower even before I saw you, and now…" When she glanced down at her pile of sweaty clothes and chuckled, he joined in.

"Yeah, we both need one now."

They washed each other leisurely beneath the shower spray, drawing pleasure from bodies that were well matched physically. Angelina loved the way his muscles rippled beneath the surface of his smooth skin when her fingers stroked over his arms, his chest, his abs and lower. He wasn't a muscle-bound weight lifter—his powerful body had a purpose more important than just showing off. Just as hers did.

She couldn't get over how much her body pleased him, an enjoyment he didn't bother to hide. Not to mention the inevitable reaction his body had to hers. But when she would have caressed his arousal, he held her off. "Not this time," he told her firmly.

He shut off the water and they toweled themselves dry in silence. Neither had any false modesty. Neither pretended not to look, to sneak peeks at each other's bodies. They looked openly, pleased at what they saw.

They fell into bed together, and Alec drew her into his arms, flush against his body. "So why?" he asked, as if their earlier conversation hadn't been interrupted by the shower they'd just taken.

She didn't pretend she didn't know what he was

asking. "Because I was excited about something and wanted to share it with you, but you were not available." That was only part of the story, and Alec obviously knew it because he waited patiently for the rest. "So I did other things. Things I would normally do on my day off. But then I found myself standing on the sidewalk outside the US embassy with no idea how I had gotten there. It was not a conscious thing—my feet just followed that path. And all at once I realized…"

"That you wanted to be with me?"

She shook her head. "More than that," she admitted in a low voice. "That I *needed* to be with you."

Alec sighed in relief as understanding finally dawned. "It's not a crime, Angel," he said softly. "Needing someone. It's not a crime to admit it, either." *Maybe for her it is,* he thought. Then he remembered what he'd told her before, and he could have kicked himself for not realizing. "I know I told you I want to be the one who gives you what you need," he said, emotion making his voice rough. "And that's the truth. But I didn't tell you how much *I* need *you.* I didn't…" The words wouldn't come easily. The words that would explain so she'd never doubt him…would never doubt *them* again.

"I never needed anyone before. Not like this. Not like you. My family—yeah. My brother Liam. But that's not the same thing at all." He was silent for a moment and she didn't say anything, just snuggled closer. Moved her hand so it was lying against his heart, and he drew courage from that silent confession.

"I didn't realize a man could need this way," he admitted. "I didn't realize *I* could need this way." It still wasn't enough. He had to break through that wall in her head, in her heart. "It's as if I've lived in a world of black and white all my life, Angel. But with you, everything is in color. Glorious, unbelievable color. Could I go back to my black-and-white world? Yeah. If I had to. I just don't want to."

His arms tightened around her. "Please don't doubt what we have together. The jobs we do... I could be dead tomorrow. So could you. But we'd survive. That's the way we're made—we're survivors." He breathed deeply. "But don't exile me back to that black-and-white world just because you're afraid of needing me."

He rolled over suddenly, taking her with him. Pinning her beneath his body. "You're the bravest woman I know," he told her fiercely. "You're not afraid of *anything*, not even death. Don't be afraid of needing me."

Aleksandrov Vishenko settled back against the leather seat of his cherished 2011 black Lincoln Town Car—the last year the luxury vehicle had been built—his hard, cold eyes fixed on the man sitting next to him in the backseat, the man he'd bought and paid for years ago.

They were alone. At least, the man *thought* they were alone, a condition he'd imposed on all their meetings from the very beginning, and Vishenko had humored him. Vishenko's chauffeur had driven his boss in the Lincoln to this deserted parking lot in the wee small hours of the morning for this arranged, illicit meeting, then had gotten out of the car and walked away, leaving them alone. Vishenko's bodyguards were hidden everywhere. They could see, but they couldn't hear. And that was good enough for Vishenko.

He hid his contempt for the other man because he

was still useful. When the man was no longer useful, he would be dead. Vishenko knew that, but the other man did not. He might *suspect*, but he didn't *know*. Vishenko had used that suspicion more than once to his own benefit.

"What do you have for me?" he asked in a voice as cold as ice.

"The wiretap has been extended," the man began in his most ingratiating voice.

"Do not bleat at me like a sheep. And do not tell me things I already know from other sources."

Intimidation sometimes worked with this man, as he yielded information he would not otherwise reveal in his fear of losing his usefulness to Vishenko.

The money Vishenko had paid him through the years was enough to supplement the man's lifestyle, not support it. Vishenko had made sure of it. He wanted him to remain with his current federal agency employer. Even though this man was one of the weapons in Vishenko's arsenal, he never let on just how important his information had become over the years or paid him what the information was really worth. He always downplayed its significance, as he was doing now. Vishenko hadn't heard the FBI's wiretap had been extended. But he knew it now.

Not that he ever said anything incriminating over the phone. He wasn't stupid. His homes—the condo in Manhattan and his estate on Long Island—as well as this car, were electronically swept for listening devices daily. Everyone who met with him was screened by his men for a body wire—neither the FBI nor the agency would ever convict him that way.

"So what do you have to tell me that is worth our meeting like this?"

"The agency has been sending out feelers again," the man said quickly. "Asking for the FBI's assistance. The two agencies haven't worked together since their joint task force was disbanded six months ago. The joint task force focused on your nephew and his super PAC, NOANC."

"Michael is in jail, and will remain in jail. And his political action committee, NOANC, is dead." Vishenko's voice grew even colder. "What does this have to do with me? The task force tried—and failed—to establish a link between Michael and me, other than the familial one. We are related, yes. But that is all. The joint FBI/agency task force could never prove otherwise."

And they never will, he thought but didn't say. He'd been extremely careful to keep his distance from Michael Vishenko's plots and schemes, the product of his nephew's uncontrollable desire for revenge against the men he held responsible for the death of his father, David Pennington.

The task force had also tried to tie Aleksandrov Vishenko to David Pennington, again with no success, because there hadn't been anything to find. Except for one minor detail. One extremely minor detail he'd almost forgotten. Which meant the task force had *nothing* on him. Unless...

Unless Caterina Mateja had surfaced. Unless she'd given the FBI or the agency—*or both*, he thought grimly—the evidence she'd stolen from him when she ran. If someone pieced together the two seemingly disparate documents, that would be the evidence the now-disbanded task force needed to bring him down. A task force that could easily be revived.

Vishenko dismissed the man and watched him as he got out of the car and walked away, furtively glancing around to make sure he wasn't spotted. Vishenko laughed softly to himself, then called his chauffeur on his cell phone just in case the chauffeur hadn't seen the other man leave.

As he was being driven back to Manhattan, Vishenko coldly reminded himself he needed to find Caterina and silence her permanently. Even if the documents surfaced, they could not be introduced as evidence without her to authenticate their source.

Failure to find Caterina was no longer an option he could afford.

Alec and Angelina dozed briefly. Then woke, ravenous. They raided her kitchen wearing nothing but T-shirts, and she was glad she'd restocked her refrigerator that afternoon. Alec's appetite for food was as unapologetically hearty as his appetite for sex.

They feasted in bed, and Angelina didn't even care about the crumbs. Crumbs could be brushed away. Watching Alec eat, watching his enjoyment of the little delicacies she'd bought with him in mind—although she hadn't admitted it to herself at the time—was another sensual pleasure she cherished.

"So tell me," she said, forking a pickled beet from the jar she held, popping it in her mouth before it could drip and making a face at the sweet tartness.

"Tell you what?"

"Why you had a hell of a day."

He grimaced and shook his head regretfully. "Sorry,

Angel. It's something I can't really discuss with you. But it was, believe me. Don't get me wrong, I love my job most of the time. But today was a hell of a day. And it's still not resolved."

"Nothing to do with what you told me, is it? About why the king brought you here?"

"No. But there *is* news on that front." He was silent for a moment, his face troubled, as if he wasn't sure how she'd take whatever he had to tell her.

"It is bad?" she asked. "Bad news?" Her eyes widened and her breath caught in her throat. "Caterina. She is dead. That is what you do not want to tell me."

He put his plate down on the bedside table, roughly pushing the lamp to one side. "No, that's not it. We don't think she's dead." He took the jar of pickled beets from her, placed it beside his plate and then held both her hands in his. "We think we might have a line on her," he explained.

"A line? What is that?"

He laughed briefly at himself. "It just means... Oh, hell, it's not something that translates easily. Literally it has to do with fishing, but figuratively it means we think we might know where she is. We're not sure it's even the same person, but...we think it might be."

"We? You mean you and Princess Mara's husband?"

"Yeah. Remember what I told you, that McKinnon was checking out your cousin for me?" She nodded. "McKinnon asked my sister, who works at his agency, to run a check on your cousin. Visas, travel records, anything and everything she could find. Keira found something else. On a totally different case. And she made the connection—easy, she says, because the name is so unusual. Caterina Mateja. Neither Caterina nor Mateja is common in the US." He paused, and she knew he was trying to find a way to tell her something he really didn't want to tell her. Because he knew it would hurt her.

"It is best to just say it, straight out," she told him. "Whatever it is, I can handle it."

He took a deep breath. "If your cousin is the Caterina Mateja that Keira tracked down, she's still alive. But how long is anyone's guess, because someone ordered a hit. And the going price is a million dollars."

"Who?" Angelina whispered. "Who wants her dead?"

Alec's face formed into grim lines. "His name is Vishenko. Aleksandrov Vishenko. McKinnon's encountered him before, and it's all bad. Really bad. Vishenko is the head of a branch of—"

"The Bratva," she said, cutting him off, her eyes growing huge as she made the connection. "The Russian mob. Operating in the US and now in Zakhar. I know."

He stared at her. "How do you know that?"

"That was why I called you today," she told him. "To tell you I interrogated the surviving cameraman. To tell you he finally gave us names. Not only the other cameraman—a Russian, Yuri Ivanovitch—but the man who was really behind the assassination attempt on the crown prince. Another Russian. Alexei Vishenko."

Chapter 13

"Son of a bitch!" Alec whispered under his breath. Just that quickly he saw everything plain. It all finally made sense. Incredible, unbelievable sense.

Vishenko and the Bratva, involved in trafficking Zakharian women into the United States—a highly profitable, illegal enterprise. Zakhar's king, whose focus was on stopping it, who'd maneuvered to bring Alec in as RSO for that very reason. Vishenko wanting the king distracted. Not dead. No, not that. What had McKinnon said about Vishenko? *"He's plowed his money into legitimate enterprises... Not as profitable, but profitable enough. And completely aboveboard..."*

Stable governments equaled stable economies. Stable economies equaled steady profits for legitimate businesses. So if Vishenko had money invested in legitimate enterprises here in Zakhar—which seemed likely—of course he wouldn't want to destabilize the economy by assassinating the king. Killing the crown prince would put a bobble in the economy, true, but it wouldn't have the same destabilizing effect as killing the king. But it *would* turn the king's attention away from the human-trafficking ring. Hadn't it already done so to a certain extent? Hadn't Angelina told him the king had diverted focus to investigate the backgrounds of *every* person on the security details guarding the royal family?

Sowing suspicion within the ranks. Not exactly divide and conquer, but close enough. Alec was a student of political history, and he'd often wondered why governments never seemed to learn the harsh lessons history taught. Why it seemed as if every generation or so, the same things came to pass, and the men and women in uniform paid the price again and again. He didn't exempt his own country from that severe judgment—the United States was often the worst offender when it came to forgetting history.

Wasn't that one of the main reasons he and Liam had joined the Diplomatic Security Service when they got out of the Marine Corps? Because diplomacy, no matter how futile it sometimes seemed, was often better than all-out war?

But this wasn't one government calling out another. This was one man who thought he was above the law, who thought he and his criminal organization could get away with murder. *Not on my watch,* Alec thought grimly. *The rule of law has to be the rule of law for everyone—governments and individuals.* Somehow he had to bring Vishenko to justice. And Caterina Mateja was the key.

He started assembling a plan in his head, automatically assigning tasks to McKinnon, Keira, Angelina and himself. Then he cursed under his breath. "I need to talk to McKinnon," he told Angelina abruptly. "And then we need to see the king."

Eleven people sat around the conference table in the same small conference room where Alec had met with the king, the king's cousin and closest confidant, and the secretary of state. The seven people Alec had wanted in attendance—the king, the three policemen working the case for Zakhar, McKinnon, Angelina and himself—had been augmented by four more. Captain Zale was there at Angelina's insistence, and Colonel Marianescu and Majors Kostya and Branko were there at the king's request.

Alec presented the known facts and the conjectures he'd drawn from them. He was careful how he disclosed what Angelina had told him, explaining that it was only after he'd given her Vishenko's name in connection with her cousin that she'd revealed his name had also come up in the investigation into the assassination attempt on the crown prince. And of course he left out completely that they'd been in bed together when they'd shared their information on Aleksandrov Vishenko. Not only was it immaterial to the investigation, but he knew it was his responsibility to shield Angelina from any criticism that could be leveled at her by the men in the room. Especially since it would be completely unwarranted.

When he was finished, he leaned back in his chair and said, "I want to add Lieutenant Mateja to my team, Your Majesty. Her cousin is the key to bringing down

Vishenko—I know it. I firmly believe Lieutenant Mateja will be critical in locating her cousin and convincing her to testify against Vishenko in the trafficking case. I realize this might put a strain on the queen's security detail, especially since we don't know how long this will take—that's why the lieutenant wanted her captain here for the discussion."

McKinnon spoke for the first time. "I don't think there will be a problem convincing my agency to let us continue using Special Agent Keira Walker's services for as long as we need her. My agency has been after Vishenko for years, and I know the head of the agency would give his eyeteeth to bring him down. So any assets we need, all we have to do is ask."

The king nodded and looked at Captain Zale. "Captain? What is your opinion?"

"Lieutenant Mateja is a critical member of the queen's security detail," he said.

Damned right, Alec couldn't help thinking. *I'm glad you finally see that.*

"But with a little cooperation from the queen," Captain Zale continued, "we can function without the lieutenant's services for as long as necessary. As I see it, bringing to justice the man who attempted to end the life of the crown prince takes precedence over nearly every other consideration."

"I agree," the king said. "And the queen will, too. You will have the cooperation you need, Captain." He turned his gaze on Majors Kostya and Branko. "Damon? Lukas? Anything to add?"

The two majors exchanged telling glances, and Alec wondered what that was all about. But the only answer they gave was, "No, Sire."

"Zax?" the king asked, but Colonel Marianescu just shook his head.

The king faced Alec again. "Your request is granted, Special Agent Jones. Lieutenant Mateja is relieved of duty as of now, and is subject to your orders until further notice." He glanced around the table. "Is there anything else, gentlemen?"

The senior policeman assigned to the case spoke up. "We have the names of seven Americans from the embassy," he said abruptly. "Six are no longer in this country."

Before the king could say anything, Alec asked sharply, "How did you get the names?"

When the policeman didn't say anything, just stared back at Alec with a steady, unwavering expression, Alec glanced at the king, hoping he would intervene and order the policeman to reveal the source of his information. "I can take the names as a starting point, sir," he explained. "But that's all. It's not evidence I can use if the names were the result of torture or some other kind of coercion."

The king's voice was dangerously soft when he said, "Torture, Special Agent Jones, is not tolerated in Zakhar any more than it is in the US."

"That may be true, sir," Alec conceded. "But coercion of any kind…"

"Not coercion," the senior policeman said now. He smiled coldly. "It was a stroke of luck. Unbelievable luck. A lower-level criminal was arrested on an unrelated drug charge. We were not even looking at him for the human-trafficking conspiracy, but he offered up what he knew in exchange for leniency on the drug charge."

Alec began to get the picture. Drugs were a very serious crime in Zakhar, even for a first offense. Zakharian judges and juries had no sympathy—the conviction rate was high and the sentences harsh. It was a huge break for them.

"This led us to five other men," the policeman continued, "all with criminal records, all of whom are now in custody. Two of those men agreed to plead to lesser charges in exchange for their testimony against the other Zakharians in the conspiracy, including certain Zakharian officials who they claim were on the take. None of the officials have been arrested, but they are being closely watched. Their complicity in the conspiracy has not been established with certainty, and we do not want to move until you are ready to do so, as well—we do not want to tip our hand."

Alec nodded his understanding, and the policeman continued in a dispassionate voice. "Both of the men have independently named seven Americans who either are, or were, stationed at the US embassy over the past nine years—men who supplied the fraudulent US visas for a price." He pulled a notepad from his pocket and referred to it. "Four of the men were Foreign Service officers at the embassy who are now gone. One is still here."

He named a name Alec recognized, instantly putting a face to the name. "Who are the others?" he asked.

The policeman read off the list of names. "Two were previous regional security officers, one of whom was your predecessor at the embassy."

A sick feeling settled in Alec's gut. Seven men. Seven corrupt officials serving at the US embassy over the past nine years. He'd known in his heart the king was right, that visa fraud *had* to be involved in this trafficking case—it was the only thing that made sense. But he'd hoped it wouldn't be this bad. That it would turn out one, maybe two, people at the embassy were involved. Not seven men over nine years.

Slippery slope, he reminded himself. How many of these men had been lured into the conspiracy by their predecessors or others they worked with, believing "everyone does it," and they'd never get caught? He would never know.

Alec pulled his own notebook from an inner jacket pocket and mechanically jotted down all seven names. His predecessor as RSO was the one that hit closest to home—he'd known the man for a long time. Not a friend, just an acquaintance. But still someone he knew personally. How many other men he knew in the DSS—men he'd worked with over the years—were also corrupt? He couldn't believe Zakhar was unique in that aspect. *Another thing I'll probably never know,* he admitted to himself.

He glanced up at the policeman. "Nothing on the ambassador?" he asked, holding his breath. He and McKinnon had pretty much cleared the ambassador in their minds based on the information McKinnon had been able to collect through his agency, but they could have missed something. And if the corruption went that high…

The policeman shook his head. "No, nothing. And we firmly believe the names we have in our possession are an all-inclusive list."

Well, that's something anyway, Alec didn't voice that thought as he tucked his notebook away. Seven corrupt officials working at one embassy would be a scandal when the press finally broke the story—*when the indictments come down and not a moment sooner,* he vowed silently—but not nearly the scandal it would be if the current and/or former ambassador to Zakhar were involved.

"No one you questioned mentioned Vishenko?" When the policeman shook his head regretfully, Alec said, "It would be too much to hope for, but I had to ask."

Silence filled the room for a minute. Then the king glanced around the table once more and asked again, "Is there anything else, gentlemen?" When no one spoke, he said, "Thank you all for coming on such short notice. You are dismissed." He stood, obviously expecting them to file out, which they did. Alec hung back because he wanted a word with the king alone, but the king said, "One moment, Lieutenant, if you please. And you, too, Special Agent Jones, if you would be so kind."

Alec exchanged glances with McKinnon. *Wait for me,* he mouthed, and McKinnon nodded before leaving the conference room.

The king turned to his bodyguards and said, "Privacy, please." The two majors also left the room, following McKinnon out.

Angelina stood at military attention, and Alec could see—because he'd come to know her so well even though they hadn't known each other very long in something as unimportant as time—that she was nervous at being asked by the king to stay. It wasn't anything in her face or manner, or even her body language, but somehow he knew she was expecting the worst.

After the door closed behind the last person to leave,

the king smiled unexpectedly. "Why is it, Lieutenant, you always fear I intend to reprimand you when I ask to speak with you? What have I done to deserve that reputation?" He didn't wait for an answer he probably figured wasn't forthcoming. "No, Lieutenant, I merely wanted to remind you of our earlier conversation regarding a fighting man's instincts. And to talk to you about your cousin. She was like your younger sister, yes?"

A look of surprise crossed Angelina's face.

"That information is in your dossier, Lieutenant. It is not a secret. It is one of the reasons Colonel Marianescu and Captain Zale picked you for the queen's security detail. One of the reasons I wholeheartedly endorsed their selection. You understand what it is to lose someone you love." He waited for that to sink in before adding, "That your cousin may not be dead, after all, that she may be in mortal peril instead, is something you will have to deal with. And if your cousin dies, you will have to grieve for her all over again."

"I know that, Sire. I…" Angelina's pale blue eyes never left the king's face. "I have accepted it."

"I understand how difficult it is to be detached when someone you love is in danger." The king's eyes—such a vivid green—seemed to darken with his words, and one hand clenched tightly. "How the desire for revenge can overwhelm even the best of intentions." After a tense moment, he visibly, forcibly relaxed. "But I have faith in you, Lieutenant. This man Vishenko must face justice for his crimes, along with everyone else involved—they must be *seen* to face justice as a deterrent to others. Killing them is easy. Bringing them to justice is not. Do not let me down. Do not let your country down."

Alec hadn't thought Angelina's spine could be any straighter, but at the king's words, pure steel seemed to enter it. "No, Sire," she promised, the light of determination in her eyes. "I will never let you down."

The king's smile returned. "Good," he said. "Very good. Thank you, Lieutenant. That is all." He waited until Angelina had left the room, with her soft yet military tread, and then he turned to Alec, whose eyes had followed Angelina's exit. "Yes, Special Agent Jones? You wished to speak privately with me?"

It had to be said. "Forgive me for speaking frankly, sir," Alec said slowly. "But I want to emphasize that while the US will cooperate fully in the investigation into the attempted assassination of your son and Vishenko's involvement in it, our primary focus has to be the human-trafficking case involving the corruption and visa fraud at our embassy." Alec put as much regret into the tone he used for his next words as he could. "Your son's case—while understandably of paramount importance to you—is ancillary to our primary investigation."

The king just stared at Alec for a moment without saying anything. "Do not take this the wrong way," he said finally, "but if you ever have children, you will understand a father's love for his child far better than you do now. You will understand the blinding rage a father can feel when his child is threatened...*and* the desire for revenge."

A tiny pang went through Alec at the king's words. A yearning for something he'd never realized was so strong in him. *If I ever have children,* he thought, his mind veering off onto a tangent with an impossible dream in the hazy distance. Angel. And children. *If. If. If.*

But the king wasn't done, and Alec pulled his attention back with an effort. "But my son is only one," the king said now, his face hardening and his voice turning frigid. "The Zakharian women who were trafficked are many. My subjects, Special Agent Jones. My *people.* Zakharians I have sworn to care for as if *they* are my children." He paused until he knew Alec grasped the depth and gravity of his concern. "Both cases are equally important to me. As long as Vishenko pays for his crimes, that is all I care about. Do we understand each other?"

Alec's admiration for the man in front of him rose once again. "Yes, sir. And for what it's worth, if I have anything to say about it, Vishenko is going down. *How* he goes down is up to him. But he's going down."

The sun was high in the sky in Denver, Colorado. It had snowed the night before, covering the earth with a powdering of snow that made the world seem fresh and new, but now the snow had turned to slush, making walking chancy at best. Caterina Mateja was carefully picking her way to the bus stop to catch a bus that would take her to the second of her three house-cleaning jobs that day.

But Caterina—who was known to her employers as Cate Jones because she'd wanted a common American name that wouldn't be remembered—wasn't really thinking about where she was putting her feet. She was adding up in her mind everything she would be paid today and what she had to budget for out of those wages.

Cate always insisted on being paid in cash, accepting with a fatalistic shrug the fact that she wasn't accumulating any credits in the American social security system. She didn't have a social security number anyway—she wasn't in this country legally, having long overstayed her temporary work visa. Which, she thought now with a cynical smile, had been fraudulently obtained to begin with. She hadn't known that at the time. Her supposed agent for the modeling contract she'd signed had arranged everything. *Nothing you need to worry your pretty head about,* he'd told her. *I will take care of it.*

But she couldn't fret about that. Couldn't change it, either. She was here in the States, with nowhere else to go. She couldn't go back to Zakhar—she had no passport. She'd frantically searched for it before running, but eventually she'd been forced to flee without it. And she had nothing to prove her identity, even if she'd ever considered applying to the Zakharian embassy—which she hadn't. Not just because she feared for her life should Aleksandrov Vishenko ever find out where she was, but because she could never return home. Could never face her family, her friends, after what she'd survived. Not even her cousin Angelina would welcome her back if she knew the truth.

She had to earn money to keep a roof over her head, food in her stomach and clothes on her back—warmer clothes, now that winter was here. She needed a new winter jacket. Well, new to her. She shopped at thrift stores for her clothes, and her next winter jacket would be no exception. If she was careful with her money, she might even be able to afford a pair of boots that weren't too worn. A pair that would last the winter, and wouldn't leak as her current boots did.

Maybe I should have picked somewhere warmer, Cate thought now. *One of the southwestern states.* But she'd been worried that in states adjacent to the Mexican border, she'd face stiff competition with other illegal immigrants for jobs that paid under the table. And she'd been homesick. She hadn't realized it until she'd stepped down from the interstate bus that had brought her to Denver, but the mountains outside Denver reminded her poignantly of Zakhar. There were times she almost felt at home here.

Caterina hadn't gone by her real name in so long, she didn't answer to it anymore. So she didn't even turn around when a harsh voice called out her name from across the street, didn't respond as if the name had anything to do with her. But it did register in her consciousness. And she knew she had mere seconds to escape death.

She continued on her way toward the bus stop with forced nonchalance, but then darted down a side alley so quickly the gunman who'd been following her was taken off guard. She slipped and fell to her knees as bullets hit the building above her head, and a ricochet sent a shower of concrete dust over the space she'd so recently occupied. Desperate, she scrambled to her feet and turned the corner, her heart pounding in her chest.

Another hail of bullets echoed through the street and rattled off the side of the building. But Caterina was no longer there. And when the gunman reached the alleyway, she was nowhere to be found.

Chapter 14

Angelina waited for Alec outside the conference room. Princess Mara's husband, Trace McKinnon, leaned leisurely against the wall, his hands in his pockets, also waiting. But his eyes were constantly on the move. And when Major Branko approached her, he straightened. It was a little thing, but telling. So was the way he removed his hands from his pockets oh so casually. She smiled to herself. *Once a bodyguard, always a bodyguard,* she thought. *It is in the blood. Even when there is no need, a bodyguard cannot help being alert. Like a bloodhound on the scent.*

"Lieutenant Mateja?" Major Branko's voice was low, pitched to carry no farther than the two of them, but as Angelina came to attention, she was aware Trace McKinnon could hear every word.

"Yes, Major?"

"Were you or were you not given a direct order by Major Kostya to keep certain information to yourself?"

"I was." Her chin tilted up.

"Then how is it Special Agent Jones knows about Aleksandrov Vishenko and the Bratva?"

"Because I told him," McKinnon said, moving toward them with an unhurried air.

Angelina could see Major Branko was torn. He obviously wanted to question her, possibly even reprimand her, but hadn't expected the king's brother-in-law to interfere. She glanced from one man to the other. If this wasn't such a serious issue, she could have laughed. Both men were sizing each other up, looking for weaknesses in the other's defenses as automatically as they breathed.

Part of her yearned to be like them. Intrepid. Nearly invincible. A challenge to other men just by their presence. But part of her was glad she *wasn't* like them. Would either of them have been able to trick a confession out of Boris Tabor? No. Being a woman had its advantages.

The sound of the conference room door opening abruptly made Angelina turn toward it, just as Alec walked through the door. *That is another advantage of being a woman,* she thought with a secret smile. She loved how he made her intensely aware of her feminine side. A side of herself she'd repressed for years, hidden from everyone except Alec. A wave of longing surged through her that she was hard-pressed to suppress, but she managed it.

He crossed the wide hallway to Angelina and McKinnon. "Thanks for waiting for me," he told them. "Is there something I can do for you, Major? Because if not, the king is alone now, and I don't think he should be."

Major Branko cast Angelina a look that said, *We will continue this discussion another time, Lieutenant. When your protectors aren't around.*

Her returning glance said, *Anytime, Major. Anywhere.*

"So what's up?" McKinnon asked after Major Branko left. "Why'd you want me to wait for you?" He glanced at his watch. "Mara's just about to put the twins to bed, and I like to be there when I can." He grinned at Alec. "Fatherhood's the best thing that's ever happened to me…not counting the princess, of course. I highly recommend it."

An enigmatic expression crossed Alec's face, a look that intrigued Angelina, and she wondered what it meant. But all he said was, "I won't keep you long. I just wanted to set up a time and place for us to meet. Tomorrow morning okay with you? My office at the embassy, say, 8 a.m.?"

"Sure. Anything you want me to do ahead of time?"

"No, I'll get the ball rolling on those seven names. Speaking of which, did you mean what you said in there about Keira?" He indicated the conference room with a thumb over his shoulder. "Will the agency really give us whatever we need, without the DSS or the State Department having to fill out reams of paperwork?"

The grin faded from McKinnon's face. "I've known Nick D'Arcy since I got out of the Corps and joined the US Marshals Service," he said. "Worked for him a lot of years, first as a marshal, then as a special agent when the agency was created, before he went to DC to head up the entire agency. I can't think of anything

D'Arcy would like more than to put Vishenko behind bars for a long time—preferably for life.

"I'll call him to satisfy the legalities, ask him to send the official word through channels to Keira, delegating her to assist you and me in this investigation. But yeah. Keira, and anything else we ask for from the agency will be forthcoming. No problem."

Alec watched McKinnon walk away at a pace that told him the other man was in a hurry to be there for his children's bedtime. And just as the king's words earlier had sent a pang through Alec's heart at the unexpected vision of children—his children, Angel's children—he realized with another shaft of pain he had no idea where Angelina stood on that subject. They'd never discussed it.

He could rationalize their relationship was too new—it wasn't the sort of topic that popped up in conversation between a man and woman who were just beginning an intimate liaison. *Oh, by the way, how do you feel about kids?* wasn't the question a man asked a woman right after he made love to her, even if he could manage to speak, which wasn't all that likely. Rationalization aside, though, he didn't know what Angelina's answer would be, didn't know if children factored into her future plans.

But even if she wanted them—even if she wanted them with *him*—he could never be an absentee father. And that was a huge deterrent. He might be able to reconcile having a long-distance relationship with Angelina after he was transferred—assuming she'd agree to something like that—but his conscience would never accept bringing children into the world who didn't know they were wanted. Cherished. Loved. Study after study had proven fathers played a crucial role in the behavioral and mental development of children. And that meant *being* there for his children.

Yeah, sometimes fathers couldn't be there when circumstances intervened. Military service, for instance. Soldiers couldn't pick and choose their battles, couldn't know when they'd be called up and sent overseas. But he couldn't deliberately father children he knew in advance would grow up without him for the most part. No way.

Which meant either convincing Angelina to give up her job, give up her life for him—follow him to his next posting, and the next, and the next—or surrendering to the idea of never having children with her.

Neither choice was acceptable. Neither choice was one he wanted to live with. And what was even worse, he had no way of knowing Angelina's opinion of either option because he was too afraid to ask.

Angelina and Alec left the palace separately. She knew he didn't like it, could tell by his mulish expression that someday soon he would rebel against her determination to keep their affair secret from everyone who knew her. The more she thought about it, the more she realized she didn't like that word. *Affair.* Didn't like the connotation. She and Alec weren't having an affair. They were...

What are we? she asked herself as she drove back to her apartment, where Alec would rendezvous with her after stopping off at his place for a change of clothes. *Lovers,* she settled on finally. *We are lovers.* That sounded a little better. "Affair" sounded cheap. Tawdry.

"Lovers" sounded more acceptable. More permanent. Not as permanent as "husband and wife," but...

That's when it hit her. She didn't want to be Alec's lover. She wanted to be his wife. She wanted that commitment from him, and wanted to commit to him in return. She wanted *permanence*. That little band of gold signifying their pledge to each other to be true and faithful. She wanted forever and a day, like the legend upon which her country was built.

Alec had exploded into her life with the force of a bomb, changing everything. Including her. And now, the thing she'd long told herself she didn't want, the thing she'd long reconciled herself to being unable to have...now she wanted it. Fervently.

Which meant only one thing. She was in love with Alec. Alec, who'd never said he loved her.

The first thing Alec did when he walked into his apartment was perform a quick electronic sweep. He'd never found any listening devices, but he always checked anyway—better safe than sorry. Then he glanced at his watch and mentally calculated the time difference between Zakhar and Denver, Colorado, where his sister worked. Satisfied he wouldn't be calling too early or too late, he punched a series of numbers into his telephone and waited a little impatiently for the call to go through.

"Keira Walker," came the crisp voice in his ear.

"Hey," he replied. "It's Alec."

"Hey yourself. So how come you only call me when it's work related? What kind of way is that to treat your only sister?"

"How'd you know?"

"Are you kidding?" She laughed her musical laugh. "Trace called Baker Street a half hour ago," she said, using Nick D'Arcy's nickname within the agency, a tip of the hat to Sherlock Holmes because D'Arcy was so omniscient. "Then Baker Street called me less than a minute after he hung up with Trace."

"So he gave you the green light to help in this investigation?"

"And then some. His words were, 'Whatever your brother asks for. And even if he doesn't ask for it, if you think he needs it, give it to him. I'm not passing up the chance to take Vishenko down—not after all these years.'"

"Wow." Alec laughed softly. "Remind me to thank him."

"So, what do you need? Besides whatever there is to find on Aleksandrov Vishenko, which I'm already working on. Oh, and by the way, did you know the FBI has a wiretap warrant on Vishenko? A warrant that was recently extended?"

"How the hell do you know that?"

"If you had a need to know, Alec, I'd tell you. But you don't. The agency has its own ways of finding things out. Just trust me when I tell you the warrant exists. Whatever they get from that wiretap, we'll know." That silenced him for a moment, until Keira repeated, "So what else do you need?"

"I've got seven names. I need everything you can find out about them. Work history, credit reports, financial data, bank accounts, especially any foreign bank accounts they might not want anyone to know about. You name it, I want it. And I want it yesterday."

"No problem. Give me the list."

He read the names and occupations from his note-book. "All except the first one used to be employed at the US embassy here in Drago. I have no idea where they're posted, but if they were dirty here, it's possible they're doing something similar wherever they are now."

"If they got away with it once…"

"Yeah, that's what I was thinking." He hoped it wasn't true, but the odds were against that. "The first name on the list is still here—make him your top priority," he told his sister. "Because if there are still fraudulent work visas being sold through my embassy, he's the guy. And I want to shut him down now."

"Got it," she said. "Any by the way, those foreign bank accounts they might not want anyone to know about? Shouldn't be a problem. We can start digging without warrants, but at some point in this investigation you're going to need one on each of your suspects. Especially for those bank accounts."

Alec thought about it for a moment. "What are my options? I'm really concerned about this getting out. McKinnon said Vishenko used to have at least one FBI agent in his pocket, and still might for that matter. Not to mention who knows all else. I don't want anyone to know they're under investigation until the indictments come out, especially Vishenko." While Alec knew that might not be possible, he at least wanted to maintain secrecy until Caterina Mateja was brought in safe and sound.

"Who knows about your investigation so far?"

"Besides the president and the secretary of state? And the king of Zakhar? Just a handful of people, including McKinnon and your husband. And now you and D'Arcy."

"D'Arcy has connections at the Department of Justice. Let me give him a call, see who he wants to approach at the DOJ about this. I'm thinking you want wiretaps on all these people, not just Vishenko. Right?"

"I hadn't thought about it, but yeah."

Keira chuckled softly in his ear. "Well, Baker Street *did* tell me to give you whatever you need, even if you don't know you need it," she murmured. "I guess that counts as one you owe me," she said, using terminology from their childhood. Then she became all business again. "You're going to need evidence to substantiate your warrant requests. Do you have any?"

Alec remembered what he'd learned at the meeting earlier tonight. "I might. I'll get McKinnon working on that first thing in the morning."

"Sounds good. This is enough for me to start on. I'll get back to you when I have anything to report. Encrypted reports sent to the embassy are okay? Or should I call?"

Alec thought rapidly. "Encrypted reports are probably okay, but call me before you send one so I know it's on the way. Supposedly, the only men involved in the fraud at the embassy are the seven names I already gave you, but you never know. I'd rather err on the side of caution."

"Works for me."

Now that his business was finished, Alec glanced at his watch again and saw how late he was going to be, but still took a minute to ask, "So how's my favorite niece?"

"Your *only* niece is a walking, talking nightmare,

a disaster waiting to happen. I shudder to think what she'll be like when she grows up. But don't tell Cody I said so. She takes after her daddy in everything. She can charm her way out of anything—or at least she thinks she can—just by smiling that winsome smile."

"Give her a kiss for me anyway." Alec hung up the phone, smiling at the thought of Alyssa. If he could have a daughter like her...

Angelina parked her little red Fiat across the street from her apartment building, locked it and hurried inside. She was worried Alec might be there before her, but she had time to get her mail and ring for the elevator before Alec walked through the front door carrying a garment bag slung over one shoulder.

He crossed the foyer with his brisk stride, slid one arm around her waist and pulled her tightly into his embrace for a long, lingering kiss. She thought about resisting for less than two seconds. Then she didn't think at all. When he finally raised his head, he said, "I've been wanting to do that ever since I left you at the palace."

Angelina glanced around to make sure no one was watching. But the lobby was empty. She smiled at Alec, a smile of promise and expectation. Then the elevator doors opened with a *ding*. She grabbed Alec's arm, pulled him inside with her and punched the button for her floor before leaning in for another kiss as the elevator doors swished shut.

Only then did a man move from the shadows where he'd been waiting for Lieutenant Mateja to return. He looked up to confirm what floor the elevator stopped on and smiled to himself. He pulled out a little notebook and made an entry, glancing at his watch to record the exact time. Then he headed out of the building, whistling a gay little Zakharian folk tune, a satisfied expression on his face.

Angelina watched Alec dress for work. She'd never really had the opportunity to watch a man go through his peculiar morning routine—so different from a woman's morning routine. They'd woken very early and had gone running together, working up a satisfying sweat. Then they had shared a shower, something that was becoming a treasured ritual.

She'd observed Alec shaving earlier, as he lathered up and scraped the stubble from his face, meticulously maneuvering the razor over the tricky patches—especially his chin—and she'd experienced momentary regret. Right before they'd pulled on their sweats and gone jogging in the pre-dawn, he'd kissed her. She'd felt that stubble as he'd nuzzled her cheek, sending shivers of awareness throughout her body. An unshaved masculine face was a potent sexual weapon.

But then, nearly everything about Alec was a potent sexual weapon.

To distract herself from that suddenly uncomfortable awareness, she asked, "So what is my assignment this morning? What do you want me to do?"

"It might not sound like much," he said as he checked the action on his gun before returning it to his shoulder holster, "but I want you to write down everything you can remember about Caterina. Every detail, no matter how small. I want to know what makes her tick. What motivates her. After that's done, I want you to talk to my sister. Keira can try to track your cousin down, and knowing everything about her will help."

"But I have not seen Caterina for eight years," Angelina exclaimed. "She was sixteen when she left Zakhar. How can what I knew of her before she disappeared tell your sister anything about her now?"

"People don't change," Alec told her, placing a comforting hand against her cheek. "You might not believe it, but most people are who they're going to be as adults by the time they're six years old. Numerous studies support this. So if you're a shy child at six, you'll be a shy adult. You might be able to overcome the outward, visible signs of shyness, but you'll still feel shy inside. The same goes for other character traits. Something in your memories of Caterina could be the key to finding her—that's what I told the king last night, and I meant it."

"This is good," she told him seriously. "This I can do." It was a challenge, but now she was fired up. Everything she could remember about Caterina—even the most painful memories—would be written down. She would even call upon her parents to jog her memory, if necessary. She would capture every little detail and try not to think of Aleksandrov Vishenko wanting her cousin dead. Getting closer by the minute. It was a race against time, but she would do whatever she could to win. If Alec believed this was the best way—the *only* way—then that was what she'd do.

He glanced at his watch. "Gotta go," he said. "McKinnon will be at the embassy in twenty-one minutes exactly—he's punctual to a fault. So kiss me as if you mean it, and get started on your assignment. Call me at the embassy if you need something."

Two minutes later, he still hadn't left, and he removed his mouth from hers with reluctance. "Guess you meant it," he murmured.

Chapter 15

The minute Alec walked out the door, Angelina picked up the phone. She was supposed to be on duty with the queen this morning, and though she'd officially been relieved of that duty, she wanted to let the queen know personally.

She identified herself to the palace operator when her call was answered, and waited patiently until she heard the queen's voice on the phone.

"Angelina?" Queen Juliana said. "I'm glad you called, because I wanted to talk to you. Andre told me about your new assignment, and I'm so glad you're involved in this investigation—although not the reason for it. Your cousin... I know how much she meant to you. Means to you," she quickly corrected. "Please don't worry about anything except finding her before Aleksandrov Vishenko does."

Angelina was touched by the queen's concern. "Thank you, Your Majesty."

"Juliana," the queen reminded her. "When it's just us, it's Juliana. Remember?" Then she returned to the issue at hand. "Andre and Alec—they're focused on the big picture, the human-trafficking case. And they're right in a way. It has to be shut down and the men responsible brought to justice. But bringing Caterina home safely is just as important, and not only because she might have evidence against Vishenko and might be willing to testify against him. You need to bring her home safely because...well...because what happened to her should never happen to *any* woman. Ever."

"Trace McKinnon was here to see you, sir," Alec's bright young administrative assistant told him the minute he entered the outer office. "He stopped in, said he was early for your meeting and would be back at eight on the dot." She looked at Alec's calendar, then added, "He's not on the schedule." There was just a hint of reproach in her voice.

"Yeah, I know," he told her ruefully. "I just arranged it last night. But I knew I didn't have anything else scheduled for this morning, not until my eleven o'clock meeting."

He started for his office door but then turned to ask a question. Before he could, his administrative assistant volunteered, "It's been swept already. I was here when the team came in."

Alec knew she wasn't referring to a cleaning team but rather to the electronics team that swept his office daily for listening devices. "You must have come in very early."

Her laugh held a trace of shyness. "I have a date to-night, and I was hoping I could leave exactly on time... maybe a few minutes early, if it's okay with you."

Alec smiled to himself. His administrative assistant, Tahra Edwards, was the person he'd had in mind when he told Angelina that a shy six-year-old would grow up to be a shy adult. Tahra—whose name rhymed with Sahara—was bright, articulate and a real go-getter where her job at the embassy was concerned, but painfully shy when it came to dealing with the opposite sex.

She was far from plain, but lacked the sophisticated veneer most young women her age wore like a shield. She was the kind of woman who appealed to his brother Liam.

"Fine with me," he said now. "You're not a clock watcher, and you've put in more than your share of OT these past few weeks helping me get up to speed. So feel free to leave early. Anyone I know?" A tinge of protectiveness made him ask the question. Not that he was responsible for Tahra, but still. *Any decent man would be concerned,* he justified to himself. *She's as vulnerable as a lamb among wolves.*

Tahra shook her head. "I don't think so—he's Zakharian."

Alec didn't know why her answer mollified him— Zakharian men could be wolves, too. But then again, Zakhar was fifty years behind the times in many ways. Men still treated women with old-fashioned courtesy here—unless the women were trying to move into jobs that had previously been reserved for men. Still, it wasn't a bad thing from Tahra's perspective. He didn't want anyone pressuring her—

Then McKinnon walked into the outer office right at

eight o'clock, and Tahra's date was driven from Alec's mind. "Come on in," he told the other man. To Tahra, he said, "I don't want to be disturbed for anything or anyone other than the ambassador. And that reminds me. Try to set up an appointment for me with him, will you? This afternoon, if possible, but if not, as soon as he's free."

Once in his office with the door closed and locked, Alec indicated one of the chairs in front of his desk and settled himself behind his desk. "Unless you object, I'm going to take the ambassador into my confidence regarding the investigation," he said, almost before they two of them were seated.

McKinnon shook his head. "No objection from me—we'd already cleared him. Last night's meeting was just confirmation."

"I agree," Alec said before moving on to the next topic. "I talked with Keira when I got back to my apartment. You didn't waste any time calling D'Arcy, did you? And apparently he didn't waste any time, either. Keira told me he'd already contacted her, told her to give us anything we need. Whether or not we ask for it."

"Yeah, sounds like D'Arcy. So I take it you already gave Keira the list of names last night?"

Alec nodded. "But I forgot to tell her I was going to ask Angeli—Lieutenant Mateja to—"

McKinnon cut him off. "You're still trying to kid me you and she aren't involved?" He snorted. "I thought you were smarter than that."

Alec stiffened. "Whatever's between me and Lieutenant Mateja doesn't have anything to do with this case," he said coldly.

"Maybe not. But I'll say the same thing you said to me back when I was falling for Mara. If it was important to the case, you'd tell me. Right?"

Something in that steady blue stare reminded him of the way he'd looked at McKinnon when he and Liam had confronted the other man about Princess Mara. Now the shoe was on the other foot, and he didn't like it. Not one bit. "I had a hell of a nerve back then, didn't I?" he admitted.

"Back then?" McKinnon laughed suddenly. "You still do. But that's okay. You get the job done, and that's all that really matters. It must run in the family." He shifted gears. "So, what were you starting to say you didn't tell Keira about Lieutenant Mateja?"

"Oh, right. I forgot to tell Keira I was going to ask Angelina to make a list of everything she could remember about her cousin. Everything that might possibly help Keira track her down. I know it's like trying to find a needle in a haystack, but—"

"But if anyone can do it, your sister can," McKinnon finished for him.

"Exactly."

"Sounds good. So what do you want me to focus on?"

"Keira's checking out the seven names. But I need notarized witness statements—or the Zakharian equivalent—from the two canaries the police have in custody if we're going to apply for search warrants, including wiretaps. I also want you to interview those two men, see what kind of witnesses they'd make in an American court." He didn't have to say it—both men knew American juries tended to distrust criminals with foreign accents. Especially criminals who were trying to cut a deal by testifying. The propensity for lying or stretching the truth to make their own sentences lighter made them less than trustworthy witnesses—or so the defense attorneys would allege. Another thing they'd have to contend with.

"And if you can, I'd like you to interview the other three Zakharians who are in custody. I don't have to tell you how to do your job—"

McKinnon cut him off. "That's right, you don't."

Alec smiled at how the tables had been turned on him in this, too. "Humor me," was all he said. When McKinnon made a gesture signifying for him to continue, he added, "I was thinking if you interviewed them all together, and they thought you spoke only English..."

"You read my mind," McKinnon said in fluent Zakharan. The two men smiled at each other in perfect understanding. "Speaking the language didn't do us a damn bit of good when the State Department wanted us to spy on Mara for them," McKinnon said judiciously, "because there wasn't anything to learn. But in this case..."

"There's nothing like having an ace up your sleeve when you're playing poker with men who'd just as soon slit your throat than let you win a pot," Alec said with a laugh. "Okay, we're on the same page there. I think that's it for now. I want—" The buzzer on Alec's phone sounded, interrupting what he was going to say. He frowned. "I told Tahra I didn't want to be interrupted unless it was the ambassador, so maybe..." He hit the speaker button. "Yes, Tahra?"

"There's someone to see you, sir," Tahra said. "I told him you were in a meeting and couldn't be disturbed, but he said it can't wait. He's quite insistent." There was an odd tone in Tahra's voice, and it was the tone more than her words that made Alec say, "I'll be right out." He disconnected and told McKinnon, "Give me a minute. Something's not right."

Alec crossed the room and jerked the door open. Captain Marek Zale was standing by Tahra's desk at military attention, an attitude that seemed to afflict all those who served in the Zakharian National Forces even when they weren't in uniform. Alec didn't know how the captain had managed to get past Security downstairs, unless Tahra had authorized his entry. From the captain's stony-eyed expression and the way he was studiously avoiding looking at Tahra, not to mention the distress and betrayal on Tahra's face, Alec put two and two together and came up with...four?

Tahra wouldn't authorize just anyone to enter this restricted area of the embassy. Which meant she had to know Captain Zale in something other than his official capacity. *Is he Tahra's mysterious Zakharian date?* Alec wondered. *Is that how he managed to convince Tahra to let him in past Security?*

And if he *was* the man Tahra was suddenly interested in, was it more than just a coincidence Captain Zale just *happened* to ask Alec's shy administrative assistant for a date? *And if I believe that,* he told himself wryly, *there's this bridge in Brooklyn...*

"You needed to see me now, Captain Zale?" he asked coolly. "It can't wait?"

The other man folded his lips tightly together as if he was keeping hasty words in. Hot words he might regret. "No," he said finally. "It cannot wait. It concerns Lieutenant Mateja."

A dart of fear shot through Alec. Had something happened to Angelina? He'd left her safely in her apartment, but what if she'd gone somewhere? *Traffic accident? He remembered telling Angelina that with the jobs they did, one of them could be dead tomorrow.* If something had happened to her... *Please, God, no. No!* But all he said out loud was, "Come into my office, Captain."

Captain Zale checked in the doorway when he saw McKinnon, who stood up, and said to Alec, "We were done, weren't we, Special Agent Jones? I'll get back to you about what we discussed." He smiled easily at the captain. "Good to see you again." Then he was gone, passing Captain Zale in the doorway and closing the door softly behind him.

Alec took a deep, calming breath and arranged his face in stoic lines, refusing to betray his reaction to whatever the other man was going to tell him. He held himself so tightly, his muscles ached. "What about Lieutenant Mateja?"

"Are you aware the lieutenant is under observation by the secret intelligence service?" the captain asked abruptly. "As are all the members of the security details since the assassination attempt?"

Alec let himself breathe, let his muscles relax against the strict control he'd exerted when he thought he was going to be told the worst, that his Angel was dead. *Not dead,* his brain whispered. *She's not dead.* For an instant nothing else mattered. Then he focused on what the captain had just said. If Zakhar's secret intelligence service had Angelina under surveillance, then that meant...

"I wasn't aware Lieutenant Mateja's personal life

was subject to military scrutiny," he said with a nonchalance he was far from feeling.

"It would not be," the captain snapped, "if you had not requested she be added to your team investigating the trafficking case. Can you not see you have compromised her?" he argued hotly. "Called her integrity into question? She is one of my best men, and now—"

Furious at having his own integrity impugned, Alec refused to let him finish. "My personal involvement with Lieutenant Mateja has absolutely nothing to do with this case, and you'd better believe it, Captain," he said in clipped tones. "It's crucial we find her cousin and convince her to testify, and Lieutenant Mateja can assist in that effort—that's the *only* reason I asked the king to put her on my team."

Both hot under the collar, both operating under intense emotion held under a tight rein, the two men stared narrow-eyed at each other for a moment. Then Alec took a mental step back from the brink. "Look," he said reasonably, realizing honesty would serve him best here. "She didn't want anyone to know—especially you—because she didn't want you to think badly of her. She's conscientious to a fault, devoted to her job and to you, and fearless in her determination to keep the queen safe."

He waited for that to register with the other man. "But she's human, and she has the right to be a woman as well as a fighting man. The king's words—'fighting man'—not mine," he added dryly. "She has the right to keep her private life private so long as it doesn't get in the way of doing her job. And it won't. You should know her well enough to know that much about her. I shouldn't have to tell you."

An expression that in anyone else would be called chagrin crossed the captain's face. "You are correct," he said stiffly after a moment. "Lieutenant Mateja is, as I stated earlier, one of my best men. I can count on the fingers of one hand men I would pick for a mission before I would pick her. And not," he was quick to add, "for any other reason than she is a woman, and there are still men in the Zakharian National Forces who resent women in the military. In every other way, she is an exemplary officer."

He laughed unexpectedly. "She even threw me once in hand-to-hand combat," he explained. "Me! She took me by surprise, of course, but still…" He shook his head in disbelief.

"Join the crowd," Alec said with a self-deprecating smile.

"You, too?" Captain Zale asked.

"Yeah. And yeah, she took me by surprise, too, but still…" The two men shared a look of commiseration.

"Your secret is safe with me," the captain assured Alec.

"Same here." Now that they'd calmed down a little, Alec ventured to say, "Your respect means a hell of a lot to her. Even when you suspected her of being involved in the assassination conspiracy, even when she thought you were unfairly blaming her for having to kill Tcholek, she defended you to me. That kind of loyalty is rare."

"I did not really suspect her," Captain Zale was quick to say. "Majors Kostya and Branko—the king's favorite bodyguards—they are the ones who raised the possibility. I knew in my heart she was innocent, but I also knew I could not prove it—not to their satisfaction. They are ruthless in their devotion to the king. So I allowed her to be questioned by them until it was obvious to all she was telling the truth.

"As for the other, you are right. I did not speak up when the majors implied a man would not have let his guard down with Tcholek. I should have. I should have told them I would have done the same with a man I had worked with so closely." A tinge of color touched his cheekbones. "That I did not speak in her defense is a shame I bear."

He breathed deeply. "Then she interrogated the remaining would-be assassin and tricked two names out of him no one else had been able to obtain." Admiration colored his words. "You should have heard her. A man could not have done what she did."

"So what are you going to do about this latest accusation of impropriety?" Alec asked. "I can talk to the king, tell him the truth about Lieutenant Mateja and me, and explain that I—"

"No." Captain Zale shook his head firmly. "I will handle it. She is my officer. My responsibility. I will handle it." He turned to go, but Alec called him back.

"Captain, wait a minute, please." When the other man turned around, Alec found himself torn. Despite the original accusation, despite the confrontation, Captain Zale had turned out to be a fairly decent guy. How to say what he felt he had to say?

Straight out, he told himself firmly. *That's the only way.* "I have to ask," he said frankly. "Tahra—my administrative assistant—you have a date with her tonight, right?"

"I *had* a date with her, yes." Captain Zale's face gave nothing away except the fact that he now believed his date was in jeopardy after he'd used his personal connection with Tahra to gain admittance to this restricted area. "When she authorized security to let me in, I let her think I came to see her."

"Tahra's very trusting," Alec told him. "Did your date with her have anything to do with me? What I mean is," he rushed to add, "if you only asked her out to pump her for information about me, please don't. She doesn't deserve that kind of treatment, and I don't want her hurt."

If anything, the captain's face turned even more wooden. "That was not why I... She is very sweet. A man would have to look far and wide to find someone like her."

He didn't say anything more, but Alec read between the lines and was satisfied. "Then on your way out, why don't you make sure your date for tonight is still on. She was really looking forward to it. I'll give you five minutes' privacy. If you can't convince Tahra of your sincerity in five minutes, you're not the man I take you for, Captain."

Alec waited for Captain Zale to leave before he picked up the phone and dialed a number he already knew by heart. "Hi," he said when Angelina answered. "How's everything going? Making progress?" He wouldn't normally call to check so soon—he didn't hover—but he had an urgent need to hear Angelina's voice. To *know* she was safe.

"Progress," she confirmed with a hint of excitement in her tone. "Yes. I had not realized I had so many memories of Caterina. Perhaps because I did not want to let myself remember them. But I already have ten pages, with many more to go."

"Great," Alec said. "Don't skip over anything. Not even the smallest detail. My sister's got a knack for figuring things out, sometimes based on the tiniest clue. Kind of like putting together a jigsaw puzzle with nothing to go on but the shape of the pieces. But the more she has to work with, the better off we are."

"I understand."

Alec hesitated. Then figured, *What the hell,* and asked, "Tell me something."

"Yes?"

"It's been bugging me for days, ever since McKinnon and I first learned Caterina might be alive. As soon as I heard there was a hit out on her, as soon as I heard how high the price tag was, I figured she either knows something or has some kind of evidence. Evidence Vishenko is afraid she'll take to the authorities. Which means wherever she is *now,* at some point she was with Vishenko."

At first, Angelina didn't respond. But then she answered Alec's unspoken question. "She would not stay with a man like Vishenko. Not by choice. Yes, she wanted more out of life than she could have here in Zakhar. And yes, she believed modeling was the way to achieve these things. But she believed in hard work. Believed in achieving success by her own efforts. She was a good girl on the brink of becoming a good woman. She would not sleep with a man for what it would get her—that is what you are thinking? That Caterina would choose the easy way?"

Alec was sorry he'd brought it up. But now that he

had… "Are you sure, Angel?" he asked softly, knowing the question would hurt no matter the answer.

Her voice didn't waver. "I know her. I know she would not any more than I would. If she was with Vishenko, it was not by her choice."

"Then why? If she was forced into prostitution and eventually escaped that life, why didn't she go to the authorities? Especially if she had evidence against Vishenko. That's what doesn't make sense. And if she couldn't bring herself to press charges—if she was afraid for her life—why didn't she just come home?"

A long silence followed. "Caterina did not come home because she was ashamed," Angelina said finally, and Alec knew she was swallowing back tears because she didn't want to admit she was crying. Again. Tears from the woman who swore she never cried. "Because she blamed herself. Because she believed everyone would blame her for what happened. Because she believed *I* would blame her."

Suddenly it all made sense to Alec. Rape victims weren't to blame for what happened to them any more than robbery victims were, or victims of home invasions. And yet the perception persisted in the minds of many that they *were* to blame. Alec wasn't naive. He'd been posted in countries where fathers and brothers of rape victims killed the *victim*—not the perpetrator—to salvage their family honor. Honor killings were still acceptable in many countries, countries with which the United States had diplomatic relations.

"I'm sorry," he said now, wishing he were there with Angelina, wishing he could hold her and somehow convey that he understood her pain and shared it.

"That is why she did not come home," Angelina

said. "She did not want me to know. Her parents were dead before she ever disappeared, but they would have blamed her just as my parents would. She did not want *anyone* to know what she had suffered. She would rather live alone for the rest of her life than admit the truth."

Determination grew in Alec. Hard. Cold. Not just to bring Vishenko down, but to rescue Caterina and help her understand *she* was the victim. That she wasn't responsible for *anything* that had happened to her. The same way he'd helped Angelina understand she wasn't responsible for the deaths of Sasha Tcholek and Yuri Ivanovitch. These things had *happened*, and they couldn't be undone. They just had to be lived with. But the blame—the blame had to be placed where it truly belonged.

"We'll find her, Angel," he promised, his heart aching for what Angelina was going through. "We'll find her. And when we do…" *She'll never have to feel ashamed again.*

"Stop right there!"

Cate froze with one hand on the front door to the rooming house in Boulder, Colorado, where she'd moved in three weeks ago, waiting for the bullets that would tear her body apart. Vishenko's men had found her again. She couldn't escape as she had at the bus stop in Denver—there was nowhere to run this time.

Six years, she thought, not bothering to utter a last-minute prayer she knew wouldn't be answered. *At least I lived six years free from him. Even if it had only been a day, one day of freedom would have been worth it after spending two years as his prisoner, and I had six years.*

"Put your hands up where we can see them. Then slowly, very slowly, turn around."

Confused—because she expected to be dead already, or at least gasping out her last breaths on the ground—Cate obeyed, putting her hands up as she slowly turned around to face whoever was behind her. A man and a woman stood there, both wearing dark blue jackets and vests over beige pants, their guns drawn and pointed at her. Emblazoned across the pocket of the vests was the word POLICE. And underneath that word was another word, one she had no trouble recognizing. ICE. And though it wasn't as bad as she'd first feared, it was bad enough.

Chapter 16

That night, Alec reviewed what Angelina had written down about her cousin. Every memory, every facet of her character, every motivation. Everything. "Okay," he told her. "This is good. I can't swear to it, but it might help find her. All we can do now is turn this over to Keira and see what she can do with it."

He put the voluminous document—which Angelina had typed on her computer, organized and cross-referenced before printing it out—to one side. Then he took her hands in his and kissed them both before sitting her down on the sofa. "We have to talk about something," he told her, settling himself next to her. Close enough so she could feel the warmth emanating from his body but just far enough away not to be touching her. And she knew instantly something was wrong.

"What is it?"

"Captain Zale came to see me today," he began, but stopped. "There's no way to say this except straight out," he told her roughly. "Captain Zale knows about us. About you and me."

"You told him?" Angelina couldn't believe it. Betrayal? From Alec?

"I didn't have to. He already knew. But yeah, I confirmed it."

"How? How did he know?"

"Apparently you, along with everyone else on the security details, are under observation by Zakhar's secret intelligence service."

She blinked but made the connection. "The assassination attempt. Of course. The king said he wanted us all investigated. I did not realize..." She glanced down at her hands. "I am sorry, Alec. I should have thought of this. I should have—"

He crushed her hands in his. "Don't apologize. If you think I give a damn who knows about us, think again." He loosened his grip but still kept possession of her hands. "I know you wanted to keep our relationship a secret, at least for a while. Especially from your captain." She still refused to look up, but she sensed his internal struggle, could hear the strain in his voice. "But I'm not ashamed, and as far as I'm concerned, the whole world can know about us. Or the whole world can go to hell."

She raised her face to his then, and saw the truth in his eyes. "I refused to lie to your captain," Alec said now, a hard edge to his voice. "When he told me he knew about us, I admitted it. But I also told him you have the right to keep your private life private, so long as it doesn't impact your job. And he knows it won't."

"Then he does not think less of me? It is not an issue?"

"Why the hell should he think less of you?" The challenge in his words was matched by his tone. "You're a woman, Angel. A living, breathing woman, not an automaton. Neither is he. In fact—" He stopped abruptly, as if he wasn't sure he should say anything more. But then he said, "In fact, I just found out he has a date tonight with my administrative assistant."

"A *date*?" Angelina couldn't believe it. "Captain *Zale*?"

Alec laughed suddenly, and then she did, too. "What's wrong with that? As far as I can tell, he's a normal man with functioning parts. You act like he's not allowed to be human."

"No, not that, but…" It still struck her as funny, and she chuckled. "He is very much a man. No question of that. He is much sought after by women, this I know— it is no secret within the ranks. But he has time only for his duty. His eyes are always on the queen." Angelina suddenly realized how this might sound, and hurried to clarify. "Not that he is interested in the queen *that* way. Please do not misunderstand."

"Don't worry," Alec assured her. "I wasn't thinking along those lines. Besides," he added dryly, "it would take an extremely brave—or reckless—man to touch *anything* belonging to your king. He doesn't strike me as the kind of man who would tolerate that, not for a second."

"That is a very sexist thing to say," she retorted. "The queen is not a *thing*, and—"

"Okay, okay," Alec said, holding up his hands, palms outward. "Forget I said it."

But Angelina could tell he was still thinking it. *So Alec is not perfect, after all,* she realized. *In some ways, he is a typical man, with typical male thinking.* It didn't make her love him any less. Just the opposite, in fact. It was somewhat endearing to know that Alec—so perfect in many ways—had his faults just like everyone else.

Then another thought crept into her mind, distracting her from consideration of Alec's few faults, and she blurted out before she meant to, "I have never known Captain Zale to *date.* Is she very beautiful, this assistant of yours?"

Alec's eyes widened in surprise, and Angelina cursed her unruly tongue. "You're jealous," he said eventually, as if he couldn't believe it.

"No, I…how can there be jealousy when there is trust?" she asked, suddenly flustered in a way she hadn't been since high school. "And I trust you. I… I am not jealous, you understand. I would merely like to know."

Alec tried to suppress the unholy glee in his expressive eyes but failed. *And that is another fault in him,* Angelina averred with a spurt of anger. *He laughs at the most inappropriate times.* But when she admitted the truth to herself, her anger faded.

"Yes, I am jealous. I do not mean to be," she said seriously. "But I…what are you doing?" Alec was stripping off his coat, his shoulder harness, undoing his tie and unbuttoning his shirt. "What are you doing?" she asked again, bewildered.

"Proving to you there's no reason to be jealous. Not of Tahra. Not of any woman." He was completely naked now, except for his socks, which he stripped off with an un-self-conscious air. He was magnificently aroused already, but his hand went to his erection, stroking it a couple of times until it swelled even larger. Impossibly larger. He bent down and retrieved a condom from his pants pocket, which he quickly rolled on. Angelina watched for a moment, then glanced up at Alec's face, trying to read his intentions in his determined expression.

"I'm all yours, Angel," he said as he pulled her to her feet. He hooked his hands underneath her armpits and lifted. She automatically wrapped her legs around his hips and grasped his shoulders for balance, feeling him hard and heavy against the crux of her thighs, as his hands moved to her hips to hold her. And just like that, she wanted him. But she wanted to be naked, too. Wanted to feel his hard warmth inside her where it belonged. Where *he* belonged.

He kissed her, putting his whole soul into it. "All yours," he murmured, grinding his pelvis against hers. Teasing her. "Every inch. Every time. All yours."

He walked into her bedroom carrying her that way and tumbled her onto the bed. He stripped off her shoes, her slacks, her panties in no time, but left the rest of her clothes untouched. He fitted himself into place, and the teasing expression disappeared. "Tell me you want me," he demanded. "Tell me."

She arched her hips upward, wanting everything he offered. Everything he was. "Yes," she panted. "Yes."

He surged into her. No foreplay, nothing to prepare her for his entry, but she was already so wet, so ready for him, all she could do was moan in pleasure at the incredible feeling of being stretched, filled, taken to a whole different plane. Then he was riding her hard and fast, so fast she couldn't catch her breath. So fast she exploded without warning, arching and crying his name as he rocked her with his deep thrusts, her body milking his uncontrollably when he exploded, too, driving himself deep with his last thrust.

They lay there like that forever, it seemed. Her legs locked around his hips, holding him tight and deep inside her. His lips found her throat and he kissed her there, just a slight movement, but enough for her to feel it. He was still shaking, tremors running through his muscles. But so was she. They were both breathing hard, depleted. And yet… Angelina tightened her pelvic muscles around his erection, and he groaned. *Not pain,* she told herself with a secret smile. *Pleasure.* So she did it again. Then again.

He groaned each time, but he didn't ask her to stop. Eventually, though, she was forced to let him go, unlock her legs and let him roll off her body to lie beside her with one arm thrown across his face. He didn't say anything, just lay there breathing hard. And that was the first inkling she had that something wasn't right.

"Alec?" She touched his arm tentatively, but he refused to remove it from his face. Then he drew a deep, shuddering breath and sat up abruptly, his arm falling away.

"It's not enough, Angel. Not for me. Not anymore."

"I do not understand."

"I can't just make love to you and pretend that's all I want." He ripped off the condom and disappeared into the bathroom. When he returned, he sat next to her on the bed and dragged a corner of the coverlet over her.

His eyes closed for a moment as an expression she didn't understand flickered across his face. His jaw tightened and he swallowed. Hard. When his eyes finally met hers, he said, "I…you want to talk sexist? I wanted to mark you as mine. I started out wanting to prove I belong to you, only to you. And then somehow, along the way, that changed. I wanted so badly to prove you belong to me. And I didn't want to wear a condom this time."

Angelina caught her breath because it sounded as if Alec was saying…

"I love you, Angel. I wouldn't admit it to myself until this morning, when Captain Zale came to see me. When I thought something had happened to you. And I realized I don't want to be a survivor if it means being without you."

"Alec—"

"I know this isn't what you wanted," he continued, cutting her off. "This isn't what you planned. I know that. But I—"

"Alec—"

"No, let me finish. I can make you happy, Angel, if you'll let me. I can—"

Angelina reached up, slid her hand around his neck and pulled him down for an endless kiss. When their lips finally parted, she murmured dreamily, "I love you, too, Alec."

He looked blown away by her confession. "You do? Since when? Why didn't you tell me?"

She laughed deep in her throat. "To answer your questions in order, yes. Since last night. At least, that is when I admitted it to myself. And I did not tell you because I did not want you to know. Not until…"

"Why didn't you want me to know?"

She could feel warmth creeping into her cheeks.

"Because I am more Zakharian than I knew, and in Zakhar a woman does not…not first, you understand." She held his gaze. "And because for years I told myself I could not have what other women have. Not and have my career, too. But that was before I met you."

His face contracted. "I told you I'm more traditional than you think I am. Not that I want you to give up your career, but I want the whole nine yards, Angel." When she shook her head, not understanding the reference, he explained, "I want the whole picture. Marriage. Children."

Angelina caught her breath. *Alec* wanted *children?* With her? She had never thought of having children before—children weren't compatible with the life she'd chosen for herself—and the sudden yearning for a child with Alec's warm, brown eyes slammed into her from nowhere.

All at once she remembered the look Queen Juliana had given her in the spring when the queen had been expecting her baby and Angelina had made some off-the-cuff remark about never having children of her own. At the time, she hadn't understood the expression of…was it amusement on the queen's face? Not exactly. More like her friend knew something Angelina didn't know, and was humoring her by not saying anything. Not contradicting Angelina's assertion that her life was perfect just as it was.

Now she understood that expression, and the thoughts behind it. Now it made sense. Because the queen had known that because Angelina had never loved a man, she'd never had the chance to feel this way before. Hadn't understood.

She did now.

She didn't need children to complete her, just as she didn't need a man to complete her. That wasn't it at all. She hadn't lied to Alec when she'd told him she'd been happy before he'd come along. Her life had been rewarding. Fulfilling. Enough to make her reasonably content. There were things she would have changed—Caterina, her parents—but not the lack of a man in her life.

That is the key, she realized now—she hadn't missed having a man in her life because she hadn't known what she was missing. But now there was Alec, and everything was different, including her. Now the desire for Alec's child rolled through her like an incoming tide. Inevitable. Not just any man's child. Only Alec's, because she loved him and wanted to give him the gift of immortality his child would bring…if he wanted it, too. And incredibly, it seemed, he did.

She touched Alec's face with a hand that didn't tremble. "Yes," she told him, sure in a way she didn't stop to question.

But Alec did. "Angel, are you sure? Your job—at some point you wouldn't be able to continue doing it if you get pregnant. I know how much it means to you, and you're already fighting prejudice here because you're a woman. If you were pregnant, there's no way they'd let you—"

She placed her fingers over his lips, stopping his words. "At some point, I could no longer be a bodyguard anyway," she told him firmly. "As we age, our reflexes slow. Our minds may stay sharp, but that split-second difference in reaction time could be critical to the person we are guarding. I accepted that a long time ago. I am twenty-nine. I told myself I would be a bodyguard only as long as I could stay in peak physical condition. Only that long and no longer. Then I would do something else. Yes, I love my job. But ten years from now…who knows if I will even make it that long?"

She smiled at him. Not a tremulous smile. A smile that conveyed rock-solid assurance in what she was doing. "I have a law degree. Did I ever tell you that? I was a junior prosecutor, but not for long, because when the king ascended the throne, he threw open the gates to something I had long dreamed of but never thought to attain—service to my country in the Zakharian National Forces.

"Then I was tapped for the queen's security detail. Dream followed dream, and my life was full. But I knew someday I would return to the law—that was always my long-term plan. I would still be serving my country as a prosecutor, and there would be great job satisfaction in bringing evildoers to justice."

She placed her hands around his face. "It will just be a little sooner than I originally planned, because now there is you, and the life I want to share with you. A life that includes your child." Her eyes held his, willing him to understand, to believe. "Not just any man's child, Alec. Yours. Can you understand the difference?"

His eyes were suddenly damp, but he blinked the moisture away. "I can understand the difference," he told her in the deep voice that never failed to move her. "Because I feel the same way."

Then he was holding her in a crushing embrace, an embrace she returned. Her heart was full—so full she couldn't believe she was the same Angelina Mateja who three months ago had never known what love between a man and a woman could be. Who three months ago thought her life was complete. Who three months ago would have scorned to think she would ever give up what she had for something else. Something better. Far, far better. Not trading her job for Alec, but trading her life without him for a life with him.

Five days later, Aleksandrov Vishenko's chief brigadier charged into Vishenko's office and wasted no time. "She has been located, *Pakhan*." He didn't have to specify a name.

Vishenko rose to his feet. "Where?" he demanded.

"After she was spotted in Denver by the man who missed taking her out"—a man whose failure to kill Caterina Mateja had been a fatal mistake—"we concentrated our search efforts there. We have just learned a woman resembling her was arrested by immigration agents a week ago and taken to a detention facility outside Denver."

"A detention facility?" Vishenko frowned. "Can you get a man inside?"

"That will not be necessary." The brigadier's smile was cold and confident. "We merely need to spread the word that the man who kills her will be deported with a fortune. There will be no shortage of volunteers."

Alec put down the report he was reading, sat back in the chair in his office at the embassy and sighed. *Damn it,* he told himself. *We're no closer than we were last week.*

That wasn't strictly true. McKinnon had turned over the witness statements to Nick D'Arcy's contact at the DOJ, and they now had search warrants and wiretap warrants on the seven former and current embassy employees. Wiretaps were already being installed. And McKinnon's interview with the three other Zakharians in custody had also borne fruit. Based on McKinnon's sworn statement as to what the three had said when they thought McKinnon didn't understand Zakharan, they were also able to obtain limited warrants on Vishenko in addition to the wiretap warrant the FBI already had.

But that was all McKinnon's doing. Alec had accomplished exactly nothing. He'd faithfully turned over Angelina's detailed report on her cousin to his sister the very next day. But so far Keira hadn't been able to come up with anything based on it. He'd known up front it had been a long shot, but…

Alec ran a hand over his face and realized he was tired. Very tired. It was late—he should have left the office hours ago. He was pushing himself too hard. He knew it, but he couldn't seem to stop. If he wasn't careful, he'd miss something because he wasn't at his best. But he wanted to get this case solved. Needed to get it solved so he could get on with the rest of his life.

Things were far from settled in his personal life. From everything Angelina had said, she wasn't envisioning leaving Zakhar. Yes, she would transition jobs when and if she got pregnant—as she'd already planned to give up her position when she could no longer function at the peak proficiency she demanded of herself—but her license to practice law was here in Zakhar. Her current job as a bodyguard on the queen's security detail and her fallback job as an attorney both required she stay in Zakhar.

She'd already met him more than halfway. Now it was his turn. He couldn't ask her to follow him from place to place, from job posting to job posting. He couldn't ask her to give up *everything*—family, friends, home, job. And country. *No,* he told himself with clear-cut determination. *Time for you to step up to the plate, Jones. Time for you to give up something for her.*

He knew what he had to do. If he left the DSS, they couldn't transfer him away from Zakhar. Angelina wouldn't need to sacrifice her career for him—he could sacrifice his career for her instead. Which meant he needed to start looking for another job. Security, maybe? A lot of US companies had offices here. Maybe security was a possibility.

He wasn't going to ask Angelina to marry him until he could support a family. Old-fashioned? Yeah, but he couldn't change *everything* about himself overnight. He'd wait to ask her until he had his new job all lined up. Until he could promise her they'd never have to leave Zakhar because of him.

But he couldn't start looking for another job until he could resign from the DSS without destroying his conscience. And that meant he had to close the trafficking case and bring everyone involved to justice. Because he'd never given up on *anything.* Ever. And he couldn't do it now—not even for Angelina.

A few months back, he'd wondered if he'd ever meet a woman who understood what it was like to kill in the line of duty. Who understood that a man could regret the *necessity* of killing, while not regretting the killing itself, and that his motivation wasn't money or power or greed, but rather the desire to make a difference and make the world a safer place.

Edward Everett Hale had said it best. *I am only one, but I am one. I cannot do everything, but I can do something. And I will not let what I cannot do interfere with what I can do. And by the grace of God, I will.*

His father had carved that quotation in wood and hung it over the fireplace mantel at home before Alec was born. His parents had instilled that maxim in all their children even before they'd learned to read. Wasn't that why every one of the Jones children had gone into the Marine Corps when they turned eighteen? And wasn't that why all of them had gone into public service of some sort after they'd left the Corps? Shane into politics. Niall into something so secret he couldn't even tell his family what he was doing. Alec and Liam into the DSS. Keira into the agency. Because even though they couldn't do everything, they could do something. They couldn't *not* do something—that was deeply ingrained in them all.

Well, he'd met her. Met the woman who understood what motivated him, because she was motivated by the same things. A woman who was just as tough as he was. Just as uncompromising. Just as strong inside, where it counted. And just as determined to make a difference.

So, yeah, now it was his turn to sacrifice something, because he wasn't giving up Angelina. Now it was his turn to—

The phone on his desk rang suddenly, startling him. He picked it up. "Alec Jones."

"It's Keira," his sister said, her excitement bubbling over in his ear. "You're not going to believe this, but we've got her."

Alec straightened in his chair. "Caterina Mateja?"

"You bet. ICE picked her up a week ago," she explained, referring to Immigration and Customs

Enforcement by their commonly used acronym. "The fake identification she gave the arresting officers says her name is Cate Jones, but…"

"Damn, you're good." The compliment slipped out. Alec didn't make a habit of praising his sister to her face—although he was quick to brag about her to others—but he couldn't help himself this time. "You sure it's her?"

"They ran her fingerprints against IAFIS, but nothing popped." *The FBI's Integrated Automatic Fingerprint Identification System,* Alec translated in his mind as Keira continued. "The same for IDENT." He wasn't exactly sure what that acronym stood for, but he wasn't about to interrupt his sister to ask. "That didn't surprise me. If the US embassy in Zakhar was issuing fraudulent visas, it's not likely they were submitting legit digital fingerprints to the FBI for the women involved. But that didn't matter. The agency has face-recognition software—so good it's classified—and I've been running random searches on every database I can access. The picture ICE took when they arrested her matches the picture on her expired work visa. She's a lot older now, but it's her. I know it's her."

"Where is she?"

"Would you believe that she's here in Denver? ICE is holding her at the Denver Contract Detention Facility. It's actually located in Aurora, but close enough."

"Holy crap. You're right, I don't believe it." He thought a moment. "Can you get her out of there? Not that I don't trust ICE, but wherever they're holding her won't keep her safe from the hit Vishenko has out on her. If he or his men find out where she is, think how easy it would be for a fellow inmate to shank her. And if she's been there a week…"

"Already in the works," Keira assured him. "The request had to come from Baker Street, but I called him as soon as I knew it was her. Two steps ahead of you, Alec," she told him with a tiny hint of superiority in her voice, and he laughed under his breath. Keira was so damned competitive, especially with her brothers. But he didn't care this time. All he cared about was getting Caterina Mateja to a place of safety, and the fact that his baby sister had solved it first wasn't important.

"So what's your plan?" Keira asked him. "Assuming ICE surrenders custody of Caterina to the agency—and I don't see why they wouldn't, given D'Arcy's clout— what's your next step?"

"I've got to question her. Find out what she knows, what evidence she has."

"D'Arcy will stash her in a safe house here in Denver, so interrogating her in private won't be a problem. But ICE says she hasn't said a word other than the name on her fake ID the whole time she's been in custody. What if she asks for an attorney when you get here? She'd be perfectly within her rights to do so. Then where are you?"

"Not going to happen." Alec was boldly confident.

"How can you be so sure?"

"Because I'll have my other secret weapon with me," he told her. "Angelina Mateja—Caterina's cousin. They were like sisters growing up. If anyone can get Caterina to open up and tell us what she knows, it'll be her cousin."

They talked for a couple more minutes, ironing out details, but as soon as Alec hung up he let out a whoop of excitement that reverberated through his office, and he pumped his fist. "Yes!"

He reached for the phone to call Angelina but changed his mind. What he had to tell her could wait until he could tell her in person. But he had one other call he had to make. He dialed a number, tapping his pen impatiently against the desktop while he waited for the switchboard at the palace to answer. When they did, he said, "Trace McKinnon, please."

Another minute passed before the phone was answered. "McKinnon."

"Are you sitting down?" Alec asked him, not even bothering to identify himself.

"Should I be?"

"Hell, yeah. We've got her."

Chapter 17

"Gone?" Aleksandrov Vishenko roared like a wounded lion to the brigadier who had dared to beard him in the lion's den of his Manhattan apartment before his day had even properly started. "What do you mean she's gone?"

"She is no longer in the detention center. Our sources say Nick D'Arcy of the agency intervened personally, and she has been spirited away—no one knows where."

"Find out," Vishenko hissed, furious that his prey had eluded him once again. Furious...and afraid. It was his worst nightmare come true—Caterina in the hands of the agency. It wasn't just the evidence Caterina had stolen about his criminal activities, though that was bad enough. If anyone made the connection between David Pennington and him from years ago, he would never escape justice. "Find her," he told his brigadier as fear clutched at his heart. "Find her *now.*"

* * *

The Zakharian Airlines plane landed in Denver only twenty minutes late, despite the snowstorm that threatened to shut down the airport.

Alec's brother-in-law, Cody Walker, was waiting for them outside, and Alec was glad to see him. He introduced Angelina to Cody, but decided to keep the personal aspect of his relationship with Angelina to himself for the time being. Not that he wasn't bursting to tell the world, but just as Angelina had wanted to keep their relationship secret for fear of being misjudged by her superiors, Alec didn't want anything screwing up their interrogation of Caterina Mateja.

"Hotel first?" Cody asked as he and Alec threw the luggage in the back of Cody's SUV. "Do you need to rest after the flight? Or do you want to go right to the safe house?"

"The safe house," Angelina interjected before Alec could respond. "It has been eight years since I have seen my cousin."

"You heard the lady," Alec told Cody.

"Then the safe house it is."

They'd only been driving for ten minutes when Cody said quietly, "Don't look now, but we have company."

Angelina's right hand went inside her jacket, but then she gave Alec a stricken look. "My gun is in my luggage."

He didn't hesitate. He bent down and retrieved the spare SIG Sauer he carried in his ankle holster and handed it to her. Then he said to Cody, "You think they're following you or us?"

"They weren't following me *to* the airport," Cody answered. "That much I can tell you for sure."

"Then they're following us. Maybe they've been following us since we left Zakhar, thinking we'll lead them right to Caterina." Alec thought for a moment. "You have someplace we can set a trap?"

Cody's eyes met Alec's in the rearview mirror. "You read my mind." He tapped a button on his SUV's steering wheel and the Bluetooth's automated voice system answered.

Caterina Mateja sat on the piano bench in the living room of the safe house, picking out a tune from memory on the keys of the piano. She had not played the piano for more than eight years, but somehow, when she sat down, it was as if her fingers had a memory all their own. From Beethoven's *Für Elise*, she moved right into one of her mother's favorites—also by Beethoven—*Moonlight Sonata*. She hit a few wrong notes, wincing each time, but she managed to put remarkable feeling into the overall piece, and the couple guarding her—who'd introduced themselves to her as Dara and Walt Barron—exchanged speaking glances.

"That was beautiful, Cate," Dara said gently when she was finished.

Cate shrugged her shoulders. She had not spoken a single word since she'd been brought to this house, not even to ask why she was there. She'd spent a week in the ICE detention center, and all she'd told them there was the name on her ID card—Cate Jones. They'd tried to question her several times—for hours on end. But she had listened to their questions in stony silence and never answered.

She'd never been arrested before, and inside she was terrified. Not just because she didn't know what was going to happen—deportation wasn't something she wanted to think about, but if they didn't know who she really was how could they know where to deport her *to*?—but also because she feared Aleksandrov Vishenko's men would find and kill her. Or worse, take her back to Vishenko.

When the two men had come to fetch her from the detention center, she'd thought the worst. That they were taking her away to turn her over to Vishenko's men. Vishenko had policemen on his payroll. She had the records. So when they'd brought her to what they referred to as a safe house and left her in the custody of the Barrons, she hadn't believed them. When they'd unlocked her handcuffs and shown her to a bedroom with its own private bath, she'd been amazed. But she still hadn't believed them.

Even when she'd been told she could change out of the prison jumpsuit into any of the clothes in the closet or dresser that took her fancy, she hadn't believed them…although she *had* changed clothes. It would be easier to escape and hide when the opportunity arose if she wasn't wearing prison-issued clothing.

She kept expecting Vishenko to show up. Kept expecting that it was all a cruel trick of some kind. She'd slept—if you could call it sleep—with the expectation that any moment Vishenko would walk through her bedroom door…and that the nightmare would begin again.

But night turned into day and no one else had appeared. Only the same two people, who claimed to be husband and wife, stood guard over her. They both wore guns, so she hadn't tried to escape. Not yet. She was biding her time. Waiting for them to relax their vigilance for an instant and then she'd be gone. She was good at it.

The SUV's windshield wipers were working over-time against the snowstorm when Cody turned right, into a middle-class suburban neighborhood. "They're still back there," he told Alec and Angelina. He drove halfway down the block and then pulled into the drive-way of a house that had seen better days. He parked and said, "Showtime."

Alec glanced over at Angelina, and she nodded. "Then let's do it," he said. The three of them exited the SUV and made their way to the front porch, rang the doorbell and waited, stomping their feet to clear the snow. When the door opened, they entered the fake safe house, and the door was closed behind them. Then they waited, with guns drawn.

Five minutes went by. Then ten. None of the agents who'd set up this trap said a word—the house was si-lent as a tomb. At the thirteen-minute mark, a voice from the top of the stairs whispered, "Here they come."

The glass in the back door was shattered by a burst of submachine-gun fire and four black-hooded men kicked the remnants of the door open and swarmed into the kitchen. Three of them made it as far as the foot of the staircase before Cody's agents tackled and cuffed them. The fourth, who'd been guarding the death squad's escape route, heard the commotion from the other room and tried to run for it, only to find his escape thwarted by Alec and Angelina, who'd circled around from the front of the house to the back porch.

"Federal agent!" Alec shouted, identifying himself

as he and Angelina confronted the hooded gunman. "Drop your weapon! Drop it!"

Cate's fingers wandered into another of her mother's favorites—Schumann this time. *Träumerei*. It had always soothed her to play it. She was almost to the end when the doorbell rang, and she froze, her heart nearly jumping out of her chest. Then she sprang to her feet. "Please," she whispered to her captors in a breathless, desperate voice. "Please…" They were the first words she'd spoken in more than a week.

She didn't run when the woman went to answer the door. What would be the point? And besides, she refused to show fear in front of *him*. Hatred, yes. And contempt. She would show him those emotions. But not fear. Never fear. She would slash her own wrists before she would let him force tears from her. She'd cried once. Begged him once. Never again.

She steeled herself to face him, locking her muscles so she wouldn't tremble. The front door opened wide, and a tall blond man walked through. Not Vishenko. He shook snow from his overcoat and stamped his boots on the rug just inside the door. He was followed by a woman who did the same thing, but she was shielded from Cate's view by the blond man's broad shoulders and the woman's coat hood. Cate's gaze was drawn to the third person to enter, another tall man, younger than the first one, but with auburn hair and a determined expression. Again not Vishenko, and Cate breathed a sigh of profound relief. Then the woman moved into view. "Caterina," she said, and all the gladness in the world was in her voice.

Cate's eyes grew big and her breath stuck in her

throat. Then the stress she'd lived under for the past week suddenly caught up with her. The terror she'd felt when the doorbell rang and she'd thought it was *him* took its toll. The blood drained away from her face when she recognized the woman. Light-headed, her muscles no longer able to support her, Cate quite simply fainted.

Angelina was the first to reach Caterina, but Alec was right behind her. He lifted Caterina's slender body in his arms, noting as he did so that for all her height, her weight was relatively insubstantial, as if she'd eaten barely enough to keep alive for years. "Where should I put her?" he asked Dara Barron.

"Probably best if you take her up to her bedroom. Let me show you."

Alec followed her, and Angelina followed him. When he laid Caterina on top of the bedspread, Angelina was right there. She stripped off her coat and dropped it heedlessly on the floor. She took her cousin's hands in hers, chafing them gently, trying to bring Caterina back to consciousness. Then he heard a choked sound from Angelina. Not tears. Rage. A Zakharan curse he recognized issued from her lips, and then she whispered in Zakharan, "Animals. Animals! What did they do to her?"

Alec frowned, not following. "What do you mean?"

"Look," she said in English. She held up Caterina's wrists, first one, then the other. That's when Alec saw the scars. Nearly identical scars almost an inch wide encircling both wrists. Old scars, from wounds long healed. But he knew how those wounds had been inflicted. Even worse, he knew why. And Angelina's rage was transferred to him.

* * *

Not quite two hours later, Alec quietly excused himself and made his way into the bathroom. His whole body seesawed back and forth in alternating spasms of hot and cold, and there was a churning in his belly he tried desperately to control. Then his face broke out in a sweat and he knew he wasn't going to make it.

He was vilely, miserably sick.

Afterward he felt much better. He ran cold water over his hands and wrists and splashed some on his face and the back of his neck after rinsing out his mouth. Still sickened by what he'd heard, he could barely stand to look at himself in the mirror. Could barely stand to know he belonged to that half of the human race who could do what had been done to Caterina.

Angelina found him there. "You are okay?" she asked gently.

"Yeah." He wiped his face and hands on a towel and looked at her in bewilderment. He would have thought she'd be as upset as he was, but she was calm. Composed. And though there was a militant light in her eyes, by no other sign did she betray she'd heard the same despicable tale he'd just heard. "How can you do it?" he asked.

"Do what?"

"Remain unmoved." He gestured toward the other room. "Hearing what happened to Caterina. How can you—"

"I am not unmoved. I want to kill him. I want to kill every man like him," she said fiercely. "But the king is right. Killing him is easy. Bringing him to justice is not. He must be *seen* to face justice. Otherwise…"

Her jaw set tightly. "He is not the only one, Alec. I have heard this kind of story before, when I first became a prosecutor. Not exactly like this, and not nearly as bad. But men have been doing things like this to women for thousands of years and will continue to do so until good men—men like you—stand up and say, *'This stops here!'*"

He put his arms around her and held her tight, feeling her heart beating in sync with his own. "This stops here," he said, fighting the unexpected restriction in his throat. "I promise you, Angel, this stops here." He vowed to do everything he could to stop not only Vishenko, but the trafficking of women everywhere. *Thank God it's included in my job description,* he told himself fervently. *Thank God fighting human trafficking is part of the DSS's mandate. Even when I'm transferred, I'll still be—*

A sudden realization deluged him like a cold shower. If he resigned from the DSS, if he took a job in the private sector, fighting human trafficking would no longer be part of his job description. If he left the DSS, those women who were counting on him to help them—women like Caterina Mateja and thousands more just like her—would look in vain for help. Not just from men like him, but from *him.*

He'd joined the DSS for a reason. A damned good reason. He wanted to make a difference. How could he have forgotten? "'I am only one, but I am one,'" he whispered to himself.

Angelina stirred in his arms. "What did you say?" she murmured.

"Nothing." He couldn't tell her. His dreams were dissolving before his eyes—dreams of her, of them, of having a child with her, of being a family—because he couldn't *not* do what he could do to save the world, or at least his little corner of it. Edward Everett Hale's words came back to him in all their stark reality, reminding him of who he was.

For just a moment he raged against his better self. Raged against a conscience that wouldn't *let* him do nothing. And by doing nothing, have his heart's desire. His arms tightened around Angelina, as if by holding her he could hold back the dictates of his conscience through the dictates of his heart.

He couldn't do it. But he couldn't tell Angelina, either. Not now. Not when she was still reeling—as he was—from Caterina's story of the two years she'd been Vishenko's prisoner. Not when they were both so emotionally ravaged by a reality far worse than they could have imagined. A reality it would always torture them to know.

Angelina was right. The king was right. Vigilante justice—so tempting, so enticing, especially in this case—wasn't the way to go. They had to take Vishenko down, but legally. Publicly. They had to put him away for life, making sure life meant *life*.

Which meant Alec had no choice. Despite what she'd been through, despite what she'd survived, despite his protective instincts kicking in and wanting him to take Caterina someplace far away where she'd never have to be afraid again, he had to convince her to testify against Vishenko. Had to somehow get through to Caterina that her evidence and her testimony were crucial to putting Vishenko away so he could never do to anyone else what he'd done to her.

Somehow.

* * *

Cate lay back against the pillows, physically and emotionally exhausted. She'd been running on adrenaline ever since she'd been brought here, and she had no reserves of physical energy left.

But it was the emotional drain that had really done her in. Telling her story—haltingly at first, then gaining momentum when neither Angelina nor Alec seemed to judge her—had brought every detail back. Details she'd hidden away from herself, just as she'd hidden away the evidence she'd stolen from Vishenko when she escaped. Details she'd sworn she'd never remember.

And yet…now she had. The memories her brain had successfully blanked out for years had returned to her as if they'd happened yesterday. And as she recounted them, she relived them. Every single one.

But she hadn't cried—she'd sworn more than eight years ago she'd never cry again, and she hadn't. Neither had Angelina. Oddly, it was Alec whose eyes grew damp as her story unfolded, Alec whose throat had worked as if he was fighting emotions he didn't know how to handle. As if he suffered as he learned the horror she'd lived through. As if he would have taken her pain if he could.

Such a good man. The kind of man she'd dreamed of all those years ago back when she'd still dreamed. But she wasn't blind. Alec loved Angelina. She could see it in his eyes, hear it in his voice when he said her cousin's name. And Angelina loved him. Not quite as openly—Angelina had never been demonstrative that way—but it was obvious to someone who knew her as well as Caterina did. The years had fallen away, as if they'd never been apart. While a small part of her was envious of her cousin, most of her rejoiced. Angelina was so *good*! She always had been. She'd been the older sister Cate had looked up to. Adored. Wanted to emulate. She deserved a man like Alec.

Cate glanced up when Angelina reentered the room, followed by Alec. She didn't know why it was, but telling Alec her story had been easier than telling Angelina. She'd looked at his face more often than her cousin's as she'd confessed everything that had happened. Everything she'd done. Maybe because Alec hadn't known her before, hadn't loved her before, as her cousin had once loved her and—as impossible as it seemed—loved her still, despite the shame Cate had brought to their family. Despite knowing the truth. All of it.

Angelina crossed the room, leaned over and kissed Cate on the cheek and then gently cradled Cate's face in her strong hands. In Zakharan, she said softly, "Alec needs to talk to you, *dernya*. Alone. Is that okay?"

Cate blinked and caught her breath at Angelina's pet name for her, a nickname from her childhood that meant *little treasure*. No one had called her that in more than eight years. She'd been no one's treasure since she'd left Zakhar.

She nodded quickly, agreeing before she could change her mind. Angelina turned to gaze at Alec, and Cate could see the question in her cousin's eyes—a question that was silently answered by the tall man who somehow had won Angelina's heart. That meant he *had* to be a good man. Angelina wouldn't love him if he wasn't.

Then Angelina kissed Cate one more time and left the room.

* * *

Alec stood by the window gazing out into the gathering darkness, watching the snow fall in a blanket of white, as he marshaled his thoughts. For a moment he wished he hadn't asked Angelina to leave. Maybe it would be easier with her there. But then he knew he'd been right to insist on doing this himself. Angelina was too close to her cousin. Too attached. She couldn't be objective, not on something like this, despite being able to listen calmly, quietly, to Caterina's story—*Cate*'s story, he reminded himself. Angelina's cousin had told them she went by Cate now, and he had to remember that.

But without Angelina's assistance, that meant it was all on him to figure out what to say to a woman who'd been to hell and back to convince her she needed to go back into hell.

Cate made it easy for him. "It is best to just say it, straight out, whatever it is."

Despite everything, Alec couldn't help laughing softly. "You sound just like Angelina," he told her, unexpected humor lightening the heavy burden on his heart as he paid her the highest compliment in his book. *And that's the key,* he realized suddenly. The key to the woman Cate was, the way to reach her. Despite her waiflike appearance, she was strong inside, where it counted. Just like Angelina. Determined not to crumble where a lesser woman would have. Tough enough to survive the hell she'd survived and fight her way out. Hadn't he told McKinnon Angelina would testify because it was the right thing to do, no matter the risk? And hadn't he said, *If Caterina's anything like her cousin, she'll do it. She'll testify?*

"I want the evidence you've got against Vishenko and everyone involved in the trafficking and prostitution ring," he said straight out. Not harshly, but a demand. "Not just that—I want anything and everything you've got on Vishenko. And I want you to testify against him. Against them."

She paled. "Why?" she asked through lips that barely parted enough to get that one word out.

Pain slashed through him, but Alec knew he couldn't soften. Knew there was a time for gentleness and compassion. This wasn't it. Cate didn't need tenderness right now. She needed to remember how strong she really was. "Because you're one," he told her in no uncertain terms.

Her head tilted to one side, and her brows drew together in a question. "I don't—"

"Edward Everett Hale wrote it more than a hundred years ago," he said before she could finish. "My parents thought it was so important they made sure every one of their children understood the concept. 'I am only one, but I am one. I cannot do everything, but I can do something. And I will not let what I cannot do interfere with what I can do. And by the grace of God, I will.'"

He paused to let that sink in. "You're one. Just as I am. Just as Angelina is. All we can do is the best we can do. Each time. Every time. And we can never give up. We *can't*. Because if we give up, if we say, 'Let someone else do it, let someone else take the risk,' then people like Vishenko win. *Not* because they're smarter than us, or better than us, but because they can make us afraid. Because we *let* them make us afraid."

"I *am* afraid," she said faintly. "Why me? Why do I have to testify?" She stumbled over her words in her haste to explain. "When…when you left the room, Angelina told me that even if Vishenko never faces justice here in the US, he will be tried in Zakhar for attempting to kill the crown prince. One of the men he hired has already confessed. So you don't need me to put him away—he will end his days in a Zakharian prison."

Alec shook his head again, wondering what else he could say to convince her she was strong enough to do this. "It's not just Vishenko. If it was, you'd be right, but it's not. We have to bring *all* the men in the conspiracy to justice—from the men who lured the Zakharian women with false promises, to the men at the US embassy who provided the fraudulent work visas for the trafficked women, to the men from the Bratva who forced the women into prostitution. We can't do it without you."

She drew a sharp, shuddering breath and gazed at him from wounded eyes. "But *he* will be there," she whispered, almost in despair.

"So will I," he promised her. "So will Angelina. We'll be there. You can't let him win—not this time. Not ever again." He reached down and touched a finger to the scar on one of her wrists. "You fought him before, Cate—this proves it. Fight him now with everything in you. We'll help you. Your cousin and I will do everything we can to help you."

His jaw tightened, and he knew in his heart of hearts he had only one final argument to put forth. If it didn't work, if he couldn't convince her… He held her gaze with his intent one. "If I could fight this battle for you, I would," he said, meaning every word. "But I can't. Only you can do it. Only you can stand up to the evil these men represent and say, 'This stops here. This stops *now*!'"

She bent over, covering her eyes with the heels of her hands. At first he thought she was crying as she dragged one ragged breath after another into her body, and his resolution was shaken. *How the hell can I ask her to do this after what she's been through?* he thought. *And how the hell can I judge her if she refuses?*

But when she finally raised her face to his, her eyes were dry. Dry, but with a determined light in them that reminded him poignantly of Angelina. "You're right," she said. "'I am only one, but I am one.' I will testify. And I'll give you all the evidence I have. I've kept it hidden for six years, thinking someday I might find the courage to use it against him."

Cate glanced down at her hands for a moment, at the scars on her wrists, and her mouth trembled. But then her lips tightened into a firm line. She breathed deeply, and Alec watched as her slender, patrician hands formed into tightly clenched fists. Somehow he knew she was remembering—and fighting the fear that memory created. Then she looked up and beyond him at something only she could see. "Someday is today," she whispered. Then her eyes met Alec's—blue-gray eyes that were so like Angelina's—dauntless courage reflected in their shining depths. "Someday is today."

Chapter 18

Five weeks later, Alec stood at the window of his office in the embassy, hands in his pockets, staring out at nothing. Would they ever have all the answers? *Probably not,* he admitted to himself. You almost never got *all* the answers.

They still didn't know who'd killed the king's cousin. The investigation into his murder inside the prison was ongoing. The Zakharian police were relentless, and he knew they weren't giving up anytime soon. The working theory was that Vishenko had ordered the hit. They just didn't have any evidence. Not yet.

What they *had* found—and Alec couldn't believe the Zakharian investigators at the time had missed it— wasn't really evidence in Prince Nikolai Marianescu's murder. But there *had* been a connection between the prince and Aleksandrov Vishenko dating back to the assassination attempts on the king and the woman who was now Zakhar's queen. The prince had been arrested, tried and convicted without anyone knowing that Vishenko could very well have been involved in that plot. Even if he hadn't played an active role, he'd probably given it his blessing. And if Prince Nikolai had succeeded in taking the throne, Vishenko would have owned him—something a career criminal at Vishenko's level would have wanted.

Another thing they didn't have all the answers for— not yet—was the connection between Vishenko and Sasha Tcholek. Angelina was adamant that Sasha just wasn't the kind of man who was motivated solely by money. So there had to be something else involved— maybe some kind of blackmail involving his family, Angelina theorized—to make him turn traitor. That investigation was still ongoing, too.

And the four gunmen arrested in the sting at the safe house where Cate *hadn't* been? They'd been Vishenko's men, no question. The FBI had identified them as members of the Bratva, all with long criminal histories. But none of them were talking. *Surprise, surprise,* Alec thought cynically. Frustrating, but only to be expected, as all four had lawyered up immediately so they couldn't even be questioned.

But that didn't matter, because one slight woman with more courage than all the men who worked for Vishenko combined was going to bring him down and put him away for life. The joint DSS–agency task force was combing through the documents Cate had turned over, and they were dynamite.

Alec glanced at his watch and realized he was going to be late meeting Angelina for dinner if he didn't get a move on. He had a table booked for six o'clock at Mischa's—their restaurant—and he couldn't be late, tonight of all nights.

Because tonight, after dinner, he was going to tell her. His conscience had been bugging him for weeks, practically since the day they returned from the States. But yesterday had been the final straw. Angelina had taken him to the royal cemetery, to the tomb of the first king and queen of Zakhar. He'd seen the movie, *King's Ransom*, so he knew the story. He even knew the English translation of the Latin inscription carved on the tomb. But he hadn't known just how much those words meant to Angelina until she'd whispered, "Two hearts as one, forever and a day." Then she'd turned to gaze at him, her heart in her eyes. And his heart had shredded.

He could put off telling her for months, maybe even a year, until he was forced to tell her. Until the DSS transferred him someplace else. But he just couldn't do that to her. He couldn't pretend everything was fine. Angelina deserved better. She deserved to know *now* that they had no future. That for them there was no forever and a day. But he knew once he told her, her smile would fade. The light would go out of her eyes. And the light would go out of his world.

She'd understand. That was the damnable thing. She'd understand when he told her he couldn't resign from the DSS because he needed to continue the fight for all the Cates out there. Just as she'd understand when he told her children weren't an option—not for him. Not for them. Not under the circumstances.

You're afraid to tell her. Just admit it.

Yeah, he was. Because he'd rather cut off his right hand—his shooting hand—than break her heart. But he *had* to tell her. He'd put it off long enough. And no matter what she decided—even if she chose to go with him when he was reassigned—their life together would never be the same. It couldn't be.

Angelina stared at Alec in the soft, wintry moonlight. They'd walked after dinner, as they usually did. But instead of walking by the river, this time he'd shepherded her to this little park not far from her apartment. Then he'd sat her down on a park bench and told her.

Her world was crumbling, but the manners she'd had drummed into her since she was a little girl said a lady never made a scene. A *lady* was always circumspect, always in control of her emotions, no matter what.

"Say something, Angel." The hard edge to Alec's voice steadied her.

"What is there to say?" she said, fiercely glad her voice didn't tremble. "You have made your decision without consulting me."

His lips tightened. "I don't have a choice, damn it!"

She forced a smile. "There is always a choice." She tucked her hair behind one ear, struggling to hold back the chaos of emotions bubbling inside her. "I understand," she said when she finally had herself under control. "You would not be the man I lo—" she chopped off what she'd started to say and replaced it with "—the man you are if you could choose otherwise."

"You don't understand," he said with desperation. "I *can't* resign. I thought I could—I was even making plans about what I could do for a living instead—but I can't. Not even for you, Angel. My job is who I am. Just as your job is who you are."

His breath made a white cloud in the cold air. "I

know you said you'd give it up for me. To build a life with me when the time came. But we're not just talking going to your fallback career in the law. You know that. Eventually I'd be transferred. How can I ask you to sacrifice everything? Your job? Your home? Your country? Yes, you love me. But do you love me that much? To give up *everything*?"

"We will never know, will we?" she asked softly. "You did not ask me."

"Angel—"

"No," she said, cutting him off. "You did not ask me." She stood, calmly rewrapped her scarf securely around her throat and walked away, her head held high.

She walked for miles. Dazed, bewildered and bereft, she huddled inside the warmth of her coat, but the chill in the air was nothing compared to the ice embedded in her heart.

Alec loved her, but not enough. Not enough to sacrifice his career. That was all she could think of as she eventually found herself at the river and made her way along the river's edge. *We jogged here,* she remembered when she came to a bend in the river. This was where she'd taken him by surprise and thrown him to the ground. Where he'd turned the tables on her so neatly. Where he'd kissed her for the first time. *You wanted him to kiss you,* she acknowledged. *You wanted him then, just as you want him now.*

She'd been drawn to Alec from the beginning. *Why?* she asked herself now. *Why Alec, and no other man?*

Because he understood her. Understood what motivated her. And loved those things in her she'd never believed a man could love in her. He loved those things in her *because he was the same way.* And she loved him for the same reasons he loved her. Because he could sacrifice what *he* wanted, what would make *him* happy, for a higher purpose.

Honor. Duty. Loyalty. Sacrifice.

Words that meant *everything* to them.

A quotation came to her from out of the blue, a line from a seventeenth-century poem by Richard Lovelace. *"I could not love thee, dear, so much, loved I not honor more."*

A memory clicked into her mind suddenly, her telling Alec in the safe house, *"...men have been doing things like this to women for thousands of years and will continue to do so until good men—men like you— stand up and say, 'This stops here!'"*

And Alec's heartfelt vow, *"I promise you, Angel, this stops here."*

She realized then that was exactly why Alec had made the choice he'd made. Because being the honorable man he was, he couldn't refuse to answer the call of duty. He couldn't *not* do whatever he could to make the world a better place, no matter the personal cost.

And he couldn't ask her to sacrifice everything for him. *Not* because he didn't love her enough, but because he did.

The question was, did she love him enough? Did she understand? *Truly* understand?

Alec stood watching the snow falling in a soft cloud outside his embassy office window and remembered how together, he and Angelina had confronted one of Vishenko's henchmen in the Denver snowstorm. They hadn't even had to discuss what to do; they'd oper-

ated on the same wavelength as only a team could before moving on to the real safe house where Cate had
been taken.

Cate and all the women like her were counting on
Alec to do everything in his power to stop men like
Vishenko. How could he let those women down?

But at the same time he remembered the devastated
expression in Angelina's eyes a week ago as she said,
"You did not ask me." She'd tried to hide it from him,
but he could read her. And though he'd never doubted
himself before, never questioned his decisions, now he
wondered, *Should* he have asked her?

The buzzer sounded and Alec moved to his desk to
answer it. "Yes, Tahra?"

"If you don't leave shortly, sir, you'll be late for your
appointment with the king." He glanced at the clock
on his desk and realized Tahra was right as usual. "I
already ordered one of the embassy limos," she continued. "It should be waiting downstairs for you in
five minutes."

"Thanks. I'll head down in a minute." He clicked
off the speakerphone, but his hand stayed poised over
the phone for a moment as he considered calling Angelina's cell. Then he discarded that as a bad idea. She
was working, and what would he say, anyway? That
he'd been wrong not to ask her to sacrifice her world
for him? That he'd been wrong not to sacrifice his
honor for her?

As he rode down in the elevator, Alec wondered
what this meeting with the king was all about. It
couldn't be related to the progress in the trafficking case—Alec and the ambassador had met with the
king and his advisers the day before yesterday in their

weekly status meeting. So it had to be something else. Try as he might, he couldn't think of a reason for the unexpected phone call he'd received that morning from the king's appointments secretary, asking for this meeting. But as an embassy diplomat, he could never refuse an invitation from a head of state.

Alec met King Andre Alexei IV in his private office, not one of the conference rooms they usually met in. He was politely shown into the large, airy room, and when the king rose to meet him, both the footman and the king's bodyguard left them alone, something that had obviously been prearranged.

"Thank you for coming, Special Agent Jones," the king began when they were both seated, but then he shook his head. "Need we be so formal? My sister calls you Alec. May I?"

"Please do, sir."

The king smiled. "I am Andre to my friends, Alec. And I have a feeling we are going to become friends."

"Sir?" Alec hadn't been expecting this. Yes, they were close in age—the king was only a year or so younger than he was. But…he was a king. Not Alec's king, but still. A king. A sovereign ruler of a sovereign nation. Even though the United States and its citizens were egalitarian, Alec had been trained in diplomacy. But nothing in his training had covered a situation like this.

"Assuming you are agreeable to a suggestion I will be making to you today," the king clarified, "we will be seeing a lot of each other over the coming years. My sister speaks very highly of you, Alec, as does her husband—both hold you in affection as well as esteem. You might already know I value their opinions."

Slight understatement, Alec thought wryly, *especially where Princess Mara is concerned,* although he didn't share that with the king.

"And then, of course," the king continued without a pause, "there is what you have accomplished in such a relatively short time. All these things speak to your character. I would welcome the opportunity to add you to my small circle of friends."

Alec drew a deep breath. "I would be honored, sir."

"Andre," the king insisted. "At least when we are in private."

It went against his training, but Alec repeated, "Andre."

The king laughed. "There, that was not so difficult, was it?" He didn't wait for an answer. "Now to the issue at hand. If you have not already received a commendation from your superiors for a job well done, you will. I have formally expressed Zakhar's sincere thanks in a letter to your president, a copy of which I have here." He picked up an envelope embellished with the state seal of Zakhar, and handed it to Alec. "It thanks the United States—in particular you and Trace McKinnon—for rooting out the corruption in the US embassy in Drago, and for bringing an end to the human-trafficking ring operating between our countries. Above and beyond the call of duty. I believe those were the words I used to describe your actions, but you can read the letter yourself when you are alone."

"Thank you, si—Andre," Alec corrected himself quickly. "But I really don't think I went above and beyond. I did what I had to do, that's all. That's all any man can do."

The king merely smiled. "So," he said pleasantly, "where do you go from here? I understand you have been posted all over the world. Other than your own country—and I truly believe every man loves his own country best—is there anyplace you have been posted that particularly appeals to you?"

"Not to sound as if I'm—" *sucking up* is what he'd been about to say, but he decided it really wasn't appropriate "—trying to flatter you," he settled for. "But Zakhar is far and away the most beautiful, the most peaceful place I've lived in the past eighteen years, except my home in Colorado. Recent events notwithstanding."

The king's eyes gleamed. "So you could see yourself living here…indefinitely?"

"When I first found out I was being posted to Zakhar, I thought I was being rewarded for something, and I still feel that way." He chuckled. "Your sister told me one of the reasons she loves Colorado is that it reminds her of Zakhar. I'm just the reverse. I love Zakhar partly because the mountains here remind me of the Colorado Rockies. So it won't be a hardship to stay here until my next transfer."

"Ah, yes," the king said. "About that…let me ask you a question, Alec. And before you answer, I would like you to consider everything very carefully." He steepled his fingers and held them to his lips for a moment, as if he wanted to choose his words wisely.

"Given your stellar accomplishments here, I would not be surprised if a promotion were offered you sometime in the next twelve months. You could accept that promotion, accept relocation to someplace else in the world. Your performance in your new location could easily lead to another promotion a few years down the road. That would not surprise me, either. You have intrinsic leadership qualities, qualities that cannot be taught. They must come from within."

Slightly embarrassed, Alec felt compelled to say, "Thank you."

"As I said, you could accept that next promotion, and put in motion a chain of events, the ultimate outcome of which cannot be predicted. Or," he said, his voice dropping a notch, "you can accept your government's appointment as the RSO here for the remainder of your career. Until you retire in the normal course of things."

When Alec just stared at him, the king said, "I have already broached the possibility with the president of the United States. I have offered in exchange unrestricted use of the missile bases your government has here for a reduced fee, for as long as you are the RSO."

"What?" Probably not the most diplomatic of responses, but Alec was too stunned to say anything else.

"Nothing has been formalized, you understand," the king was quick to point out. "Nothing *can* be unless you give your assent to the agreement. But your president seemed…amenable." The king smiled as if he couldn't help it. "*Eager* is perhaps a better word. He is sure a deal can be worked out that will be mutually beneficial to all parties concerned."

The first thing Alec thought of was Angelina. Of how his staying in Zakhar permanently would affect the two of them. He'd never be reassigned, and he wouldn't have to sacrifice his honor to stay here. He would still be able to keep the vow he'd made to Angelina and to himself—*this stops here.*

He could author a case study based on his experience at the US embassy in Drago, pointing out the danger signs for other embassies to watch for—not just US embassies but those of their allies, as well—and how to prevent what had happened here from happening anywhere else. He could be a guest lecturer—not just at the DSS training center in DC, but everywhere women were at risk.

And he could be an advocate within the DSS for a stronger focus on fighting human trafficking, not just in Zakhar, but around the world.

Then there were the children he'd reluctantly acknowledged he would never have—*could* never have—because he could never allow himself to be an absentee father. Now he wouldn't be. Now children were back in the realm of possibility. Children Angelina wanted as much as he did.

"What do you get out of this?" Alec asked abruptly, needing a moment to consider this incredible offer. To figure out exactly what it meant for everyone concerned, not just for him. And why it was being offered. "What's in it for you? For Zakhar?"

The king smiled his faint smile. "Zakhar gets an incorruptible man at the US embassy. And after the two previous RSOs—corrupt men who made possible a terrible crime against the women of Zakhar—that is not a small thing."

Alec wasn't convinced. "That's not good enough, sir," he said, automatically using the more formal designation rather than the king's given name. The king raised his chin and his eyes narrowed, as if he was being accused of lying. "I'm sorry, sir. That explanation might be true, but it doesn't cover something of this magnitude. You'd be signing away treaty rights indefinitely. And I need to know why." He hurried to add, "You must know if I accept this offer, I couldn't owe you anything for it. I couldn't accept it under those conditions. My loyalty can't be bought, and it can't be divided."

The smile that had disappeared from the king's face when Alec told him his explanation wasn't good enough returned. "Loyalty that can be bought is worth no more than a wife who can be bought," he said in a soft, meaningful voice. "No, Alec, I am not trying to buy your loyalty. I am merely trying to repay my debt. Oh, not to you," he clarified when Alec started to speak. "To Lieutenant Mateja."

Alec wasn't surprised the king knew about their relationship, given what Captain Zale had told him regarding Zakhar's secret intelligence service. But he *was* surprised the king knew the depth of their attachment. "How did you—" he began, but then stopped short.

"How did I know?" The king picked up a letter from the center of his desk and handed it to Alec. "Because of this."

Alec skimmed the few sentences, then shook his head in disbelief and began reading it again. Then read it a third time, his thoughts in turmoil.

"Lieutenant Mateja resigned her commission yesterday," the king told him. "I take it you were unaware she intended to do so?"

Alec shook his head, still in shock. "I had no idea." His Angel had resigned her commission for him. He hadn't asked her, couldn't have brought himself to ask her. But she'd done it anyway. Because she loved him enough to sacrifice everything for him. Because she understood—*really* understood—the sacrifice of his own happiness he was willing to make to be a force for good in the world.

"She gave that letter to her captain, who turned it over to Colonel Marianescu," the king continued. "My cousin called her in to discuss it at length, and pried the full story out of her. Then he came to see me."

"I don't under—"

"I owe Lieutenant Mateja a debt that can never be repaid with money," the king explained. "And not with honors, a promotion or anything of that nature. She saved the life of my son. Priceless. I would sacrifice my own life for him, but she made that unnecessary. If I can give her the one thing she cannot give herself without tremendous sacrifice—a life with the man she loves—then I will have repaid her for what she has done for the queen and me."

The king smiled. "*And* I keep Lieutenant Mateja here in Zakhar. Captain Zale has agreed to take over as head of my son's security detail, a post for which he is eminently qualified. I also plan—but please keep this to yourself for the time being—to promote Lieutenant Mateja to head the queen's security detail in Captain Zale's place. Even more than my son, my wife is the most precious thing in my world. I would give anything to keep her safe. I would also give anything to make her happy. She is particularly attached to Lieutenant Mateja, especially after the lieutenant saved our son's life, and counts her as a friend."

His smile deepened. "As I said, this way I not only

keep Lieutenant Mateja in Zakhar, keep her guarding my wife, but I give her everything her heart desires—her job and you. Can you put a price on those things, Alec? I cannot."

When the king put it that way, it made perfect sense. Alec realized once again the king was a brilliant tactician. He'd divined the problem and had devised an ingenious solution. All that was necessary for this to work was for Alec to sacrifice certain career possibilities. A sacrifice that was no sacrifice, all things considered.

He'd be doing a job he loved—making the world a safer place—for the rest of his professional career, with the woman he loved at his side. A woman who loved him as fiercely as he loved her, who was willing to sacrifice everything for him. A woman who *understood*.

That made his choice easy. "I accept," he told the king. "Assuming you can swing it with the State Department and the DSS, I accept."

Angelina hurried inside her apartment building's front door to escape the cold, stamped her boots on the rug and impatiently brushed the snow from her hair. After a quick check of her empty mailbox, she headed for the elevator, only to find a discreet out-of-order sign taped by the button.

She sighed. It wasn't the first time and wouldn't be the last. She loved her apartment in this older building, especially because of the breathtaking view of the royal palace on the hill and the river winding its way through Drago. But sometimes the inconveniences—such as the elevator breaking down with regularity, or the hot water turning ice-cold without warning—made her yearn for something more modern, more reliable. Although she'd long since accepted the sacrifices she had to make for her charming home, that didn't stop her from muttering maledictions as she began the trek up eight flights of stairs.

Then she consoled herself with the reminder that she needed the exercise anyway. She'd had to cut her jog short this morning because the overnight snowdrifts hadn't been cleared yet, and the footing had been hazardous in the extreme.

Still, Angelina was glad when she reached the seventh-floor landing and knew she had only one more flight to go. She turned the corner, her hand on the railing, and stopped short at the sight of Alec sitting on the top step, his head and shoulder propped against the wall. Fast asleep.

Her heart had already been pounding from exertion, but seeing her indomitable Alec waiting for her, his face soft and vulnerable in sleep, kicked her pulse into overdrive and sent a wave of tenderness through her body. She knew—because she'd suffered from the same lack of sleep as he obviously had—that his decision to break things off with her had cost him dearly since she'd last seen him a week ago. Mentally. Emotionally. Physically.

She also knew there could only be one reason why he was here—somehow he'd found out she'd resigned her commission before she could tell him. And he'd come here to…tell her what? That he wasn't worth the sacrifice? That he couldn't accept it?

Alec had unilaterally decided to end their relationship the first time around. And though she understood why—because of the way he'd been raised—it was time he learned there were some things he was going to have to compromise on. And a life-altering decision was something that had to be made by both of them...together.

The stairwell door on the bottom floor slammed shut, and faint footsteps mounting the stairs could be heard in the distance. Alec jolted awake, his hand reaching for his SIG Sauer in the same instinctive move Angelina herself would have made.

Their eyes met across the distance that separated them. But instead of the despairing expression she remembered from the last time she'd seen him, now his face glowed with hope. And Angelina's hope was kindled, too.

She rushed up the stairs, but Alec met her halfway, his arms closing around her in a bear hug that lifted her feet from the ground and threatened to crack her ribs. He did nothing else, just held her tight, not saying a word. But the tiny flame of hope in her heart was fanned into a blaze.

Angelina didn't know how long they stood there on the stairs, lost in each other's embrace, but when the footsteps mounting the stairwell below them grew closer, she murmured, "This is not the place. My apartment, yes?"

Somehow they made it into her apartment without letting each other go. And as soon as the door closed behind them Alec was kissing her as if his life depended on it. Angelina matched him kiss for kiss, understanding his fierce need the way she understood *him*.

When Alec finally released her long enough for them both to catch their breaths, he pressed his forehead against hers and his eyes squeezed shut. When they opened again she saw that same dampness in them she'd seen when he'd listened to Caterina's story unfolding. Only this time the emotions he was fighting weren't painful to watch. This time they gladdened her heart.

"You resigned for me," he whispered.

"Yes. And no."

He pulled back slightly and his brows twitched together. "I don't understand."

She smiled a little at his bewilderment. "I resigned because I love you, but not *only* because I love you. I also resigned because this is work that *must* be done, and *you* must do it." She drew a deep breath. "Even though I always intended to eventually resume my career in the law, Alec, it was not an easy decision. Even though I have been seeking job counseling from some of my former law professors, it broke my heart to resign now. But I did not want to put it off, because—"

Air gusted out of Alec's lungs. "That's just it, Angel. You're not going to believe this, but neither of us has to resign. Neither of us has to sacrifice our honor...our duty...to be together."

Her smile faded. "Now *I* do not understand."

Alec explained. Quickly. Succinctly. "So you see, there's no need for you to resign after all. And the king refuses to accept your resignation anyway." Then he said in a low voice, "I love you, Angel. No one will ever love you more than I do. Please believe that. I just *couldn't* ask you to give up everything for me—"

"Because you love me," she said swiftly, cutting him off. "Yes, I know. But I also know your love is rooted in honor, the same as mine. You could not love me otherwise."

"You *do* understand." His words were barely above a whisper.

"Of course. The same way you understand me. You could not love me if I were not who I am. And I could not love you if you were anything other than the man you are." She cradled his face in her hands and kissed him.

When his lips finally left hers—reluctantly—he said, "When I read your resignation letter, I knew you loved me more than I ever dreamed possible. But more important, I knew you understood." His brown eyes were very dark, very serious. "God—through the king—has given us a second chance, Angel. Has given *me* a second chance at happiness." A trace of uncertainty colored his next words. "Please tell me we can start over. Please tell me you want there to be an *us* as much as I do."

Tenderness welled up in her heart, because uncertainty and Alec was a rare combination. Just as she had certainty of purpose, so did he—and she loved that about him. Uncompromising. Unyielding. Invincible. He would always demand the best of himself…and of her. Warrior heart calling to warrior heart.

"We are not starting over," she corrected him, another smile beginning to form, a sure one this time. "We are merely beginning a new chapter."

Epilogue

"Indictments were handed down today in a federal courtroom in Washington, DC, in a human-trafficking conspiracy case that could have far-reaching repercussions," announced CNN correspondent Carly Edwards, standing on the steps of the courthouse. "Named in the indictments were seven current or former employees of the US embassy in Zakhar, a country that is critically important to the United States' strategic plan for NATO and Europe. Also named in the indictments was Aleksandrov Vishenko—" a mug shot of Vishenko appeared briefly "—reputed to be the head of a New York City–based branch of the Russian Brotherhood—also known as the Russian Mafia—and a half dozen alleged associates. Sources tell us that at the same time the indictments were sought here, nine men were indicted in Drago, the capital of Zakhar, for their participation in the alleged conspiracy. Trial dates have yet to be set. Back to you, Tom."

The news anchor in the studio said, "Thank you, Carly. In other news today…"

Alec clicked on the *X* in the top right-hand corner of his internet browser, closing the window. He wasn't interested in the other news from home—he'd only wanted to hear the story about today's indictments.

It gave Alec particular satisfaction to hear the CNN correspondent saying Aleksandrov Vishenko's name— the only name reported in the story—along with the words *Also named in the indictments…*

American jurisprudence being what it was, the trials were at least six months away, probably more. The sixth amendment to the US Constitution referred to the right of the *accused* to a speedy trial. It said nothing about the prosecution or the rights of the victims. Defense teams often sought to push trials out as far as they could, especially if their clients were out on bail. All those indicted today were eligible for bail, and while the judge could set bail as high as he legally could, Aleksandrov Vishenko, at least, would make bail. That was a given.

Caterina Mateja was currently residing inside the royal palace in Drago. It was far safer for her than staying in the States, although she'd have to travel back and forth to the United States between now and the trials. The defense teams had the right to take her deposition, although Alec would be damned before he let them intimidate her, even though he was sure they'd try. The prosecution team would want to prep her for trial, too, so she would have to go there as needed.

When she was in the States she'd be closely guarded

by US marshals, but Alec would never know a minute's peace until she was safely back in Drago. Her blood would be on his hands if anything happened to her, since he was the one who'd convinced her to testify against Vishenko and the others. At least while she was here she was as safe as she could be. The king had arranged tight security, and Alec could keep a watchful eye on her, too. So could Angelina.

He laughed softly to himself. If Angelina's behavior around Caterina was any indication, she'd be a terrific mother to their children. A little *over*protective, maybe, but it would be his job to help her know where to draw the line. The old traditional split of parental duties might not apply so much anymore, and with Angelina's assistance he would work to overcome the example set by his father in that regard. But some things would never change—involved, hands-on fathers still instilled self-confidence, self-esteem and, most important, self-discipline in their children. He could hardly wait.

He'd finally met Angelina's parents when Cate had returned to Zakhar, and he'd understood almost immediately why Angelina hadn't been eager to introduce them to him—their moral outrage over the "shame" Cate had brought to their family told him all he needed to know about them. He shook his head, still unable to fathom how parents like Angelina's had managed to produce an extraordinary woman like her.

A slight movement behind him alerted him to Angelina's presence even before she spoke. "Is everything okay?" she asked him in the deep, rich contralto that had enthralled him when he'd first heard it. It always would. "What did the news say?"

He turned around to face her. "Nothing new. I just wanted to hear it again."

The glimmer of a smile touched her lips. "Soon," she said with satisfaction. "Soon they will begin to pay."

"Not as soon as they would if the trials were being held here," he reminded her. "But it *will* happen— we'll make sure of it." He stepped toward her, and she walked into his embrace. "'I am one,'" he reminded her in a low voice.

"As am I." They held each other close, both of them giving the encouragement and support the other needed. When they finally drew apart, Alec kept his hands on her shoulders and asked, "So how was your day, *Captain* Mateja?"

She flushed. The promotion was recent enough that he knew she still found immense satisfaction in hearing her new rank, which was why he made a point of mentioning it as often as he could. "Busy," she said. "I had not realized all the administrative work involved in managing the queen's security detail. Just coordinating all the schedules takes far too much time. And then, of course, I had to stop and see Caterina—Cate."

She shook her head ruefully. "I cannot always remember to call her Cate, even though she prefers that name now. And even if I do, she will be Caterina to me, I think, no matter what." Her expression turned wistful. "Caterina means pure. When she first told me she wished to be called Cate, I wondered if…"

"If she didn't want to be reminded of what she thinks she no longer is?" he finished for her.

She nodded reluctantly. "We have told her many times there is no shame in what happened to her."

"But she doesn't believe us." Alec smiled sadly. "Yeah, I know." He pulled Angelina back into his arms and held her tight. "We just have to keep telling her. And showing her. Someday she'll believe. I have to believe that. Maybe when she testifies. Maybe when she faces Vishenko in court and tells her story to the jury—maybe then she'll finally realize the shame is his, not hers."

"You are such a good man," she told him softly, laying her head on his shoulder for just a moment. Then she chuckled to herself, surprising him. Their eyes met, and hers were brimming over with humor and a little glint of teasing. "That is what Cate says. I think, perhaps, she has a little crush on you."

"What?" Alec was too startled at first to say anything else. Then he protested, "But I've never done anything to… You know I haven't… She knows that I—"

"Yes, she knows you love me." The humor faded from her face and the wistfulness returned. "I think that is why she feels it is safe to let herself care about you a little—because she knows you will never ask more of her than she can give…*that* way."

She caressed his cheek with one hand. Her left hand. The one wearing his engagement ring, soon to be joined by a wedding ring. *One more month,* he promised himself. He caught her hand in his and pressed a kiss into her palm. A tender kiss that soon turned into more. He reluctantly let her go. "Did you eat with Cate?" he asked. "You were so late I went ahead and fixed myself something, but if you're hungry I could—"

She smiled the smile she kept for him alone. A private smile that promised unbearable delight. "I am hungry, yes," she told him. But as she said the words, she was taking his hand and walking backward into the bedroom, drawing him with her. "I am *always* hungry for you." She fell onto the bed, pulled him down on top of her and squirmed a little until his erection was nestled between her thighs. Telling him without words exactly what she was hungry for.

The scent of her soap teased his nostrils, and he breathed deeply, enjoying her nearness. He smiled down at her—a wolfish smile he didn't bother to hide. A smile that conveyed exactly what he was hungry for, too. But he did nothing else, perfectly willing to wait, because his Angel would make the first move if he didn't. She'd take the lead the first time. Then it would be his turn.

He took primitive satisfaction in knowing she was his just as he was hers—what was that phrase she liked to use? Forever and a day, that was it.

Forever and a day.

Angelina was a romantic at heart, no matter how much she tried to deny it, and that poetic phrase she used proved it. Alec was more prosaic. He could no more stop loving her than he could voluntarily stop breathing—he would love her throughout eternity. If that translated as forever and a day in Angelina's book, that was fine with him.

* * * * *

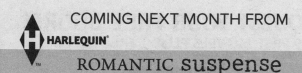
#1863 PROTECTING THE COLTON BRIDE
The Coltons of Oklahoma • by Elle James
Megan Talbot needs money—fast—and the only way to get
her inheritance is to marry. Her wealthy rancher boss has his
own agenda when he proposes a marriage of convenience,
but as Megan is targeted by an assassin, family secrets must
be exposed.

#1864 A WANTED MAN
Cold Case Detectives • by Jennifer Morey
Haunted by his past, Kadin Tandy moves to Wyoming to open
his own investigative firm. His new client, Penny Darden,
suspects someone close to her is a killer. As they hunt for
answers and she falls for the rugged PI, they both learn the
depths of healing, love...and true danger.

#1865 AGENT ZERO
by Lilith Saintcrow
He's the most dangerous man terminally ill Holly Candless
will ever meet—and he'll do anything to keep her safe. But
it's a race against time, since only a top secret government
program stands between her and a slow, sure death....

#1866 THE SECRET KING
Conspiracy Against the Crown • by C.J. Miller
After a tragic loss and an ensuing royal battle, the princess of
Acacia must choose between her heart and her duty. But the
man who comes to protect her and whom she starts to love
has a dark, twisted secret that could destroy them both.

REQUEST YOUR FREE BOOKS!
2 FREE NOVELS PLUS 2 FREE GIFTS!

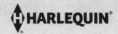

ROMANTIC suspense

Sparked by danger, fueled by passion

YES! Please send me 2 FREE Harlequin® Romantic Suspense novels and my 2 FREE gifts (gifts are worth about $10). After receiving them, if I don't wish to receive any more books, I can return the shipping statement marked "cancel." If I don't cancel, I will receive 4 brand-new novels every month and be billed just $4.74 per book in the U.S. or $5.49 per book in Canada. That's a savings of at least 12% off the cover price! It's quite a bargain! Shipping and handling is just 50¢ per book in the U.S. and 75¢ per book in Canada.* I understand that accepting the 2 free books and gifts places me under no obligation to buy anything. I can always return a shipment and cancel at any time. Even if I never buy another book, the two free books and gifts are mine to keep forever.

240/340 HDN GH3P

Name	(PLEASE PRINT)	
Address		Apt. #
City	State/Prov.	Zip/Postal Code

Signature (if under 18, a parent or guardian must sign)

Mail to the **Reader Service:**
IN U.S.A.: P.O. Box 1867, Buffalo, NY 14240-1867
IN CANADA: P.O. Box 609, Fort Erie, Ontario L2A 5X3

Want to try two free books from another line?
Call 1-800-873-8635 or visit www.ReaderService.com.

* Terms and prices subject to change without notice. Prices do not include applicable taxes. Sales tax applicable in N.Y. Canadian residents will be charged applicable taxes. Offer not valid in Quebec. This offer is limited to one order per household. Not valid for current subscribers to Harlequin Romantic Suspense books. All orders subject to credit approval. Credit or debit balances in a customer's account(s) may be offset by any other outstanding balance owed by or to the customer. Please allow 4 to 6 weeks for delivery. Offer available while quantities last.

Your Privacy—The Reader Service is committed to protecting your privacy. Our Privacy Policy is available online at www.ReaderService.com or upon request from the Reader Service.

We make a portion of our mailing list available to reputable third parties that offer products we believe may interest you. If you prefer that we not exchange your name with third parties, or if you wish to clarify or modify your communication preferences, please visit us at www.ReaderService.com/consumerchoice or write to us at Reader Service Preference Service, P.O. Box 9062, Buffalo, NY 14240-9062. Include your complete name and address.

HRS15

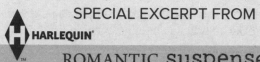
"Why don't we get married?"

Even though she'd known it was coming, it still hit her square in the chest. The air rushed from her lungs and a tsunami of feelings washed over her. A surge of joy made her heart beat so fast she felt faint. She crested that wave and slid into the undertow of reality. "A marriage of convenience?"

"Exactly." Daniel reached for her hands.

When she hid them behind her back, he dropped his arms. "It wouldn't have to be forever. Just long enough to satisfy the stipulations of your grandmother's will and save your horses, and that would help me get past the Kennedy gauntlet. We could leave tomorrow, spend a night in Vegas, find a chapel and it would be over in less than five minutes."

With her heart smarting, Megan forced a shaky smile. "Way to sweep a girl off her feet."

He waved his hand and Halo tossed her head. "If you want, I can make an official announcement in front of my family."

Megan shook her head. "No."

"No, you won't marry me?"

"No." She pushed past him to pace down the center of the barn. "Your plan is insane."

"Do you have a better one?" he asked. "I'm all ears."

The plan was the same as the one she'd been thinking of before Daniel had woken up. Only when she'd dreamed it up, it didn't sound as cold and impersonal as Daniel's proposal. Somewhere in the back of her mind she'd hoped that marriage to Daniel would be something more than one of convenience.

After yesterday's kiss, she wasn't sure she could be around Daniel for long periods of time without wanting another. And another.

Don't miss
PROTECTING THE COLTON BRIDE
by New York Times *bestselling author Elle James.*
Available September 2015

www.Harlequin.com

Love the Harlequin book you just read?

Your opinion matters.

Review this book on your favorite book site, review site, blog or your own social media properties and share your opinion with other readers!